JEFFREY EUGENIDES is the author of three novels. His first, *The Virgin Suicides*, published in 1993, was made into a film by Sofia Coppola. *Middlesex* appeared in 2002, going on to win the Pulitzer Prize for Fiction, the WELT-Leteraturpreis and the Santiago de Compostela Literary Prize from Spain. *Middlesex* was also a finalist for the National Book Critics Circle Award, the International IMPAC Dublin Literary Award and France's Prix Médicis. In 2011, Eugenides published *The Marriage Plot*, which became a finalist for the National Book Critics Circle Award and was named as the best novel of that year by independent booksellers in the United States. *The Marriage Plot* also won the Prix Fitzgerald and the Madame Figaro Literary Prize in France. Eugenides is a professor of creative writing in the Lewis Center for the Arts at Princeton University. His work has been translated into thirty-five languages.

From the reviews of *The Virgin Suicides*:

'Weaves a sinuous spell … shot through with sneaky black humour … intoxicating'                                   *Esquire*

'A subtle and ingenious talent'                          *Sunday Telegraph*

'Humour prevails throughout but doesn't deflate the disturbing elements of the tale'                                   *Variety*

'Bold and resonant'                              *Independent on Sunday*

Also by Jeffrey Eugenides

*Middlesex*
*My Mistress's Sparrow Is Dead* (editor)
*The Marriage Plot*
*Fresh Complaint*

# JEFFREY EUGENIDES

## THE VIRGIN SUICIDES

COLLINS
MODERN
CLASSICS

4th Estate
An imprint of HarperCollins*Publishers*
1 London Bridge Street
London SE1 9GF

www.4thestate.co.uk

HarperCollins*Publishers*
1st Floor, Watermarque Building, Ringsend Road
Dublin 4, Ireland

Published as a Collins Modern Classics paperback in 2021 Previously
published by 4th Estate in 2013
First published in Great Britain by Bloomsbury Publishing plc in 1993

6

A catalogue record for this book is
available from the British Library

ISBN 978-0-00-848516-0

Printed and Bound in the UK using 100% Renewable Electricity at
CPI Group (UK) Ltd

**MIX**
Paper from
responsible sources
**FSC™ C007454**

This book is produced from independently certified FSC™ paper
to ensure responsible forest management.

For more information visit: www.harpercollins.co.uk/green

*For Gus and Wanda*

# ONE

On the morning the last Lisbon daughter took her turn at
suicide—it was Mary this time, and sleeping pills, like
Therese—the two paramedics arrived at the house knowing exactly where the knife drawer was, and the gas oven,
and the beam in the basement from which it was possible
to tie a rope. They got out of the EMS truck, as usual moving much too slowly in our opinion, and the fat one said
under his breath, "This ain't TV, folks, this is how fast we
go." He was carrying the heavy respirator and cardiac unit
past the bushes that had grown monstrous and over the
erupting lawn, tame and immaculate thirteen months
earlier when the trouble began.

Cecilia, the youngest, only thirteen, had gone first,
slitting her wrists like a Stoic while taking a bath, and
when they found her, afloat in her pink pool, with the yellow eyes of someone possessed and her small body giving
off the odor of a mature woman, the paramedics had

been so frightened by her tranquillity that they had stood mesmerized. But then Mrs. Lisbon lunged in, screaming, and the reality of the room reasserted itself: blood on the bath mat; Mr. Lisbon's razor sunk in the toilet bowl, marbling the water. The paramedics fetched Cecilia out of the warm water because it quickened the bleeding, and put a tourniquet on her arm. Her wet hair hung down her back and already her extremities were blue. She didn't say a word, but when they parted her hands they found the laminated picture of the Virgin Mary she held against her budding chest.

That was in June, fish-fly season, when each year our town is covered by the flotsam of those ephemeral insects. Rising in clouds from the algae in the polluted lake, they blacken windows, coat cars and streetlamps, plaster the municipal docks and festoon the rigging of sailboats, always in the same brown ubiquity of flying scum. Mrs. Scheer, who lives down the street, told us she saw Cecilia the day before she attempted suicide. She was standing by the curb, in the antique wedding dress with the shorn hem she always wore, looking at a Thunderbird encased in fish flies. "You better get a broom, honey," Mrs. Scheer advised. But Cecilia fixed her with her spiritualist's gaze. "They're dead," she said. "They only live twenty-four hours. They hatch, they reproduce, and then they croak. They don't even get to eat." And with that she stuck her hand into the foamy layer of bugs and cleared her initials: *C.L.*

We've tried to arrange the photographs chronologically,

though the passage of so many years has made it difficult. A few are fuzzy but revealing nonetheless. Exhibit #1 shows the Lisbon house shortly before Cecilia's suicide attempt. It was taken by a real estate agent, Ms. Carmina D'Angelo, whom Mr. Lisbon had hired to sell the house his large family had long outgrown. As the snapshot shows, the slate roof had not yet begun to shed its shingles, the porch was still visible above the bushes, and the windows were not yet held together with strips of masking tape. A comfortable suburban home. The upper-right second-story window contains a blur that Mrs. Lisbon identified as Mary Lisbon. "She used to tease her hair because she thought it was limp," she said years later, recalling how her daughter had looked for her brief time on earth. In the photograph Mary is caught in the act of blow-drying her hair. Her head appears to be on fire but that is only a trick of the light. It was June 13, eighty-three degrees out, under sunny skies.

When the paramedics were satisfied they had reduced the bleeding to a trickle, they put Cecilia on a stretcher and carried her out of the house to the truck in the driveway. She looked like a tiny Cleopatra on an imperial litter. We saw the gangly paramedic with the Wyatt Earp mustache come out first—the one we'd call "Sheriff" when we got to know him better through these domestic tragedies—and then the fat one appeared, carrying the back end of the stretcher and stepping daintily across the lawn, peering at his police-issue shoes as though looking out for dog shit, though later, when we were better acquainted with the machinery, we knew he was checking the blood pressure gauge. Sweating and fumbling, they moved toward the shuddering, blinking truck. The fat one tripped on a lone croquet wicket. In revenge he kicked it; the wicket sprang loose, plucking up a spray of dirt, and fell with a ping on the driveway. Meanwhile, Mrs. Lisbon burst onto the porch, trailing Cecilia's flannel nightgown, and let out a long wail that stopped time. Under the molting trees and above the blazing, overexposed grass those four figures paused in tableau: the two slaves offering the victim to the altar (lifting the stretcher into the truck), the priestess brandishing the torch (waving the flannel nightgown), and the drugged virgin rising up on her elbows, with an otherworldly smile on her pale lips.

Mrs. Lisbon rode in the back of the EMS truck, but Mr. Lisbon followed in the station wagon, observing the speed limit. Two of the Lisbon daughters were away from home, Therese in Pittsburgh at a science convention, and Bonnie at music camp, trying to learn the flute after giving up the piano (her hands were too small), the violin (her chin hurt), the guitar (her fingertips bled), and the trumpet (her upper lip swelled). Mary and Lux, hearing the siren, had run home from their voice lesson across the street with Mr. Jessup. Barging into that crowded bathroom, they registered the same shock as their parents at the sight of Cecilia with her spattered forearms and pagan nudity. Outside, they hugged on a patch of uncut grass that Butch, the brawny boy who mowed it on Saturdays, had missed.

Across the street, a truckful of men from the Parks Department attended to some of our dying elms. The EMS siren shrieked, going away, and the botanist and his crew withdrew their insecticide pumps to watch the truck. When it was gone, they began spraying again. The stately elm tree, also visible in the foreground of Exhibit #1, has since succumbed to the fungus spread by Dutch elm beetles, and has been cut down.

The paramedics took Cecilia to Bon Secours Hospital on Kercheval and Maumee. In the emergency room Cecilia watched the attempt to save her life with an eerie detachment. Her yellow eyes didn't blink, nor did she flinch when they stuck a needle in her arm. Dr. Armonson stitched up her wrist wounds. Within five minutes of the transfusion he declared her out of danger. Chucking her under her chin, he said, "What are you doing here, honey? You're not even old enough to know how bad life gets."

And it was then Cecilia gave orally what was to be her only form of suicide note, and a useless one at that, because she was going to live: "Obviously, Doctor," she said, "you've never been a thirteen-year-old girl."

The Lisbon girls were thirteen (Cecilia), and fourteen (Lux), and fifteen (Bonnie), and sixteen (Mary), and seventeen (Therese). They were short, round-buttocked in denim, with roundish cheeks that recalled that same dorsal softness. Whenever we got a glimpse, their faces looked indecently revealed, as though we were used to seeing women in veils. No one could understand how Mr. and

Mrs. Lisbon had produced such beautiful children. Mr. Lisbon taught high-school math. He was thin, boyish, stunned by his own gray hair. He had a high voice, and when Joe Larson told us how Mr. Lisbon had cried when Lux was later rushed to the hospital during her own suicide scare, we could easily imagine the sound of his girlish weeping.

Whenever we saw Mrs. Lisbon we looked in vain for some sign of the beauty that must have once been hers. But the plump arms, the brutally cut steel-wool hair, and the librarian's glasses foiled us every time. We saw her only rarely, in the morning, fully dressed though the sun hadn't come up, stepping out to snatch up the dewy milk cartons, or on Sundays when the family drove in their paneled station wagon to St. Paul's Catholic Church on the Lake. On those mornings Mrs. Lisbon assumed a queenly iciness. Clutching her good purse, she checked each daughter for signs of makeup before allowing her to get in the car, and it was not unusual for her to send Lux back inside to put on a less revealing top. None of us went to church, so we had a lot of time to watch them, the two parents leached of color, like photographic negatives, and then the five glittering daughters in their homemade dresses, all lace and ruffle, bursting with their fructifying flesh.

Only one boy had ever been allowed in the house. Peter Sissen had helped Mr. Lisbon install a working model of the solar system in his classroom at school, and in return Mr. Lisbon had invited him for dinner. He told us the girls had kicked him continually under the table, from every direction, so that he couldn't tell who was doing it. They gazed at him with their blue febrile eyes and smiled, showing their crowded teeth, the only feature of the Lisbon girls we could ever find fault with. Bonnie was the only one who didn't give Peter Sissen a secret look or kick. She only said grace and ate her food silently, lost in the piety of a fifteen-year-old. After the meal Peter Sissen asked to go to the bathroom, and because Therese and Mary were both in the downstairs one, giggling and whispering, he had to use the girls', upstairs. He came back to us with stories of bedrooms filled with crumpled panties, of stuffed animals hugged to death by the passion of the girls, of a crucifix draped with a brassiere, of gauzy chambers of canopied beds, and of the effluvia of so many young girls becoming women together in the same cramped space. In the bathroom, running the faucet to cloak the sounds of his search, Peter Sissen found Mary Lisbon's secret cache of cosmetics tied up in a sock under the sink: tubes of red lipstick and the second skin of blush and base, and the depilatory wax that informed us she had a mustache we had never seen. In fact, we didn't know whose makeup Peter Sissen had found until we saw Mary Lisbon two weeks later on the pier with a crimson mouth that matched the shade of his descriptions.

He inventoried deodorants and perfumes and scouring pads for rubbing away dead skin, and we were surprised to learn that there were no douches anywhere because we had thought girls douched every night like brushing their teeth. But our disappointment was forgotten in the next second when Sissen told us of a discovery that went beyond our wildest imaginings. In the trash can was one Tampax, spotted, still fresh from the insides of one of the Lisbon girls. Sissen said that he wanted to bring it to us, that it wasn't gross but a beautiful thing, you had to see it, like a modern painting or something, and then he told us he had counted twelve boxes of Tampax in the cupboard. It was only then that Lux knocked on the door, asking if he had died in there, and he sprang to open it. Her hair, held up by a barrette at dinner, fell over her shoulders now. She didn't move into the bathroom but stared into his eyes. Then, laughing her hyena's laugh, she pushed past him, saying, "You done hogging the bathroom? I need something." She walked to the cupboard, then stopped and folded her hands behind her. "It's private. Do you mind?" she said, and Peter Sissen sped down the stairs, blushing, and after thanking Mr. and Mrs. Lisbon, hurried off to tell us that Lux Lisbon was bleeding between the legs that very instant, while the fish flies made the sky filthy and the streetlamps came on.

When Paul Baldino heard Peter Sissen's story, he swore that he would get inside the Lisbons' house and see things even more unthinkable than Sissen had. "I'm going to watch those girls taking their showers," he vowed. Already, at the age of fourteen, Paul Baldino had the gangster gut and hit-man face of his father, Sammy "the Shark" Baldino, and of all the men who entered and exited the big Baldino house with the two lions carved in stone beside the front steps. He moved with the sluggish swagger of urban predators who smelled of cologne and had manicured nails. We were frightened of him, and of his imposing doughy cousins, Rico Manollo and Vince Fusilli, and not only because his house appeared in the paper every so often, or because of the bulletproof black limousines that glided up the circular drive ringed with laurel trees imported from Italy, but because of the dark circles under his eyes and his mammoth hips and his brightly polished black shoes which he wore even playing baseball. He had also snuck into other forbidden places in the past, and though the information he brought back wasn't always reliable, we were still impressed with the bravery of his reconnaissance. In sixth grade, when the girls went into the auditorium to see a special film, it was Paul Baldino who had infiltrated the room, hiding in the old voting booth, to tell us what it was about. Out on the playground we kicked gravel and waited for him, and when he finally appeared, chewing a toothpick and playing with the gold ring on his finger, we were breathless with anticipation.

"I saw the movie," he said. "I know what it's about. Listen to this. When girls get to be about twelve or so"— he leaned toward us—"their tits bleed."

Despite the fact that we now knew better, Paul Baldino still commanded our fear and respect. His rhino's hips had gotten even larger and the circles under his eyes had deepened to a cigar-ash-and-mud color that made him look acquainted with death. This was about the time the rumors began about the escape tunnel. A few years earlier, behind the spiked Baldino fence patrolled by two identical white

German shepherds, a group of workmen had appeared one morning. They hung tarpaulins over ladders to obscure what they did, and after three days, when they whisked the tarps away, there, in the middle of the lawn, stood an artificial tree trunk. It was made of cement, painted to look like bark, complete with fake knothole and two lopped limbs pointing at the sky with the fervor of amputee stubs. In the middle of the tree, a chainsawed wedge contained a metal grill.

Paul Baldino said it was a barbecue, and we believed him. But, as time passed, we noticed that no one ever used it. The papers said the barbecue had cost $50,000 to install, but not one hamburger or hot dog was ever grilled upon it. Soon the rumor began to circulate that the tree trunk was an escape tunnel, that it led to a hideaway along the river where Sammy the Shark kept a speedboat, and that the workers had hung tarps to conceal the digging. Then, a few months after the rumors began, Paul Baldino began emerging in people's basements, through the storm sewers. He came up in Chase Buell's house, covered with a gray dust that smelled like friendly shit; he squeezed up into Danny Zinn's cellar, this time with a flashlight, baseball bat, and a bag containing two dead rats; and finally he ended up on the other side of Tom Faheem's boiler, which he clanged three times.

He always explained to us that he had been exploring the storm sewer underneath his own house and had gotten lost, but we began to suspect he was playing in his father's escape tunnel. When he boasted that he would see the Lisbon girls taking their showers, we all believed he was going to enter the Lisbon house the same way he had entered the others. We never learned exactly what happened, though the police interrogated Paul Baldino for over an hour. He told them only what he told us. He said he had crawled into the sewer duct underneath his own basement and had started walking, a few feet at a time. He described the surprising size of the pipes, the coffee cups and cigarette butts left by workmen, and the charcoal drawings of naked women that resembled cave paintings. He told how he had chosen tunnels at random, and how as he passed under people's houses he could smell what they were cooking. Finally he had come up through the sewer grate in the Lisbons' basement. After brushing himself off, he went looking for someone on the first floor, but no one was home. He called out again and again, moving through the rooms. He climbed the stairs to the second floor. Down the hall, he heard water running. He approached the bathroom door. He insisted that he had knocked. And then Paul Baldino told how he had stepped into the bathroom and found Cecilia, naked, her wrists oozing blood, and how after overcoming his shock he had run downstairs to call the police first thing, because that was what his father had always taught him to do.

The paramedics found the laminated picture first, of course, and in the crisis the fat one put it in his pocket. Only at the hospital did he think to give it to Mr. and Mrs. Lisbon. Cecilia was out of danger by that point, and her

parents were sitting in the waiting room, relieved but confused. Mr. Lisbon thanked the paramedic for saving his
daughter's life. Then he turned the picture over and saw
the message printed on the back:

> *The Virgin Mary has been appearing in our city,*
> *bringing her message of peace to a crumbling world.*
> *As in Lourdes and Fatima, Our Lady has granted*
> *her presence to people just like you. For information*
> *call 555-MARY*

Mr. Lisbon read the words three times. Then he said
in a defeated voice, "We baptized her, we confirmed her,
and now she believes this crap."

It was his only blasphemy during the entire ordeal.
Mrs. Lisbon reacted by crumpling the picture in her fist
(it survived; we have a photocopy here).

Our local newspaper neglected to run an article on the
suicide attempt, because the editor, Mr. Baubee, felt such
depressing information wouldn't fit between the front-
page article on the Junior League Flower Show and the
back-page photographs of grinning brides. The only news-
worthy article in that day's edition concerned the cemetery
workers' strike (bodies piling up, no agreement in sight),
but that was on page 4 beneath the Little League scores.

After they returned home, Mr. and Mrs. Lisbon shut
themselves and the girls in the house, and didn't say a
word about what had happened. Only when pressed by
Mrs. Scheer did Mrs. Lisbon refer to "Cecilia's accident,"

acting as though she had cut herself in a fall. With precision and objectivity, however, already bored by blood, Paul Baldino described to us what he had seen, and left no doubt that Cecilia had done violence to herself.

Mrs. Buck found it odd that the razor ended up in the toilet. "If you were cutting your wrists in the tub," she said, "wouldn't you just lay the razor on the side?" This led to the question as to whether Cecilia had cut her wrists while already in the bath water, or while standing on the bath mat, which was bloodstained. Paul Baldino had no doubts: "She did it on the john," he said. "Then she got into the tub. She sprayed the place, man."

Cecilia was kept under observation for a week. The hospital records show that the artery in her right wrist was completely severed, because she was left-handed, but the gash in her left wrist didn't go as deep, leaving the underside of the artery intact. She received twenty-four stitches in each wrist.

She came back still wearing the wedding dress. Mrs. Patz, whose sister was a nurse at Bon Secours, said that Cecilia had refused to put on a hospital gown, demanding that her wedding dress be brought to her, and Dr. Hornicker, the staff psychiatrist, thought it best to humor her. She returned home during a thunderstorm. We were in Joe Larson's house, right across the street, when the first clap of thunder hit. Downstairs Joe's mother shouted to close all the windows, and we ran to ours. Outside a deep vacuum stilled the air. A gust of wind stirred a paper bag, which lifted, rolling, into the lower branches of the trees.

Then the vacuum broke with the downpour, the sky grew black, and the Lisbons' station wagon tried to sneak by in the darkness.

We called Joe's mother to come see. In a few seconds we heard her quick feet on the carpeted stairs and she joined us by the window. It was Tuesday and she smelled of furniture polish. Together we watched Mrs. Lisbon push open her car door with one foot, then climb out, holding her purse over her head to keep dry. Crouching and frowning, she opened the rear door. Rain fell. Mrs. Lisbon's hair fell into her face. At last Cecilia's small head came into view, hazy in the rain, swimming up with odd thrusting movements because of the double slings that impeded her arms. It took her a while to get up enough steam to roll to her feet. When she finally tumbled out she lifted both slings like canvas wings and Mrs. Lisbon took hold of her left elbow and led her into the house. By that time the rain had found total release and we couldn't see across the street.

In the following days we saw Cecilia a lot. She would sit on her front steps, picking red berries off the bushes and eating them, or staining her palms with the juice. She always wore the wedding dress and her bare feet were dirty. In the afternoons, when sun lit the front yard, she would watch ants swarming in sidewalk cracks or lie on her back in fertilized grass staring up at clouds. One of her sisters always accompanied her. Therese brought science books onto the front steps, studying photographs of deep space and looking up whenever Cecilia strayed to the edge of the yard. Lux spread out beach towels and lay suntanning while Cecilia scratched Arabic designs on her own leg with a stick. At other times Cecilia would accost her guard, hugging her neck and whispering in her ear.

Everyone had a theory as to why she had tried to kill herself. Mrs. Buell said the parents were to blame. "That girl didn't want to die," she told us. "She just wanted out of that house." Mrs. Scheer added, "She wanted out of that decorating scheme." On the day Cecilia returned from the hospital, those two women brought over a Bundt cake in sympathy, but Mrs. Lisbon refused to acknowledge any calamity. We found Mrs. Buell much aged and hugely fat, still sleeping in a separate bedroom from her husband, the Christian Scientist. Propped up in bed, she still wore pearled cat's-eye sunglasses during the daytime, and still rattled ice cubes in the tall glass she claimed contained only water; but there was a new odor of afternoon indolence to her, a soap-opera smell. "As soon as Lily and I took over that Bundt cake, that woman told the girls to go upstairs. We said, 'It's still warm, let's all have a piece,' but she took the cake and put it in the refrigerator. Right in front of us." Mrs. Scheer remembered it differently. "I hate to say it, but Joan's been potted for years. The truth is, Mrs. Lisbon thanked us quite graciously. Nothing seemed wrong at all. I started to wonder if maybe it was true that the girl had only fallen and cut herself. Mrs. Lisbon invited us out to the sun room and we each had a piece of cake. Joan disappeared at one point. Maybe she went back home to have another belt. It wouldn't surprise me."

We found Mr. Buell just down the hall from his wife, in a bedroom with a sporting theme. On the shelf stood a photograph of his first wife, whom he had loved ever since divorcing her, and when he rose from his desk to greet us, he was still stooped from the shoulder injury faith had never quite healed. "It was like anything else in this sad society," he told us. "They didn't have a relationship with God." When we reminded him about the laminated picture of the Virgin Mary, he said, "Jesus is the one she should have had a picture of." Through the wrinkles and unruly white eyebrows we could discern the handsome face of the man who had taught us to pass a football so many years ago. Mr. Buell had been a pilot in the Second World War. Shot down over Burma, he led his men on a hundred-mile hike through the jungle to safety. He never accepted any kind of medicine after that, not even aspirin. One winter he broke his shoulder skiing, and could only be convinced to get an X-ray, nothing more. From that time on he winced when we tried to tackle him, and raked leaves one-handed, and no longer flipped daredevil pancakes on Sunday mornings. Otherwise he persevered, and always gently corrected us when we took the Lord's name in vain. In his bedroom, the shoulder had fused into a graceful humpback. "It's sad to think about those girls," he said. "What a waste of life."

The most popular theory at the time held Dominic Palazzolo to blame. Dominic was the immigrant kid staying with relatives until his family got settled in New Mexico. He was the first boy in our neighborhood to wear sunglasses, and within a week of arriving, he had fallen in love. The object of his desire wasn't Cecilia but Diana Porter, a girl with chestnut hair and a horsey though pretty face who lived in an ivy-covered house on the lake. Unfortunately, she didn't notice Dominic peering through the fence as she played fierce tennis on the clay court, nor as she lay, sweating nectar, on the poolside recliner. On our corner, in our group, Dominic Palazzolo didn't join in conversations about baseball or busing, because he could speak only a few words of English, but every now and then he would tilt his head back so that his sunglasses reflected sky, and would say, "I love her." Every time he said it he seemed delivered of a profundity that amazed him, as though he had coughed up a pearl. At the beginning of June, when Diana Porter left on vacation to Switzerland, Dominic was stricken. "Fuck the Holy Mother," he said, despondent. "Fuck God." And to show his desperation and the validity of his love, he climbed onto the roof of his relatives' house and jumped off.

We watched him. We watched Cecilia Lisbon watching from her front yard. Dominic Palazzolo, with his tight pants, his Dingo boots, his pompadour, went into the house, we saw him passing the plate-glass picture windows downstairs; and then he appeared at an upstairs window, with a silk handkerchief around his neck. Climbing onto the ledge, he swung himself up to the flat roof. Aloft, he looked frail, diseased, and temperamental, as we expected a European to look. He toed the roof's edge like a high diver, and whispered, "I love her," to himself as he dropped past the windows and into the yard's calculated shrubbery.

He didn't hurt himself. He stood up after the fall, having proved his love, and down the block, some maintained, Cecilia Lisbon developed her own. Amy Schraff, who knew Cecilia in school, said that Dominic had been all she could talk about for the final week before commencement. Instead of studying for exams, she spent study halls looking up ITALY in the encyclopedia. She started saying "*Ciao*," and began slipping into St. Paul's Catholic Church on the Lake to sprinkle her forehead with holy water. In the cafeteria, even on hot days when the place was thick with the fumes of institutional food, Cecilia always chose the spaghetti and meatballs, as though by eating the same food as Dominic Palazzolo she could be closer to him. At the height of her crush she purchased the crucifix Peter Sissen had seen decorated with the brassiere.

The supporters of this theory always pointed to one central fact: the week before Cecilia's suicide attempt, Dominic Palazzolo's family had called him to New Mexico. He went telling God to fuck Himself all over again because New Mexico was even farther from Switzerland, where, right that minute, Diana Porter strolled under summer trees, moving unstoppably away from the world he was going to inherit as the owner of a carpet cleaning service. Cecilia had unleashed her blood in the bath, Amy Schraff said, because the ancient Romans had done that when life became unbearable, and she thought when

Dominic heard about it, on the highway, amid the cactus, he would realize that it was she who loved him.

The psychiatrist's report takes up most of the hospital record. After talking with Cecilia, Dr. Hornicker made the diagnosis that her suicide was an act of aggression inspired by the repression of adolescent libidinal urges. To each of three wildly different ink blots, she had responded, "A banana." She also saw "prison bars," "a swamp," "an Afro," and "the earth after an atomic bomb." When asked why she had tried to kill herself, she said only, "It was a mistake," and clammed up when Dr. Hornicker persisted. "Despite the severity of her wounds," he wrote, "I do not think the patient truly meant to end her life. Her act was a cry for help." He met with Mr. and Mrs. Lisbon and recommended that they relax their rules. He thought Cecilia would benefit by "having a social outlet, outside the codification of school, where she can interact with males her own age. At thirteen, Cecilia should be allowed to wear the sort of makeup popular among girls her age, in order to bond with them. The aping of shared customs is an indispensable step in the process of individuation."

From that time on, the Lisbon house began to change. Almost every day, and even when she wasn't keeping an eye on Cecilia, Lux would suntan on her towel, wearing the swimsuit that caused the knife sharpener to give her a fifteen-minute demonstration for nothing. The front door was always left open, because one of the girls was always running in or out. Once, outside Jeff Maldrum's house, playing catch, we saw a group of girls dancing to rock and roll in his living room. They were very serious about learning the right ways to move, and we were amazed to learn that girls danced together for fun, while Jeff Maldrum only rapped the glass and made kissing noises until they pulled down the shade. Before they disappeared we saw Mary Lisbon in the back near the bookcase, wearing bell-bottomed blue jeans with a heart embroidered on the seat.

There were other miraculous changes. Butch, who cut the Lisbon grass, was now allowed inside for a glass of water, no longer having to drink from the outside faucet. Sweaty, shirtless, and tattooed, he walked right into the kitchen where the Lisbon girls lived and breathed, but we never asked him what he saw because we were scared of his muscles and his poverty.

We assumed Mr. and Mrs. Lisbon were in agreement about the new leniency, but when we met with Mr. Lisbon years later, he told us his wife had never agreed with the psychiatrist. "She just gave in for a while," he said. Divorced by that time, he lived alone in an efficiency apartment, the floor of which was covered with shavings from his wood carvings. Whittled birds and frogs crowded the shelves. According to Mr. Lisbon, he had long harbored doubts about his wife's strictness, knowing in his heart that girls forbidden to dance would only attract husbands with bad complexions and sunken chests. Also, the odor of all those cooped-up girls had begun to annoy him. He felt at times as though he were living in the bird house at the zoo. Everywhere he looked he found hairpins and fuzzy combs, and because so many females roamed the house they forgot he was a male and discussed their menstruation openly in front of him. Cecilia had just gotten her period, on the same day of the month as the other girls, who were all synchronized in their lunar rhythms. Those five days of each month were the worst for Mr. Lisbon, who had to dispense aspirin as though feeding the ducks and comfort crying jags that arose because a dog was killed on TV. He said the girls also displayed a dramatic womanliness during their "monthly time." They were more languorous, descended the stairs in an actressy way, and kept saying with a wink, "Cousin Herbie's come for a visit." On some nights they sent him out to buy more Tampax, not just one box but four or five, and the young store clerks with their thin mustaches would smirk. He loved his daughters, they were precious to him, but he longed for the presence of a few boys.

That was why, two weeks after Cecilia returned home, Mr. Lisbon persuaded his wife to allow the girls to throw the first and only party of their short lives. We all received invitations, made by hand from construction paper, with balloons containing our names in Magic Marker. Our amazement at being formally invited to a house we had only visited in our bathroom fantasies was so great that we had to compare one another's invitations before we believed it. It was thrilling to know that the Lisbon girls knew our names, that their delicate vocal cords had pronounced their syllables, and that they meant something in their lives. They had had to labor over proper spellings and to check our addresses in the phone book or by the metal numbers nailed to the trees.

As the night of the party approached, we watched the house for signs of decorating or other preparations, but saw none. The yellow bricks retained their look of a church-run orphanage and the silence of the lawn was absolute. The curtains didn't rustle, nor did a van deliver six-foot submarine sandwiches or drums of potato chips.

Then the night arrived. In blue blazers, with khaki trousers and clip-on neckties, we walked along the sidewalk in front of the Lisbon house as we had so many times before, but this time we turned up the walk, and climbed the front steps between the pots of red geraniums, and rang the doorbell. Peter Sissen acted as our leader, and even looked slightly bored, saying again and again, "Wait'll you see this." The door opened. Above us, the face of Mrs. Lisbon took form in the dimness. She told us to come in, we bumped against each other getting through the doorway, and as soon as we set foot on the hooked rug in the foyer we saw that Peter Sissen's descriptions of the house had been all wrong. Instead of a heady atmosphere of feminine chaos, we found the house to be a tidy, dry-looking place that smelled faintly of stale popcorn. A piece of needlepoint saying "Bless This Home" was framed over the arch, and to the right, on a shelf above the radiator, five pairs of bronzed baby shoes preserved for all time the unstimulating stage of the Lisbon girls' infancy. The dining room was full of stark colonial furniture. One wall had a painting of Pilgrims plucking a turkey. The living room revealed orange carpeting and a brown vinyl sofa. Mr. Lisbon's La-Z-Boy flanked a small table on which sat the partially completed model of a sailing ship, without rigging and with the busty mermaid on the prow painted over.

We were directed downstairs to the rec room. The steps were metal-tipped and steep, and as we descended, the light at the bottom grew brighter and brighter, as though we were approaching the molten core of the earth. By the time we reached the last step it was blinding. Fluorescent lights buzzed overhead; table lamps burned on every surface. The green and red linoleum checkerboard flamed beneath our buckled shoes. On a card table, the punch bowl erupted lava. The paneled walls gleamed, and for the first few seconds the Lisbon girls were only a patch of glare like a congregation of angels. Then, however, our eyes got used to the light and informed us of something we had never realized: the Lisbon girls were all different people. Instead of five replicas with the same blond hair and puffy cheeks we saw that they were distinct beings, their personalities beginning to transform their faces and reroute their expressions. We saw at once that Bonnie, who introduced herself now as Bonaventure, had the sallow complexion and sharp nose of a nun. Her eyes watered and she was a foot taller than any of her sisters, mostly because of the length of her neck which would one day hang from the end of a rope. Therese Lisbon had a heavier face, the cheeks and eyes of a cow, and she came forward to greet us on two left feet. Mary Lisbon's hair was darker; she had a widow's peak and fuzz above her upper lip that suggested her mother had found her depilatory wax. Lux Lisbon was the only one who accorded with our image of the Lisbon girls. She radiated health and mischief. Her dress fit tightly, and when she came forward to shake our hands, she secretly moved one finger to tickle our palms, giving off at the same time a strange gruff laugh. Cecilia was wearing, as usual, the wedding dress with the shorn hem. The dress was vintage 1920s. It had sequins on the bust she didn't fill out, and someone, either Cecilia herself or the owner of the used clothing store, had cut off the bottom of the dress with a jagged stroke so that it ended above Cecilia's chafed knees. She sat on a barstool, staring into her punch glass, and the shapeless bag of a dress fell over her. She had colored her lips with red crayon, which gave her face a deranged harlot look, but she acted as though no one were there.

We knew to stay away from her. The bandages had been removed, but she was wearing a collection of bracelets to hide the scars. None of the other girls had any bracelets on, and we assumed they'd given Cecilia all they had. Scotch tape held the undersides of the bracelets to Cecilia's skin, so they wouldn't slide. The wedding dress bore spots of hospital food, stewed carrots and beets. We got our punch and stood on one side of the room while the Lisbon girls stood on the other.

We had never been to a chaperoned party. We were used to the parties our older brothers threw with our parents out of town, to dark rooms vibrating with heaps of bodies, musical vomiting, beer kegs beached on ice in the bathtub, riots in the hallways, and the destruction of living room sculpture. This was all different. Mrs. Lisbon ladled out more glasses of punch while we watched Therese and Mary play dominoes, and across the room Mr. Lisbon opened his tool kit. He showed us his ratchets, spinning them in his hand so that they whirred, and a long sharp tube he called his router, and another covered with putty he called his scraper, and one more with a pronged end he said was his gouger. His voice was hushed as he spoke about these implements, but he never looked at us, only at the tools themselves, running his fingers over their lengths or testing their sharpness with the tender bulb of his thumb. A single vertical crease deepened in his forehead, and in the middle of his dry face his lips grew moist.

Through all this Cecilia remained on her stool.

We were happy when Joe the Retard showed up. He arrived on his mother's arm, wearing his baggy Bermuda shorts and his blue baseball cap, and as usual he was grinning with the face he shared with every other mongoloid. He had his invitation tied with a red ribbon around his wrist, which meant that the Lisbon girls had spelled out his name as well as our own, and he came murmuring with his oversize jaw and loose lips, his tiny Japanese eyes, his smooth cheeks shaved by his brothers. Nobody knew exactly how old Joe the Retard was, but for as long as we could remember he had had whiskers. His brothers used to take him onto the porch with a bucket to shave him, yelling for him to keep still, saying if they slit his throat it wouldn't be their fault, while Joe turned white and became as motionless as a lizard. We also knew that retards didn't live long and aged faster than other people, which explained the gray hairs peeking out from under Joe's baseball cap. As children we had expected that Joe the Retard would be dead by the time we became adolescents, but now we were adolescents and Joe was still a child.

Now that he had arrived we were able to show the Lisbon girls all the things we knew about him, how his ears wiggled if you scratched his chin, how he could only say "Heads" when you flipped a coin, never "Tails," because that was too complicated, even if we said, "Joe, try tails," he would say, "Heads!" thinking he won every time because we let him. We had him sing the song he always sang, the one Mr. Eugene taught him. He sang, "Oh, the monkeys have no tails in Sambo Wango, oh, the monkeys have no tails in Sambo Wango, oh, the monkeys have no tails, they were bitten off by whales," and we clapped, and the Lisbon girls clapped, Lux clapped, and leaned against Joe the Retard, who was too dense to appreciate it.

The party was just beginning to get fun when Cecilia slipped off her stool and made her way to her mother. Playing with the bracelets on her left wrist, she asked if she could be excused. It was the only time we ever heard her speak, and we were surprised by the maturity of her voice. More than anything she sounded old and tired. She kept pulling on the bracelets, until Mrs. Lisbon said, "If that's what you want, Cecilia. But we've gone to all this trouble to have a party for you."

Cecilia tugged the bracelets until the tape came unstuck. Then she froze. Mrs. Lisbon said, "All right. Go up, then. We'll have fun without you." As soon as she had permission, Cecilia made for the stairs. She kept her face to the floor, moving in her personal oblivion, her sunflower eyes fixed on the predicament of her life we would never understand. She climbed the steps to the kitchen, closed the door behind her, and proceeded through the upstairs hallway. We could hear her feet right above us. Halfway up the staircase to the second floor her steps made no more noise, but it was only thirty seconds later that we heard the wet sound of her body falling onto the fence that ran alongside the house. First came the sound of wind, a rushing we decided later must have been caused by her wedding dress filling with air. This was brief. A human body falls fast. The main thing was just that: the fact of a person taking on completely physical properties, falling at the speed of a rock. It didn't matter whether her brain continued to flash on the way down, or if she regretted what she'd done, or if she had time to focus on the fence spikes shooting toward her. Her mind no longer existed in any way that mattered. The wind sound huffed, once, and then the moist thud jolted us, the sound of a watermelon breaking open, and for that moment everyone remained still and composed, as though listening to an orchestra, heads tilted to allow the ears to work and no belief coming in yet. Then Mrs. Lisbon, as though alone, said, "Oh, my God."

Mr. Lisbon ran upstairs. Mrs. Lisbon ran to the top and stood holding the banister. In the stairwell we could see her silhouette, the thick legs, the great sloping back, the big head stilled with panic, the eyeglasses jutting into space and filled with light. She took up most of the stairs and we were hesitant to go around her until the Lisbon girls did. Then we squeezed by. We reached the kitchen. Through a side window we could see Mr. Lisbon standing in the shrubbery. When we came out the front door we saw that he was holding Cecilia, one hand under her neck and the other under her knees. He was trying to lift her off the spike that had punctured her left breast, traveled through her inexplicable heart, separated two vertebrae without shattering either, and come out her back, ripping the dress and finding the air again. The spike had gone through so fast there was no blood on it. It was perfectly clean and Cecilia merely seemed balanced on the pole like a gymnast. The fluttering wedding dress added to this circusy effect. Mr. Lisbon kept trying to lift her off, gently, but even in our ignorance we knew it was hopeless and that despite Cecilia's open eyes and the way her mouth kept contracting like that of a fish on a stringer it was just nerves and she had succeeded, on the second try, in hurling herself out of the world.

# TWO

We didn't understand why Cecilia had killed herself the first time and we understood even less when she did it twice. Her diary, which the police inspected as part of the customary investigation, didn't confirm the supposition of unrequited love. Dominic Palazzolo was mentioned only once in that tiny rice-paper journal illuminated with colored Magic Markers to look like a Book of Hours or a medieval Bible. Miniature designs crowded the pages. Bubblegum angels swooped from top margins, or scraped their wings between teeming paragraphs. Maidens with golden hair dripped sea-blue tears into the book's spine. Grape-colored whales spouted blood around a newspaper item (pasted in) listing arrivals to the endangered species list. Six hatchlings cried from shattered shells near an entry made on Easter. Cecilia had filled the pages with a profusion of colors and curlicues, Candyland ladders and striped shamrocks, but the entry about Dominic read,

"Palazzolo jumped off the roof today over that rich bitch, Porter. How stupid can you be?"

The paramedics came back again, the same two, though it took us a while to recognize them. Out of fear and politeness we had moved across the street to sit on the hood of Mr. Larson's Oldsmobile. As we made our exit, none of us had said a word except for Valentine Stamarowski, who called across the lawn, "Thank you for the party, Mr. and Mrs. Lisbon." Mr. Lisbon was still sunk in bushes up to his waist, his back jerking as though he were trying to pull Cecilia up and off, or as though he were sobbing. On the porch Mrs. Lisbon made the other girls face the house. The sprinkler system, timed to go on at 8:15 P.M., spurted into life just as the EMS truck appeared at the end of the block, moving at about fifteen miles an hour, without flashing lights or siren, as though the paramedics already knew it was hopeless. The skinny one with the mustache climbed out first, then the fat one. They got the stretcher immediately, instead of first checking on the victim, a lapse which we later learned from medical professionals violated procedure. We didn't know who had called the paramedics or how they knew they were no more than undertakers that day. Tom Faheem said Therese had gone inside and called, but the rest of us remember the remaining four Lisbon girls immobile on the porch until after the EMS truck arrived. No one else on our street was aware of what had happened. The identical lawns down the block were empty. Someone was barbecuing somewhere. Behind Joe Larson's house we could hear a birdie being batted back and forth, endlessly, by the two greatest badminton players in the world.

The paramedics moved Mr. Lisbon aside so they could examine Cecilia. They found no pulse, but went ahead trying to save her anyway. The fat one hacksawed the fence stake while the skinny one got ready to catch her, because it was more dangerous to pull Cecilia off the barbed end than to leave it piercing her. When the stake snapped loose, the skinny one fell back under Cecilia's released weight. Then he regained his footing, pivoted, and slipped her onto the stretcher. As they carried her away, the sawed-off stake lifted the sheet like a tent post.

By this time it was nearly nine o'clock. From the roof of Chase Buell's house where we congregated after getting out of our dress-up clothes to watch what would happen next, we could see, over the heaps of trees throwing themselves into the air, the abrupt demarcation where the trees ended and the city began. The sun was falling in the haze of distant factories, and in the adjoining slums the scatter of glass picked up the raw glow of the smoggy sunset. Sounds we usually couldn't hear reached us now that we were up high, and crouching on the tarred shingles, resting chins in hands, we made out, faintly, an indecipherable backward-playing tape of city life, cries and shouts, the barking of a chained dog, car horns, the voices of girls calling out numbers in an obscure tenacious game—sounds of the impoverished city we never visited, all mixed and muted, without sense, carried on a wind from that place. Then: darkness. Car lights moving in the distance. Up close, yellow house lights coming on, revealing families around televisions. One by one, we all went home.

There had never been a funeral in our town before, at least not during our lifetimes. The majority of dying had happened during the Second World War when we didn't exist and our fathers were impossibly skinny young men in black-and-white photographs—dads on jungle airstrips, dads with pimples and tattoos, dads with pinups, dads who wrote love letters to the girls who would become our mothers, dads inspired by K rations, loneliness and glandular riot in malarial air into poetic reveries that ceased entirely once they got back home. Now our dads were middle-aged, with paunches, and shins rubbed hairless from years of wearing pants, but they were still a long way from death. Their own parents, who spoke foreign languages and lived in converted attics like buzzards, had the finest medical care available and were threatening to live on until the next century. Nobody's grandfather had died, nobody's grandmother, nobody's parents, only a few dogs: Tom Burke's beagle, Muffin, who choked on Bazooka Joe bubble gum, and then that summer, a creature who in dog years was still a puppy—Cecilia Lisbon.

The cemetery workers' strike hit its sixth week the day she died. Nobody had given much thought to the strike, nor to the cemetery workers' grievances, because most of us had never been to a cemetery. Occasionally we heard gunshots coming from the ghetto, but our fathers insisted it was only cars backfiring. Therefore, when the newspapers reported that burials in the city had completely stopped, we didn't think it affected us. Likewise, Mr. and Mrs. Lisbon, only in their forties, with a crop of young daughters, had given little thought to the strike, until those same daughters began killing themselves.

Funerals continued, but without the consummation of burial. Caskets were carted out beside undug plots; priests performed eulogies; tears were shed; after which the caskets were taken back to the deep freeze of the mortuary to await a settlement. Cremation enjoyed a rise in popularity. Mrs. Lisbon, however, objected to this idea, fearing it was heathen, and even pointed to a biblical passage that suggested the dead will rise bodily at the Second Coming, no ashes allowed.

Only one cemetery existed in our suburb, a drowsy field owned by various denominations over the years, from Lutheran through Episcopalian to Catholic. It contained three French Canadian fur trappers, a line of bakers named Kropp, and J. B. Milbank, who invented a local soft drink resembling root beer. With its leaning headstones, its red gravel drive in the shape of a horseshoe, and its many trees nourished by well-fed carcasses, the cemetery had filled up long ago in the time of the last deaths. Because of this, the funeral director, Mr. Alton, was forced to take Mr. Lisbon on a tour of possible alternatives.

He remembered the trip well. The days of the cemetery strike weren't easily forgotten, but Mr. Alton also confessed, "It was my first suicide. A young kid, too. You couldn't use the same sort of condolences. I was kind of sweating it out, to tell you the truth." On the West Side they visited a quiet cemetery in the Palestinian section, but Mr. Lisbon didn't like the foreign sound of the muezzin calling the people to prayer, and had heard that the neighbors still ritually slaughtered goats in their bathtubs. "Not here," he said, "not here." Next they toured a small Catholic cemetery that looked perfect, until, coming to the back, Mr. Lisbon saw two miles of leveled land that reminded him of photographs of Hiroshima. "It was Poletown," Mr. Alton told us. "GM bought out like twenty-five thousand Polacks to build this huge automotive plant. They knocked down twenty-four city blocks, then ran out of money. So the place was all rubble and weeds. It was desolate, sure, but only if you were looking out the back fence." Finally they arrived at a public nondenominational cemetery located between two freeways, and it was here that Cecilia Lisbon was given all the final funerary rites of the Catholic Church except interment. Officially, Cecilia's death was listed in church records as an "accident," as were the other girls' a year later. When we asked Father Moody about this, he said, "We didn't want to quibble. How do you know she didn't slip?" When we brought up the sleeping pills, and the noose, and the rest of it, he said, "Suicide, as a mortal sin, is a matter of intent. It's very difficult to know what was in those girls' hearts. What they were really trying to do."

Most of our parents attended the funeral, leaving us home to protect us from the contamination of tragedy. They all agreed the cemetery was the flattest they had ever

seen. There were no headstones or monuments, only granite tablets sunk into the earth, and, on V.F.W. graves, plastic American flags abused by rain, or wire garlands holding
dead flowers. The hearse had trouble getting through the
gate because of the picketing, but when the strikers
learned the deceased's age, they parted, and even lowered
their angry placards. Inside, neglect resulting from the
strike was obvious. Dirt was piled around some graves. A
digging machine stood frozen with its jaws piercing the
sod, as though the union's call had come in the middle of
burying someone. Family members acting as caretakers
had made touching attempts to spruce up loved ones' final
resting places. Excessive fertilizer had scorched one plot a
blazing yellow. Excessive watering had turned another into
a marsh. Because water had to be carried in by hand (the
sprinkler system had been sabotaged), a trail of deep footprints from grave to grave made it appear the dead were
walking around at night.

The grass hadn't been cut in nearly seven weeks. Mourn-
ers stood ankle-deep as the pallbearers carried out the coffin. Because of the low teenage mortality rate, mortuary
suppliers built few caskets to their middling size. They
manufactured a small quantity of infant caskets, little bigger than bread boxes. The next size up was full-size, more
than Cecilia required. When they had opened her casket
at the Funeral Home, all anyone had seen was the satin pillow and the ruffled cushioning of the casket's lid. Mrs.
Turner said, "For a minute I thought the thing was empty."
But then, making only a shallow imprint because of her

eighty-six pounds, pale skin and hair blending with white satin, Cecilia emerged from the background like a figure in an optical illusion. She was dressed not in the wedding gown, which Mrs. Lisbon had thrown away, but in a beige dress with a lace collar, a Christmas gift from her grandmother which she had refused to wear in life. The open section of lid revealed not only her face and shoulders, but her hands with their bitten nails, her rough elbows, the twin prongs of her hips, and even her knees.

Only the family filed past the coffin. First the girls walked past, each dazed and expressionless, and, later, people said we should have known by their faces. "It was like they were giving her a wink," Mrs. Carruthers said. "They should have been bawling, but what did they do? Up to the coffin, peek in, and away. Why didn't we see it?" Curt Van Osdol, the only kid at the Funeral Home, said he would have copped a last feel, right there in front of the priest and everybody, if only we had been there to appreciate it. After the girls passed by, Mrs. Lisbon, on her husband's arm, took ten stricken steps to dangle her weak head over Cecilia's face, rouged for the first and last time ever. "Look at her nails," Mr. Burton thought he heard her say. "Couldn't they do something about her nails?"

And then Mr. Lisbon replied: "They'll grow out. Fingernails keep growing. She can't bite them now, dear."

Our own knowledge of Cecilia kept growing after her death, too, with the same unnatural persistence. Though she had spoken only rarely and had had no real friends, everybody possessed his own vivid memories of Cecilia. Some of us had held her for five minutes as a baby while Mrs. Lisbon ran back into the house to get her purse. Some of us had played in the sandbox with her, fighting over a shovel, or had exposed ourselves to her behind the mulberry tree that grew like deformed flesh through the chain-link fence. We had stood in line with her for smallpox vaccinations, had held polio sugar cubes under our tongues with her, had taught her to jump rope, to light snakes, had stopped her from picking her scabs on numerous occasions, and had cautioned her against touching her mouth to the drinking fountain at Three Mile Park. A few of us had fallen in love with her, but had kept it to ourselves, knowing that she was the weird sister.

Cecilia's bedroom—when we finally obtained a description from Lucy Brock—confirmed this assessment of her character. In addition to a zodiac mobile, Lucy found a collection of potent amethysts, as well as a pack of Tarot cards under Cecilia's pillow that still smelled of her incense and hair. Lucy checked—because we asked her to—to see if the sheets had been cleaned, but she said they hadn't. The room had been left intact as an exhibit. The window from which Cecilia jumped was still open. In the top bureau drawer, Lucy found seven pairs of underpants, each dyed black with Rit. She also found two pairs of immaculate high-tops in the closet. Neither of these things surprised us. We had long known about Cecilia's black underwear because whenever she'd stood up on her bicycle pedals to gain speed we had looked up her dress. We'd also often seen her on the back steps, scrubbing her high-tops with a toothbrush and cup of Ivory Liquid.

Cecilia's diary begins a year and a half before her suicide. Many people felt the illuminated pages constituted a hieroglyphics of unreadable despair, though the pictures looked cheerful for the most part. The diary had a lock, but David Barker, who got it from Skip Ortega, the plumber's assistant, told us that Skip had found the diary next to the toilet in the master bathroom, its lock already jimmied as though Mr. and Mrs. Lisbon had been reading it themselves. Tim Winer, the brain, insisted on examining the diary. We carried it to the study his parents had built for him, with its green desk lamps, contour globe, and gilt-edged encyclopedias. "Emotional instability," he said, analyzing the handwriting. "Look at the dots on these *i*'s. All over the place." And then, leaning forward, showing the blue veins beneath his weakling's skin, he added: "Basically, what we have here is a dreamer. Somebody out of touch with reality. When she jumped, she probably thought she'd fly."

We know portions of the diary by heart now. After we got it up to Chase Buell's attic, we read portions out loud. We passed the diary around, fingering pages and looking anxiously for our names. Gradually, however, we learned that although Cecilia had stared at everybody all the time, she hadn't thought about any of us. Nor did she think about herself. The diary is an unusual document of adolescence in that it rarely depicts the emergence of an unformed ego. The standard insecurities, laments, crushes, and daydreams are nowhere in evidence. Instead, Cecilia writes of her sisters and herself as a single entity. It's often difficult to identify which sister she's talking about, and many strange sentences conjure in the reader's mind an image of a mythical creature with ten legs and five heads, lying in bed eating junk food, or suffering visits from affectionate aunts. Most of the diary told us more about how the girls came to be than why they killed themselves. We got tired of hearing about what they ate ("Monday, February 13. Today we had frozen pizza . . ."), or what they wore, or which colors they favored. They all detested creamed corn. Mary had chipped her tooth on the monkey bars and had a cap. ("I *told* you," Kevin Head said, reading that.) And so we learned about their lives, came to hold collective memories of times we hadn't experienced, harbored private images of Lux leaning over the side of a ship to stroke her first whale, and saying, "I didn't think they would stink so much," while Therese answered, "It's the kelp in their baleens rotting." We became acquainted with starry skies the girls had gazed at while camping years before, and the boredom of summers traipsing from backyard to front to back again, and even a certain indefinable smell that arose from toilets on rainy nights, which the girls called "sewery." We knew what it felt like to see a boy with his shirt off, and why it made Lux write the name Kevin in purple Magic Marker all over her three-ring binder and even on her bras and panties, and we understood her rage coming home one day to find that Mrs. Lisbon had soaked her things in Clorox, bleaching all the

"Kevins" out. We knew the pain of winter wind rushing up your skirt, and the ache of keeping your knees together in class, and how drab and infuriating it was to jump rope while the boys played baseball. We could never understand why the girls cared so much about being mature, or why they felt compelled to compliment each other, but sometimes, after one of us had read a long portion of the diary out loud, we had to fight back the urge to hug one another or to tell each other how pretty we were. We felt the imprisonment of being a girl, the way it made your mind active and dreamy, and how you ended up knowing which colors went together. We knew that the girls were our twins, that we all existed in space like animals with identical skins, and that they knew everything about us though we couldn't fathom them at all. We knew, finally, that the girls were really women in disguise, that they understood love and even death, and that our job was merely to create the noise that seemed to fascinate them.

As the diary progresses, Cecilia begins to recede from her sisters and, in fact, from personal narrative of any kind. The first person singular ceases almost entirely, the effect akin to a camera's pulling away from the characters at the end of a movie, to show, in a series of dissolves, their house, street, city, country, and finally planet, which not only dwarfs but obliterates them. Her precocious prose turns to impersonal subjects, the commercial of the weeping Indian paddling his canoe along a polluted stream, or the body counts from the evening war. In its last third the diary shows two rotating moods. In romantic passages Cecilia despairs over the demise of our elm trees. In cynical entries she suggests the trees aren't sick at all, and that the deforesting is a plot "to make everything flat." Occasional references to this or that conspiracy theory crop up—the Illuminati, the Military-Industrial complex—but she only feints in that direction, as though the names are so many vague chemical pollutants. From invective she shifts without pause into her poetic reveries again. A couplet about summer from a poem she never finished is quite nice, we think:

> *The trees like lungs filling with air*
> *My sister, the mean one, pulling my hair*

The fragment is dated June 26, three days after she returned from the hospital, when we used to see her lying in the front-yard grass.

Little is known of Cecilia's state of mind on the last day of her life. According to Mr. Lisbon, she seemed pleased about her party. When he went downstairs to check on the preparations, he found Cecilia standing on a chair, tying balloons to the ceiling with red and blue ribbons. "I told her to get down. The doctor said she shouldn't hold her hands over her head. Because of the stitches." She did as commanded, and spent the rest of the day lying on the rug in her bedroom, staring up at her zodiac mobile and listening to the odd Celtic records she'd gotten through a mailorder house. "It was always some soprano singing about marshes and dead roses." The melancholic music alarmed Mr. Lisbon, comparing it as he did to the optimistic tunes of his own youth, but, passing down the hall, he realized that it was certainly no worse than Lux's howling rock music or even the inhuman screech of Therese's ham radio.

From two in the afternoon on, Cecilia soaked in the bathtub. It wasn't unusual for her to take marathon baths, but after what had happened the last time, Mr. and Mrs. Lisbon took no chances. "We made her leave the door open a crack," Mrs. Lisbon said. "She didn't like it, of course. And now she had new ammunition. That psychiatrist had said Ceel was at the age where she needed a lot of privacy." Throughout the afternoon, Mr. Lisbon kept coming up with excuses to pass by the bathroom. "I'd wait to hear a splash, then I'd go on past. We'd taken everything sharp out of there, of course."

At four-thirty, Mrs. Lisbon sent Lux up to check on Cecilia. When she came back downstairs, she seemed unconcerned, and nothing about her demeanor suggested she had an inkling about what her sister would do later that day. "She's fine," Lux said. "She's stinking up the place with those bath salts."

At five-thirty, Cecilia got out of the bath and dressed for the party. Mrs. Lisbon heard her going back and forth between her sisters' two bedrooms (Bonnie shared with Mary, Therese with Lux). The rattling of her bracelets comforted her parents because it allowed them to keep track of her movements like an animal with a bell on its collar. From time to time during the hours before we arrived, Mr. Lisbon heard the tinkling of Cecilia's bracelets as she went up and down the stairs, trying on different shoes.

According to what they told us later on separate occasions and in separate states, Mr. and Mrs. Lisbon didn't find Cecilia's behavior strange during the party. "She was always quiet with company," Mrs. Lisbon said. And perhaps because of their lack of socializing, Mr. and Mrs. Lisbon remembered the party as a successful event. Mrs. Lisbon, in fact, was surprised when Cecilia asked to be excused. "I thought she was having a nice time." Even at this point, the other girls didn't act as though they knew what was about to happen. Tom Faheem recalls Mary telling him about a jumper she wanted to buy at Penney's. Therese and Tim Winer discussed their anxiety over getting into an Ivy League college.

From clues later discovered, it appears Cecilia's ascent to her bedroom was not as quick as we remember it. She took time, for instance, between leaving us and reaching the upstairs to drink juice from a can of pears (she left the can on the counter, punctured with only one hole in disregard of Mrs. Lisbon's prescribed method). Either before or after drinking the juice, she went to the back door. "I thought they were sending her on a trip," Mrs. Pitzenberger said. "She was carrying a suitcase."

No suitcase was ever found. We can only explain Mrs. Pitzenberger's testimony as the hallucination of a bifocal wearer, or a prophecy of the later suicides where luggage played such a central motif. Whatever the truth, Mrs.

Pitzenberger saw Cecilia close the back door, and it was only seconds later that she climbed the stairs, as we so distinctly heard from below. She flipped on the lights in her bedroom as she entered, though it was still light out. Across the street, Mr. Buell saw her open her bedroom window. "I waved to her, but she didn't see me," he told us. Just then his wife groaned from the other room. He didn't hear about Cecilia until after the EMS truck had come and gone. "Unfortunately, we had problems of our own," he said. He went to check on his sick spouse just as Cecilia stuck her head out the window, into the pink, humid, pillowing air.

# THREE

Flower arrangements arrived at the Lisbon house later than was customary. Because of the nature of the death, most people decided not to send flowers to the Funeral Home, and in general everybody put off placing their orders, unsure whether to let the catastrophe pass in silence or to act as though the death were natural. In the end, however, everybody sent something, white roses in wreaths, clusters of orchids, weeping peonies. Peter Loomis, who delivered for FTD, said flowers crammed the Lisbons' entire living room. Bouquets exploded from chairs and lay scattered across the floor. "They didn't even put them in vases," he said. Most people opted for generic cards that said "With Sympathy" or "Our Condolences," but some of the Waspier types, accustomed to writing notes for all occasions, labored over personal responses. Mrs. Beards used a quote from Walt Whitman we took to murmuring to one another: "All goes onward and outward, nothing collapses, / and to die is different from what any one supposed, and luckier." Chase Buell peeked at his own mother's card as he slipped it under the Lisbons' door. It read: "I don't know what you're feeling. I won't even pretend."

A few people braved personal calls. Mr. Hutch and Mr. Peters walked over to the Lisbon house on separate occasions, but their reports differed little. Mr. Lisbon invited them in, but before they could broach the painful subject, he sat them down in front of the baseball game. "He kept talking about the bullpen," Mr. Hutch said. "Hell, I pitched in college. I had to straighten him out on a few essentials. First of all, he wanted to trade Miller, though he was our only decent closer. I forgot what I'd gone over there to do." Mr. Peters said, "The guy was only half there. He kept turning the tint control up, so that the infield was practically blue. Then he'd sit back down. Then he'd get up again. One of the girls came in—can you tell them apart?—and brought us a couple beers. Took a swig from his before handing it over."

Neither of the men mentioned the suicide. "I wanted to, I really did," said Mr. Hutch. "I just never got around to it."

Father Moody showed more perseverance. Mr. Lisbon welcomed the cleric as he had the other men, ushering him to a seat before the baseball game. A few minutes later, as though on cue, Mary served beers. But Father Moody wasn't deflected. During the second inning, he said, "How about we get the Mrs. down here? Have a little chat."

Mr. Lisbon hunched toward the screen. "Afraid she's not seeing anybody right now. Under the weather."

"She'll see her priest," Father Moody said.

He stood up to go. Mr. Lisbon held up two fingers. His eyes were watering. "Father," he said. "Double-play ball, Father."

Paolo Conelli, an altar boy, overheard Father Moody tell Fred Simpson, the choirmaster, how he had left "that strange man, God forgive me for saying so, but He made him that way," and climbed the front stairs. Already the house showed signs of uncleanliness, though they were nothing compared to what was to come later. Dust balls lined the steps. A half-eaten sandwich sat atop the landing where someone had felt too sad to finish it. Because Mrs. Lisbon had stopped doing laundry or even buying detergent, the girls had taken to washing clothes by hand in the bathtub, and when Father Moody passed their bathroom, he saw shirts and pants and underthings draped over the shower curtain. "It sounded quite pleasant, actually," he said. "Like rain." Steam rose from the floor, along with the smell of jasmine soap (weeks later, we asked the cosmetics lady at Jacobsen's for some jasmine soap *we* could smell). Father Moody stood outside the bathroom, too bashful to enter that moist cave that existed as a common room between the girls' two shared bedrooms. Inside, if he hadn't been a priest and had looked, he would have seen the throne-like toilet where the Lisbon girls defecated publicly, the bathtub they used as a couch, filling it with pillows so that two sisters could luxuriate while another curled her hair. He would have seen the radiator stacked with glasses and Coke cans, the clamshell soap dish employed, in a pinch, as an ashtray. From the age of twelve Lux spent hours in the john smoking cigarettes, exhaling either out the window or into a wet towel she then hung outside. But Father Moody saw none of this. He only passed through the tropical air current and that was all. Behind him he felt the colder drafts of the house, circulating dust motes and that particular family smell every house had, you knew it when you came in—Chase Buell's house smelled like skin, Joe Larson's like mayonnaise, the Lisbons' like stale popcorn, we thought, though Father Moody, going there after the deaths had begun, said, "It was a mix between a funeral parlor and broom closet. All those flowers. All that dust." He wanted to step back into the current of jasmine, but as he stood, listening to rain beading bathroom tiles and washing away the girls' footprints, he heard voices. He made a quick circuit of the hallway, calling out for Mrs. Lisbon, but she didn't respond. Returning to the top of the stairs, he had started down when he saw the Lisbon girls through a partly open doorway.

"At that point, those girls had no intention of repeating Cecilia's mistake. I know everyone thinks it was a plan, or that we handled it poorly, but they were just as shocked as I was." Father Moody rapped softly on the door and asked for permission to enter. "They were sitting on the floor together, and I could tell they'd been crying. I think they were having some kind of slumber party. They had pillows all over. I hate to mention it, and I remember scolding myself for even thinking it at the time, but it was unmistakable: they hadn't bathed."

We asked Father Moody whether he had discussed Cecilia's death or the girls' grief, but he said he hadn't. "I brought it up a few times, but they didn't take up the subject. I've learned you can't force it. The time has to be right and the heart willing." When we asked him to sum up his impression of the girls' emotional state at that point, he said, "Buffeted but not broken."

In the first few days after the funeral, our interest in the Lisbon girls only increased. Added to their loveliness was a new mysterious suffering, perfectly silent, visible in the blue puffiness beneath their eyes or the way they would sometimes stop in midstride, look down, and shake their heads as though disagreeing with life. Grief made them wander. We heard reports of the girls walking aimlessly through Eastland, down the lighted mall with its timid fountains and hot dogs impaled beneath heat lamps. Now and then they fingered a blouse, or dress, but bought nothing. Woody Clabault saw Lux Lisbon talking to a motorcycle gang outside Hudson's. One biker asked her to go for a ride, and after looking in the direction of her house more than ten miles away, she accepted. She hugged his waist. He kicked the machine into life. Later, Lux was seen walking home alone, carrying her shoes.

In the Kriegers' basement, we lay on a strip of leftover carpeting and dreamed of all the ways we could soothe the

Lisbon girls. Some of us wanted to lie down in the grass with them, or play the guitar and sing them songs. Paul Baldino wanted to take them to Metro Beach so they could all get a tan. Chase Buell, more and more under the sway of his father the Christian Scientist, said only that the girls needed "help not of this world." But when we asked him what he meant, he shrugged and said, "Nothing." Nevertheless, when the girls walked by, we often found him crouching by a tree, moving his lips with his eyes closed.

Not everyone thought about the girls, however. Even before Cecilia's funeral, some people could talk of nothing but the dangerousness of the fence she'd jumped on. "It was an accident waiting to happen," said Mr. Frank, who worked in insurance. "You couldn't get a policy to cover it."

"Our kids could jump on it, too," Mrs. Zaretti insisted during coffee hour following Sunday Mass. Not long after, a group of fathers began digging the fence out free of charge. It turned out the fence stood on the Bateses' property. Mr. Buck, a lawyer, negotiated with Mr. Bates about the fence's removal and didn't speak to Mr. Lisbon at all. Everyone assumed, of course, that the Lisbons would be grateful.

We had rarely seen our fathers in work boots before, toiling in the earth and wielding brand-new root clippers. They struggled with the fence, bent over like Marines hoisting the flag on Iwo Jima. It was the greatest show of common effort we could remember in our neighborhood, all those lawyers, doctors, and mortgage bankers locked arm in arm in the trench, with our mothers bringing out orange Kool-Aid, and for a moment our century was noble again. Even the sparrows on the telephone lines seemed to be watching. No cars passed. The industrial fog of our city made the men resemble figures hammered into pewter, but by late afternoon they still couldn't uproot the fence. Mr. Hutch got the idea of hacksawing the bars as the paramedics had, and for a while the men took turns sawing, but their paper-pushing arms gave out quickly. Finally they tied the fence to the back of Uncle Tucker's four-wheel-drive Bronco. Nobody cared that Uncle Tucker didn't have a license (driving examiners always smelled booze on him, even if he quit drinking three days before the test they still smelled it evaporating from his pores). Our fathers just cried, "Hit it!" and Uncle Tucker floored his accelerator, but the fence didn't budge. By midafternoon they abandoned the effort and took up a collection to hire a professional hauling service. An hour later, a lone man showed up in a tow truck, attached a hook to the fence, pressed a button to make his giant winch revolve, and with a deep earth sound, the murdering fence came loose. "You can see blood," Anthony Turkis said, and we looked to see if the blood that hadn't been there at the time of the suicide had arrived after the fact. Some said it was on the third spike, some said the fourth, but it was as impossible as finding the bloody shovel on the back of *Abbey Road* where all the clues proclaimed that Paul was dead.

None of the Lisbons helped with the fence removal. From time to time, however, we saw their faces blinking at the windows. Just after the truck pulled the fence free, Mr. Lisbon himself came out the side door and coiled up a garden hose. He didn't move to the trench. He raised one hand in a neighborly salute and returned inside. The man lashed the fence, in sections, to his truck and—getting paid for it—gave Mr. Bates the worst lawn job we'd ever seen. We were amazed our parents permitted this, when lawn jobs usually justified calling the cops. But now Mr. Bates didn't scream or try to get the truck's license plate, nor did Mrs. Bates, who had once wept when we set off firecrackers in her state-fair tulips—they said nothing, and our parents said nothing, so that we sensed how ancient they were, how accustomed to trauma, depressions, and wars. We realized that the version of the world they rendered for us was not the world they really believed in, and that for all their caretaking and bitching about crabgrass they didn't give a damn about lawns.

After the truck drove away, our fathers gathered around the hole once more, staring down at wriggling earthworms, kitchen spoons, the one rock Paul Little swore was an Indian arrowhead. They leaned on shovels, mopping brows, even though they hadn't done anything. Everyone felt a lot better, as though the lake had been cleaned up, or the air, or the other side's bombs destroyed. There wasn't much you could do to save us, but at least the fence was gone. Despite the devastation of his lawn, Mr. Bates did some edging, and the old German couple appeared in their grape arbor to drink dessert wine. As usual they wore their

Alpine hats, Mr. Hessen's with a tiny green feather, while their schnauzer sniffed at the end of his leash. Grapes burst above their heads. Mrs. Hessen's humped back dove and surfaced amid her swelling rosebushes as she sprayed.

At some point, we looked up into the sky to see that all the fish flies had died. The air was no longer brown but blue. Using kitchen brooms, we swept bugs from poles and windows and electrical lines. We stuffed them into bags, thousands upon thousands of insect bodies with wings of raw silk, and Tim Winer, the brain, pointed out how the fish flies' tails resembled those of lobsters. "They're smaller," he said, "but possess the same basic design. Lobsters are classified in the phylum *Arthropoda*, same as insects. They're bugs. And bugs are only lobsters that have learned to fly."

No one ever understood what got into us that year, or why we hated so intensely the crust of dead bugs over our lives. Suddenly, however, we couldn't bear the fish flies carpeting our swimming pools, filling our mailboxes, blotting out stars on our flags. The collective action of digging the trench led to cooperative sweeping, bag-carting, patio-hosing. A score of brooms kept time in all directions as the pale ghosts of fish flies dropped from walls like ash. We examined their tiny wizards' faces, rubbing them between our fingers until they gave off the scent of carp. We tried to light them but they wouldn't burn (which made the fish flies seem deader than anything). We hit bushes, beat rugs, turned on windshield wipers full blast. Fish flies clogged sewer grates so that we had to stuff them down with sticks.

Crouching over sewers, we could hear the river under the city flowing away. We dropped rocks and listened for the splash.

We didn't stop with our own houses. Once our walls were clean, Mr. Buell told Chase to start cleaning bugs off the Lisbon house. Because of his religious beliefs, Mr. Buell often went the extra mile, raking ten feet into the Hessens' yard, or shoveling their walk and even throwing down rock salt. It wasn't odd for him to tell Chase to start sweeping the Lisbons' house, even though they lived across the street and not next door. Because Mr. Lisbon only had daughters, boys and men had gone over in the past to help him drag away lightning-struck limbs, and as Chase approached, holding his broom over his head like a regimental banner, nobody said a word. Then, however, Mr. Krieger told Kyle to go over and sweep some, and Mr. Hutch sent Ralph, and soon we were all over at the Lisbon house, brushing walls and scraping away bug husks. They had even more than we did, the walls an inch thick, and Paul Baldino asked us the riddle, "What smells like fish, is fun to eat, but isn't fish?"

Once we got to the Lisbons' windows, our new inexplicable feelings for the girls came to the fore. As we slapped off bugs, we saw Mary Lisbon in the kitchen, holding a box of Kraft Macaroni & Cheese. She appeared to be contemplating whether or not to open it. She read the directions, turned the box over to look at the vivid picture of the noodles, and then put the box back on the counter. Anthony Turkis, pressing his face to the window, said,

"She should eat something." She picked up the box again. Hopefully, we watched. But then she turned and disappeared.

Outside it grew dark. Lights came on down the block, but not in the Lisbon house. We couldn't see in any better, and in fact the glass panes began to reflect our own gaping faces. It was only nine o'clock, but everything confirmed what people had been saying: that since Cecilia's suicide the Lisbons could hardly wait for night to forget themselves in sleep. Up in a bedroom window, Bonnie's three votive candles glimmered in a reddish haze, but otherwise the house absorbed the shadows of night. Insects started up in their hiding places all around, vibrating the minute we turned our backs. Everyone called them crickets, but we never found any in the sprayed bushes or aerated lawns, and had no idea what they looked like. They were merely sound. Our parents had been more intimate with crickets. For them the buzzing apparently didn't sound mechanical. It came from every direction, always from a height just above our heads, or just below, and always with the suggestion that the insect world felt more than we did. As we stood charmed into stillness, listening to the crickets, Mr. Lisbon came out the side door and thanked us. His hair looked even grayer than usual, but grief hadn't altered the highness of his voice. He had on overalls, one knee covered by sawdust. "Feel free to use the hose," he said, and then he looked at the Good Humor truck passing by, the jingle of the bell seemed to trigger a memory, he smiled, or winced—we couldn't tell which—and returned inside.

We went with him only later, invisibly, with the ghosts of our questions. Apparently, as he stepped back inside, he saw Therese come out of the dining room. She was stuffing her mouth with candy—M&M's, by the colors—but stopped immediately on seeing him. She swallowed an unchewed chunk. Her high forehead glowed in the light from the street and her cupid's lips were redder, smaller, and more shapely than he remembered, especially in contrast to her cheeks and chin, which had gained weight. Her eyelashes were crusted, as though recently glued shut. At that moment Mr. Lisbon had the feeling that he didn't know who she was, that children were only strangers you agreed to live with, and he reached out in order to meet her for the first time. He rested his hands on her shoulders, then dropped them to his sides. Therese brushed the hair out of her face, smiled, and began walking slowly up the stairs.

Mr. Lisbon went on his usual nighttime rounds, checking to see that the front door was locked (it wasn't), that the garage light was off (it was), and that none of the burners on the stove had been left on (none had). He turned off the light in the first-floor bathroom, where he found Kyle Krieger's retainer in the sink, left from when he'd taken it out during the party to eat cake. Mr. Lisbon ran the retainer under water, examining the pink shell form-fitted to the roof of Kyle's mouth, the crenellations in the plastic that encircled the turret of his teeth, the looping front wire bent at key spots (you could see plier marks) to provide modulated pressure. Mr. Lisbon knew his parental and neighborly duty entailed putting the retainer in a Ziploc bag, calling the Kriegers, and telling them their expensive orthodontal device was in safe keeping. Acts like these—simple, humane, conscientious, forgiving—held life together. Only a few days earlier he would have been able to perform them. But now he took the retainer and dropped it in the toilet. He pressed the handle. The retainer, jostled in the surge, disappeared down the porcelain throat, and, when waters abated, floated triumphantly, mockingly, out. Mr. Lisbon waited for the tank to refill and flushed again, but the same thing happened. The replica of the boy's mouth clung to the white slope.

At that point something flashed in the corner of his eye. "I thought I saw somebody, but when I looked, there was nothing there." Nor did he see anything as he came around the back hall into the foyer and up the front stairs. On the second floor he listened at the girls' doors, but heard only Mary coughing in her sleep, Lux playing a radio softly, singing along. He stepped into the girls' bathroom. A beam of light from the risen moon penetrated the window, lighting up a portion of mirror. Amid smudged fingerprints, a small circle had been wiped clean where his daughters contemplated their images, and above the mirror itself Bonnie had taped a white construction-paper dove. Mr. Lisbon parted his lips in a grimace and saw in the clean circle the one dead canine tooth beginning to turn green on the left side of his mouth. The doors to the girls' shared bedrooms were not completely closed. Breathings and murmurings issued from them. He listened to the sounds as though they could tell him what the girls were feeling and how to comfort them. Lux switched her radio off, and everything was silent. "I couldn't go in," Mr. Lisbon confessed to us years later. "I didn't know what to say." Only as he left the bathroom, heading for the oblivion of sleep himself, did Mr. Lisbon see Cecilia's ghost. She was standing in her old bedroom, dressed in the wedding dress again, having somehow shed the beige dress with the lace collar she'd worn in her coffin. "The window was still open," Mr. Lisbon said. "I don't think we'd ever remembered to shut it. It was all clear to me. I knew I had to close that window or else she'd go on jumping out of it forever."

According to his story, he didn't cry out. He didn't want to make contact with the shade of his daughter, to learn why she had done herself in, to ask forgiveness, or to rebuke her. He merely rushed forward, brushing past, to close the window. As he did, however, the ghost turned, and he saw that it was only Bonnie, wrapped in a bedsheet. "Don't worry," she said, quietly. "They took the fence out."

In a handwritten note displaying the penmanship perfected during his graduate school days in Zurich, Dr. Hornicker called Mr. and Mrs. Lisbon in for a second consultation, but they didn't go. Instead, from what we observed during the remainder of the summer, Mrs. Lisbon once more took charge of the house while Mr. Lisbon receded into a mist. When we saw him after that, he had the sheepish look of a poor relation. By late August, in the weeks of preparation before school, he began leaving by the back door as though sneaking out. His car would whine inside the garage and, when the automatic door rose, would emerge tentatively, lopsided like an animal missing a leg. Through the windshield we could see Mr. Lisbon at the wheel, his hair still wet and his face sometimes dabbed with shaving cream, but he made no expression when the tailpipe hit the end of the driveway, sending up sparks, as it did every time. At six o'clock he returned home. As he came up the drive, the garage door shuddered to engulf him, and then we wouldn't see him until the next morning, when the clanging tailpipe announced his departure.

The only extensive contact with the girls occurred late in August, when Mary showed up without an appointment at Dr. Becker's orthodontal office. We talked to him years later, while dozens of plaster dental casts grinned crookedly down at us from glass cabinets. Each set of teeth bore the name of the unfortunate child who'd been made to swallow the cement, and the sight took us back to the medieval torture of our own orthodontal histories. Dr. Becker spoke for some time before we paid attention, for once again we could feel him hammering metal clasps over our molars, or stringing our upper and lower teeth together with rubber bands. Our tongues searched out pockets of scar tissue left by jutting back braces, and even fifteen years later the fissures still seemed sweet with blood. But Dr. Becker was saying, "I remember Mary because she came in without her parents. No kid had ever done that before. When I asked her what she wanted, she put two fingers in her mouth and pulled up her front lip. Then she said, 'How much?' She was worried her parents wouldn't be able to pay."

Dr. Becker declined to give Mary Lisbon an estimate. "Bring your mother in and we'll talk about it," he said. In fact, the process would have been extensive, as Mary, like her sisters, appeared to have two extra canine teeth. Disappointed, she lay back in the dentist's chair, her feet raised, while a silver tube chirred water into a sucking cup. "I had to leave her sitting in the chair," Dr. Becker said. "I had five other kids waiting. Later my nurse told me she heard the girl crying."

The girls didn't appear as a group until Convocation. On September 7, a day whose coolness dampened hopes for an Indian summer, Mary, Bonnie, Lux, and Therese came to school as though nothing had happened. Once again, despite their closed ranks, we could see the new differences among them, and we felt that if we kept looking hard enough we might begin to understand what they were feeling and who they were. Mrs. Lisbon hadn't taken the girls to buy new school clothes, so they wore last year's. Their prim dresses were too tight (despite everything, the girls had continued to develop) and they looked uncomfortable. Mary had spruced up her outfit with accessories: a bracelet bunch of wooden cherries the same bright red as her scarf. Lux's school tartan, too short by now, exposed her naked knees and an inch of thigh. Bonnie wore a tent-like something, with meandering trim. Therese had on a white dress that looked like a lab coat.

Nevertheless, the girls filed in with an unexpected dignity as a hush fell over the auditorium. Bonnie had picked a simple bouquet of late-season dandelions from the school green. She held them under Lux's chin to see if she liked butter. Their recent shock was undetectable, but sitting down they left a folding seat empty as though saving it for Cecilia.

The girls didn't miss a single day of classes, nor did Mr. Lisbon, who taught with his usual enthusiasm. He continued to pump students for answers by pretending to strangle them, and scratched out equations in a cloud of chalk dust. At lunchtime, however, rather than going to the teachers' lounge, he began to eat in his classroom, bringing a cafeteria apple and plate of cottage cheese back to his desk. He showed other odd behavior. We saw him walking along the Science Wing, conversing with spider plants hanging from the geodesic panes. After the first week, he taught from his swivel chair, wheeling back and forth to the blackboard and never standing up, explaining that this was because of his blood-sugar level. After school, as assistant soccer coach, he stood behind the goal, listlessly calling out the score, and when practice finished, wandered the chalk-dusted field, collecting soccer balls in a soiled canvas bag.

He drove to school alone, an hour earlier than his late-sleeping, bused-in daughters. Entering the main door, past the suit of armor (our athletic teams were called the Knights), he went straight into his classroom where the nine planets of our solar system hung from perforated ceiling panels (sixty-six holes in each square, according to Joe Hill Conley, who counted them during class). Nearly invisible white strings attached the planets to a track. Each day they rotated and revolved, the whole cosmos controlled by Mr. Lisbon, who consulted an astronomy chart and turned a crank next to the pencil sharpener. Beneath the planets hung black-and-white triangles, orange helices, blue cones with detachable noses. On his desk Mr. Lisbon displayed a Soma cube, solved for all time in a ribbon of Scotch tape. Beside the blackboard a wire clamp held five sticks of chalk so that he could draw sheet music for his male singing group. He had been a teacher so long he had a sink in his room.

The girls, on the other hand, entered through the side door, past the bed of dormant daffodils tended each spring by the headmaster's slim, industrious wife. Scattering to separate lockers, they reunited in the cafeteria during juice break. Julie Freeman had been Mary Lisbon's best friend, but after the suicide they stopped talking. "She was a neat kid, but I just couldn't deal with it. She sort of freaked me out. Also I was starting to go out with Todd by then." The sisters walked with poise down the halls, carrying books over their chests and staring at a fixed point in space we couldn't see. They were like Aeneas, who (as we translated him into existence amid the cloud of Dr. Timmerman's B.O.) had gone down to the underworld, seen the dead, and returned, weeping on the inside.

Who knew what they were thinking or feeling? Lux still giggled stupidly, Bonnie fingered the rosary deep in the pocket of her corduroy skirt, Mary wore her suits that made her resemble the First Lady, Therese kept her protective goggles on in the halls—but they receded from us, from the other girls, from their father, and we caught sight of them standing in the courtyard, under drizzle, taking bites from the same doughnut, looking up at the sky, letting themselves get slowly drenched.

We spoke to them in snatches, each of us adding a sentence to a communal conversation. Mike Orriyo was first. His locker was next to Mary's, and one day he peeked over its rim and said, "How's it going?" Her head was bent forward, throwing her hair over her face, and he wasn't sure she'd heard him until she mumbled, "Not bad." Without turning to meet his eyes, she slammed the metal locker shut and moved away, clutching her books. After a few steps she tugged down the back of her skirt.

The next day he waited for her and, when she opened her locker, added a new phrase: "I'm Mike." This time Mary said something distinct through her hair: "I know who you are. I've only been at this school for like my whole life." Mike Orriyo wanted to say something more, but when she finally turned to face him, he went mute. He stood staring at her, opening his mouth uselessly, until she said, "You don't have to talk to me."

Other guys were more successful. Chip Willard, the detention king, walked up to Lux as she was sitting in a pool of sunshine—it was one of the last warm days of the year—and while we watched from a second-story dormer, he sat down beside her. Lux was wearing her school tartan and white kneesocks. Her Top-Siders looked new. Before Willard had walked up, she'd been idly rubbing them in the dirt. Then she spread her legs out, propped her hands behind her back, and turned her face toward the last rays of the season. Willard moved into her sun and spoke. She brought her legs together, scratched one knee, and drew them apart. Willard settled his bulk on the soft ground. He leaned toward her, grinning, and even though he had never said anything intelligent within our hearing, he made Lux laugh. He seemed to know what he was doing, and we were astounded at the knowledge he had gained in the basements and bleachers of his delinquency. He crumpled a dead leaf over Lux's head. Bits fell down the back of her shirt and she hit him. The next thing we knew, they were walking together around back of the school, out past the tennis courts, through the row of memorial elms, and to the towering fence that marked the property of the mansions on the private drive beyond.

It wasn't only Willard. Paul Wanamaker, Kurt Siles, Peter McGuire, Tom Sellers, and Jim Czeslawski all had their few days of going steady with Lux. It was well known that Mr. and Mrs. Lisbon didn't allow their daughters to date, and that Mrs. Lisbon in particular disapproved of dances, proms, and the general expectation that teenagers should be allowed to paw one another in backseats. Lux's brief unions were clandestine. They sprouted in the dead time of study halls, bloomed on the way to the drinking fountain, and were consummated in the hot box above the auditorium, amid uncomfortable theatrical lights and cables. The boys met Lux in transit on sanctioned errands, in the aisle of the pharmacy while Mrs. Lisbon waited outside in the car, and once, in the most daring rendezvous, in the station wagon itself, for the fifteen minutes Mrs. Lisbon stood in line at the bank. But the boys who snuck off with Lux were always the stupidest boys, the most selfish and abused at home, and they made terrible sources of information. No matter what we asked, they responded with lewd assertions such as, "Squeezebox is all right. Let me tell you," or, "You want to know what happened? Smell my fingers, man." That Lux consented to meet them in the dells and thickets of our school grounds only showed too well her disequilibrium. We asked whether she spoke about Cecilia, but the boys always said they'd hadn't exactly been talking if you know what I mean.

The only reliable boy who got to know Lux during that time was Trip Fontaine, but his sense of honor kept us in the dark for years. Only eighteen months before the suicides, Trip Fontaine had emerged from baby fat to the delight of girls and women alike. Because we had known him as a pudgy boy whose teeth slanted out of his open, trolling mouth like those of a deep-sea fish, we had been slow to recognize his transformation. In addition, our fathers and older brothers, our decrepit uncles, had assured us that looks didn't matter if you were a boy. We weren't on the lookout for handsomeness appearing in our midst, and believed it counted for little until the girls we knew, along with their mothers, fell in love with Trip Fontaine. Their desire was silent yet magnificent, like a thousand daisies attuning their faces toward the path of the sun. At first we hardly noticed the wadded notes dropped through the grating of Trip's locker, nor the equatorial breezes pursuing him down the hall from so much heated blood; but finally, confronted with clusters of clever girls blushing at Trip's approach, or yanking their braids to keep from smiling too much, we realized that our fathers, brothers, and uncles had been lying, and that no one was ever going to love us because of our good grades. Years later, from the one-horse detoxification ranch where Trip Fontaine had gone to dry out on the last of his ex-wife's savings, he recalled the red-hot passions that had erupted at a time when he was growing his first chest hair. It began during a trip to Acapulco, when his father and his father's boyfriend went for a stroll on the beach, leaving Trip to fend for himself on the hotel grounds. (Exhibit #7, a snapshot taken during that trip, shows a bronzed Mr. Fontaine posing with Donald, the two of them squeezed thigh-to-thigh within the palmy Montezuma throne of a hotel patio chair.) At the no-drinking-age bar, Trip met Gina Desander, recently divorced, who ordered him his first piña colada. Always a gentleman, Trip Fontaine imparted to us upon his return only the most proper details of Gina Desander's life, that she was a dealer in Las Vegas and taught him to win at blackjack, that she wrote poetry and ate raw coconut with a Swiss Army knife. Only years later, looking over the desert with ruined eyes, his chivalry no longer able to protect a woman by that time in her fifties, did Trip confess that Gina Desander had been "my first lay."

It explained a lot. It explained why he never took off the puka-shell necklace she'd given him. It explained the travel poster over his bed showing a man soaring over Acapulco Bay on a kite pulled by a speedboat. It explained why he changed his manner of dress the year before the suicides, going from schoolboy shirts and pants to Western outfits, shirts with pearl buttons, decorative pocket flaps and shoulder stitching, every item chosen in order to resemble the Las Vegas men who stood arm in arm with Gina Desander in the wallet photographs she showed Trip during their seven-days-and-six-nights package tour together. At thirty-seven, Gina Desander had envisioned the hunk of masculinity latent in Trip Fontaine's chubby Speedoed form, and during her week with him in Mexico, she chiseled him into the shape of a man. We could only imagine what went on in her hotel room, with Trip drunk on spiked pineapple juice, watching Gina Desander deal rapid-fire in the middle of her stripped bed. The sliding door to the small concrete balcony had come off its track. Trip, being the man, had tried to fix it. The dressers and bedside tables were littered with the detritus of last night's room party—empty glasses, tropical swizzle sticks, washed-up orange rinds. With his vacation tan Trip must have looked much as he did in late summer, circulating in his swimming pool, his nipples like two pink cherries embedded in brown sugar. Gina Desander's reddish, slightly creased skin flamed in age like leaves. Ace of hearts. Ten of clubs. Twenty-one. You win. She stroked his hair, dealt again. He never told us any details, not even later, when we were all adult enough to understand. But we looked on it as a wonderful initiation by a merciful mother, and though it remained a secret, the night conveyed on Trip the mantle of a lover. When he returned we heard his new deep voice sounding a foot above our heads, apprehended without understanding the tight seat of his jeans, smelled his cologne and compared our own cheese-colored skin to his. But his musky scent, the coconut-oil smoothness of his face, the golden grains of intractable sand still glittering in his eyebrows didn't affect us as it did the girls who, one by one, and then in groups, swooned.

He received letters emblazoned with ten different sets of lips (the lines of each pucker distinct as a fingerprint). He stopped studying for tests because of all the girls who came over to cram with him in bed. He spent his time keeping up his tan, floating on an air mattress around his bathtub-size swimming pool. The girls were right in choosing to love Trip, because he was the only boy who could keep his mouth shut. By nature Trip Fontaine possessed the discretion of the world's great lovers, seducers greater than Casanova because they didn't leave behind twelve volumes of memoirs and we don't even know who they were. On the football field, or naked in the locker room, Trip Fontaine never spoke of the pieces of pie, carefully wrapped in tinfoil, that showed up inside his locker, nor of the hair ribbons gartered to his car antenna, nor even of the tennis sneaker dangling by one seamy lace from his rearview mirror, in the toe of which a sweaty note read, "The score is love: love. Your serve, Trip."

The halls began to reverberate with his whispered name. While we called him "the Tripster" or "Fountainhead," the girls spoke only of Trip, Trip, that was the whole conversation, and when he was chosen "Best-looking," "Best Dressed," "Best Personality," and "Best Athlete" (even though none of us had voted for him out of spite and he wasn't even that coordinated), we realized the extent of the girls' infatuation. Even our own mothers spoke of his good looks, inviting him to stay for dinner, disregarding his longish oily hair. Before long he lived like a pasha, accepting tribute at the court of his synthetic coverlet: small bills filched from mothers' purses, bags of dope, graduation rings, Rice Krispie treats wrapped in wax paper, vials of amyl nitrite, Asti Spumante bottles, assorted cheeses from the Netherlands, occasionally the odd chunk of hash. The girls came bearing typed and footnoted term papers, "Chick Notes" they'd compiled so that Trip could read a single page on each book. Over time, from the bounty of their offerings he compiled his museum display of "Great Reefers of the World," each sample housed in an empty spice jar lined along his bookshelf, from "Blue Hawaiian" to "Panama Red," with many stops in the brownish territories between, one of which looked and smelled like carpet. We didn't know much about the girls who went to Trip Fontaine's, only that they drove their own cars and always took in something from the trunk.

They were the jangly-earring type, with hair bleached at the fringes and cork-heeled shoes that tied around their ankles. Carrying salad bowls covered with printed dish towels, they walked bowleggedly over the lawn, snapping gum and smiling. Upstairs, in bed, they spoon-fed Trip, wiping his mouth with the bedsheet before tossing the bowls onto the floor and melting in his arms. From time to time Mr. Fontaine passed by, on his way to or from Donald's room, but the iffiness of his own conduct prevented him from questioning the susurrations coming from under his son's door. The two of them, father and son, lived like roommates, stumbling upon each other in their matching peacock robes, bitching over who used up the coffee, but by afternoon they drifted in the pool together, bumping the sides, compatriots in the search for a little passion on earth.

They had the most lustrous father-and-son tans in the city. Even Italian contractors, working in the sun day after day, couldn't achieve their mahogany hue. At dusk, Mr. Fontaine's and Trip's skins appeared almost bluish, and, putting on their towel turbans, they looked like twin Krishnas. The small, circular, aboveground pool abutted the backyard fence, its swells sometimes dousing the neighbors' dog. Marinated in baby oil, Mr. Fontaine and Trip boarded their air mattresses equipped with backrests and drink holders, and drifted beneath our tepid northern sky as though it were the Costa del Sol. We watched them, in stages, turning the color of shoe polish. We suspected Mr. Fontaine of lightening his hair, and the brightness of their teeth grew painful to look at. At parties, wild-eyed girls would clutch us just because we knew Trip, and after a while we saw that they were as distraught at the hands of love as we were. Mark Peters, going out to his car one night, felt someone grab his leg. Looking down, he saw Sarah Sheed, who confessed she had such a huge crush on Trip she couldn't walk. He still remembers the panic-stricken way she looked up at him, a big healthy girl renowned for her chest size, lying lame as a cripple in the dewy grass.

No one knew how Trip and Lux had met, or what they had said to each other, or whether the attraction was mutual. Even years later, Trip was reticent on the subject, in accord with his vows of faithfulness to the four hundred and eighteen girls and women he had made love to during his long career. He would only tell us, "I've never gotten over that girl, man. Never." In the desert, with the shakes, he had sickly-looking wads of yellow skin under his eyes, but the eyes themselves clearly looked back to a verdant time. Gradually, through incessant coaxing, and owing in large part to the recovering substance abuser's need to talk nonstop, we managed to cobble together the story of their love.

It began on a day when Trip Fontaine attended the wrong history class. During fifth-period study hall, as was his custom, Trip Fontaine had gone out to his car to smoke the marijuana he took as regularly as Peter Petrovich, the diabetic kid, took insulin. Three times a day Petrovich showed up at the nurse's office for his injections, always using the hypodermic needle himself like the most craven of junkies, though after shooting up he would play the concert piano in the auditorium with astounding artistry, as though insulin were the elixir of genius. Likewise, Trip Fontaine went to his car three times a day, at ten-fifteen, twelve-fifteen, and three-fifteen, as though he wore a wristwatch like Petrovich's that beeped at dose time. He always parked his Trans Am at the lot's far end, facing the school to spot any approaching teachers. The car's raked hood, sleek roof, and sloping rear end gave it the look of an aerodynamic scarab. Though signs of age had begun to mar its golden finish, Trip had repainted the black racing stripes and shined the spiky hubcaps that looked like weapons. Inside, the leather bucket seats retained idiosyncratic perspiration marks—you could see where Mr. Fontaine had rested his head in traffic jams, the chemicals in his hair spray turning the brown leather a light purple. The faint aroma of his "Boots and Saddle" air freshener still clung to the air, though by that time the car was permeated more with the smell of Trip's musk and reefer. The racing-car doors shut with a hermetic seal, and Trip used to say you could get higher in his car than anywhere because you kept breathing in the captured smoke. Every juice break, lunch, and study hall, Trip Fontaine sauntered out to his car and submerged himself in the steam bath. Fifteen minutes later, when he opened the door, the smoke would churn out as though from a chimney, dispersing and curling to the music—usually Pink Floyd or Yes—which Trip kept playing as he went about checking his engine and polishing his hood (the ostensible reasons for his trips to the parking lot). After shutting up his car, Trip walked behind the school to air out his clothes. He kept a spare box of mints hidden in the knothole of one memorial tree (planted for Samuel O. Hastings, graduate of the class of 1918). From classroom windows girls watched him, out under the trees, alone and irresistible, sitting cross-legged like an Indian, and even before he got up they could picture the light dirt stains on each buttock. It was always the same: Trip Fontaine rose to full height, adjusted the frames of his aviator sunglasses, flicked back his hair, zipped the breast pocket of his brown leather jacket, and started forward on the juggernaut of his boots. He came down the corridor of memorial trees, across the back green, past the beds of ivy, and into the school's rear door.

No boy was ever so cool and aloof. Fontaine gave off the sense of having graduated to the next stage of life, of having his hands thrust into the heart of the real world, whereas the rest of us were still memorizing quotations and grade-grubbing. Though he retrieved his books from his locker, we knew they were only props and that he was destined for capitalism and not scholarship, as his drug deals already augured. On that day he would always remember, however, a September afternoon when the leaves had just begun turning, Trip Fontaine came in to see Mr. Woodhouse the headmaster approaching down the hall. Trip was used to running into figures of authority while stoned, and he told us he never suffered from paranoia. He couldn't explain why the sight of our headmaster, with his flood pants and canary yellow socks, caused his pulse to rise and a light sweat to break out on the back of his neck just then. Nevertheless, in one nonchalant motion, Trip entered the nearest classroom to escape.

He didn't notice a single face as he took a seat. He saw neither teacher nor students, and was aware only of the heavenly light in the room, an orange glow from the autumnal foliage outside. The room seemed full of a sweet viscous liquid, a honey nearly light as air, which he breathed in. Time slowed down, and in his left ear the ringing of the cosmic Om started up clear as a telephone. When we suggested these details had been laced with the same THC in his blood, Trip Fontaine thrust a finger into the air, the only time his hands stopped shaking during the entire interview. "I know what it's like to be high," he said. "This was different." In the orange light the students' heads looked like sea anemones, undulating quietly, and the silence of the room was that of the ocean floor. "Every second is eternal," Trip told us, describing how as he sat in his desk the girl in front of him, for no apparent reason, had turned around and looked at him. He couldn't say she was beautiful because all he could see were her eyes. The rest of her face—the pulpy lips, the blond sideburn fuzz, the nose with its candy-pink translucent nostrils—registered dimly as the two blue eyes lifted him on a sea wave and held him suspended. "She was the still point of the turning world," he told us, quoting Eliot, whose *Collected Poems* he had found on the shelf of the detoxification center. For the eternity that Lux Lisbon looked at him, Trip Fontaine looked back, and the love he felt at that moment, truer than all subsequent loves because it never had to survive real life, still plagued him, even now in the desert, with his looks and health wasted. "You never know what'll set the memory off," he told us. "A baby's face. A bell on a cat's collar. Anything."

They didn't exchange a single word. But in the weeks that followed, Trip spent his days wandering the halls, hoping for Lux to appear, the most naked person with clothes on he had ever seen. Even in sensible school shoes she shuffled as though barefoot, and the baggy apparel Mrs. Lisbon bought for her only increased her appeal, as though after undressing she had put on whatever was handy. In corduroys her thighs rubbed together, buzzing, and there was always at least one untidy marvel to unravel him: an untucked shirttail, a sock with a hole, a ripped seam showing underarm hair. She carted her books from class to class but never opened them. Her pens and pencils looked as temporary as Cinderella's broom. When she smiled, her mouth showed too many teeth, but at night Trip Fontaine dreamed of being bitten by each one.

He didn't know the first step in pursuing her because he'd always been the one pursued. Little by little, from the girls who came up to his bedroom, he learned where Lux lived, though he had to be discreet in his questions in order to avoid provoking their jealousy. He began driving by the Lisbon house in hopes of getting a glimpse of her, or the consolation prize of a sister. Unlike us, Trip Fontaine never mixed up the Lisbon girls, but from the outset saw Lux as their shining pinnacle. He opened the windows of his Trans Am as he drove by, turning up his eight-track so that she might hear his favorite song in her bedroom. Other times, unable to control the riot in his gut, he floored the accelerator, leaving behind as a love token only the smell of burning rubber.

He didn't understand how she had bewitched him, nor why having done so she promptly forgot his existence, and in desperate moods he asked his mirror why the only girl he was crazy about was the only girl not crazy about him. For a long time he resorted to his time-tested methods of attracting girls, brushing his hair back as Lux passed, or clomping his boots up on the desktop, and once he even lowered his tinted glasses to give her the boon of his eyes. But she didn't look.

The truth was, even the wimpiest boys were more adept than Trip at asking girls out, because their sparrows' chests and knock-knees had taught them perseverance, whereas Trip had never even had to dial a girl's phone number. It was all new to him: the memorization of strategic speeches, the trial runs of possible conversations, the yogic deep breathing, all leading up to the blind, headlong dive into the staticky sea of telephone lines. He hadn't suffered the eternity of the ring about to be picked up, didn't know the heart rush of hearing that incomparable voice suddenly linked with his own, the sense it gave of being too close to even see her, of being actually *inside her ear.* He had never felt the pain of lackluster responses, the dread of "Oh . . . hi," or the quick annihilation of "Who?" His beauty had left him without cunning, and so in despair he confessed his passion to his father and Donald. They understood his predicament, and after calming him with a snifter of Sambuca, gave him advice only two people experienced with the burden of secret love could have given. First of all, they told him on no account to call Lux on the telephone. "It's all subtlety," Donald said. "It's all nuance." Rather than making overt declarations, they suggested that Trip speak to Lux only about the most mundane things, the weather, school assignments, anything that gave him an opportunity to communicate with the silent but unerring language of eye contact. They made him get rid of his tinted lenses, and keep his hair out of his face with hair spray. The next day Trip Fontaine took a seat in the Science Wing and waited for Lux to pass by on the way to her locker. The rising sun turned the honeycomb panels the color of a blush. Each time the ramp doors opened, Trip saw Lux's face float forward, before her eyes, nose, and mouth rearranged into the face of some other girl. He took this as a bad omen, as though Lux were continually disguising herself in order to evade him. He feared she would never come, or, worse, that she would.

After a week without seeing her, he decided to take extraordinary measures. The next Friday afternoon he left his carrel in the Science Wing to go to assembly. It was the first assembly he had attended in three years, because skipping assembly was easier than skipping any other period, and Trip preferred to spend the time smoking the hookah pipe running from his glove compartment. He had no idea where Lux would sit, and lingered at the drinking fountain, intending to follow her in. Against the advice of his father and Donald, he put on sunglasses to conceal his staring down the hall. Three times his heart jumped at the decoys of Lux's sisters, but Mr. Woodhouse had already introduced the day's speaker—a local television meteorologist— by the time Lux came out of the girls' bathroom. Trip Fontaine saw her with a concentration so focused he ceased to exist. The world at that moment contained only Lux. A fuzzy aura surrounded her, a shimmering as of atoms breaking apart, brought on, we later decided, from so much blood draining out of Trip's head. She passed right by him without noticing, and in that instant he smelled not cigarettes as he expected, but watermelon gum.

He followed her into the colonial clarity of the auditorium with its Monticello dome, Doric pilasters, and imitation gas lanterns we used to fill with milk. He sat next to her in the last row, and though he avoided looking at her, it was no use: with organs of sense he hadn't realized he possessed, Trip Fontaine felt Lux beside him, registered her body temperature, heartbeat, respiration rate, all the pumping and flow of her body. The auditorium lights dimmed as the weatherman began showing slides, and soon they were in the dark together, alone despite four hundred students and forty-five teachers. Paralyzed by love, Trip didn't move once as tornadoes flashed on the screen, and it was fifteen minutes before he got up the courage to place a sliver of forearm along the armrest. Once he did, an inch of space still separated them, so over the next twenty minutes, with infinitesimal advances that made his whole body sweat, Trip Fontaine moved his arm toward hers. As all other eyes watched Hurricane Zelda tear toward a coastal Caribbean town, the hairs on Trip's arm brushed Lux's, and electricity surged through the new circuit. Without turning, without breathing, Lux responded with equal pressure, then Trip applied more, she responded, and so on and so on, until they were joined at the elbow. Right then, it happened: a prankster in front, cupping his hands over his mouth, made a farting noise, and the room rippled with laughter. Lux blanched, pulling her arm away, but Trip Fontaine took the opportunity to whisper the first words he had ever spoken in her ear: "That must've been Conley," he said. "His ass is grass."

In response, she didn't so much as nod. But Trip, still leaning toward her, continued: "I'm going to ask your old man if I can take you out."

"Fat chance," said Lux, not looking at him. The lights came up, and all around them students began clapping. Trip waited for the applause to peak before he spoke again. Then he said, "First I'm going to come over and watch the tube at your house. This Sunday. Then I'm going to ask you out." Again he waited for her to speak, but the only sign she'd heard came from her hand which, turning palm up, suggested he could do what he liked. Trip stood up to go, but before doing so leaned over the back of his vacated seat as the words he'd been keeping down for weeks came pouring out.

"You're a stone fox," he said, and took off.

Trip Fontaine became the first boy after Peter Sissen to enter the Lisbon house alone. He did so simply by telling Lux when he would arrive and leaving her to tell her parents. None of us could explain how we had missed him, especially as he insisted during his interview that he had taken no stealthy measures, driving up in plain sight and parking his Trans Am in front of an elm stump so it wouldn't get covered with sap. He'd had his hair cut for the occasion, and instead of a Western getup wore a white shirt and black pants like a caterer. Lux met him at the door and, without saying much (she was keeping track of her knitting), led him to his assigned seat in the living room. He sat on the couch beside Mrs. Lisbon, with Lux on her other side. Trip Fontaine told us the girls paid him little attention, certainly less than a school heartthrob would expect. Therese sat in the corner, holding a stuffed iguana and explaining to Bonnie what iguanas ate, how they reproduced, and what their natural habitat was like. The only sister who spoke to Trip was Mary, who kept offering to refill his Coke. A Walt Disney special was on, and the Lisbons watched it with the acceptance of a family accustomed to bland entertainment, laughing together at the same lame stunts, sitting up during the rigged climaxes. Trip Fontaine didn't see any signs of twistedness in the girls, but later he did say, "You would have killed yourself just to have something to do." Mrs. Lisbon oversaw Lux's knitting. Before the channel could be changed, she consulted *TV Guide* to judge the program's suitability. The curtains were thick as canvas. A few spindly plants sat on the windowsill, and this differed so much from his own leafy living room (Mr. Fontaine was a gardening buff) that Trip would have felt he was on a dead planet had it not been for the pulsing life of Lux at the sofa's other end. He could see her bare feet every time she put them up on the coffee table. The soles were black, her toenails flecked with pink polish. Each time they appeared, Mrs. Lisbon tapped them with a knitting needle, driving them back under the table.

And that was all that happened. Trip didn't get to sit next to Lux, nor speak to her, nor even look at her, but the bright nearby fact of her presence burned in his mind. At ten o'clock, taking a cue from his wife, Mr. Lisbon slapped Trip on the back and said, "Well, son, we usually hit the hay about now." Trip shook his hand, then Mrs. Lisbon's colder one, and Lux stepped forward to escort him out. She must have seen the situation was futile, because she hardly looked at him during the short trip to the door. She walked with her head down, digging in her ear for wax, and looked up as she opened the door to give him a sad smile that promised only frustration. Trip Fontaine left crushed, knowing that all he could hope for was another night on the sofa beside Mrs. Lisbon. He walked across the lawn, unmown since Cecilia died. He sat in his car, gazing at the house, watching as downstairs lights traded places with those upstairs, and then, one by one, went out. He thought about Lux getting ready for bed, and just the idea of her holding a toothbrush excited him more than the full-fledged nudity he saw in his own bedroom nearly every night. He laid his head back on the headrest and opened his mouth to ease the constriction in his chest, when suddenly the air inside the car churned. He felt himself grasped by his long lapels, pulled forward and pushed back, as a creature with a hundred mouths started sucking the marrow from his bones. She said nothing as she came on like a starved animal, and he wouldn't have known who it was if it hadn't been for the taste of her watermelon gum, which after the first few torrid kisses he found himself chewing. She was no longer wearing pants but a flannel nightgown. Her feet, wet from the lawn, gave off a pasture smell. He felt her clammy shins, her hot knees, her bristly thighs, and then with terror he put his finger in the ravenous mouth of the animal leashed below her waist. It was as though he had never touched a girl before; he felt fur and an oily substance like otter insulation. Two beasts lived in the car, one above, snuffling and biting him, and one below, struggling to get out of its damp cage. Valiantly he did what he could to feed them, placate them, but the sense of his insufficiency grew, and after a few minutes, with only the words "Gotta get back before bed check," Lux left him, more dead than alive.

Even though that lightning attack lasted only three minutes, it left its mark on him. He spoke of it as one might of a religious experience, a visitation or vision, any rupture into this life from beyond that cannot be described in words. "Sometimes I think I dreamed it," he told us, recalling the voracity of those hundred mouths that had sucked out his juice in the dark, and even though he went on to enjoy an enviable love life, Trip Fontaine confessed it was all anticlimactic. Never again were his intestines yanked with such delectable force, nor did he ever again feel the sensation of being entirely wetted by another's saliva. "I felt like a stamp," he said. Years later he was still amazed by Lux's singleness of purpose, her total lack of inhibitions, her mythic mutability that allowed her to possess three or four arms at once. "Most people never taste that kind of love," he said, taking courage amid the disaster of his life. "At least I tasted it once, man." In comparison, the loves of his early manhood and maturity were docile creatures with smooth flanks and dependable outcries. Even during the act of love he could envision them bringing him hot milk, doing his taxes, or presiding tearfully at his deathbed. They were warm, loving, hot-water-bottle women. Even the screamers of his adult years always hit false notes, and no erotic intensity ever matched the silence in which Lux flayed him alive.

We never learned whether Mrs. Lisbon caught Lux as she tried to sneak back inside, but for whatever reason, when Trip tried to make another date to come sit on the couch, Lux told him she was grounded, and that her mother had forbidden any future visits. At school, Trip Fontaine was cagey about what had passed between them, and though stories circulated about their sneaking off into various enclosures, he insisted the only time they ever touched was in the car. "At school, we could never find a place to go. Her old man kept a close eye on her. It was agony, man. Fucking agony."

In Dr. Hornicker's opinion, Lux's promiscuity was a commonplace reaction to emotional need. "Adolescents tend to seek love where they can find it," he wrote in one of the many articles he hoped to publish. "Lux confused the sexual act with love. For her, sex became a substitute for the comfort she needed as a result of her sister's suicide." A few of the boys did provide details that supported this theory. Willard said that once, while they lay together in the field house, Lux asked him if he thought what they had done was dirty. "I knew what to say. I said no. Then she grabs my hand and goes, 'You like me, don't you?' I didn't say anything. It's best to keep chicks guessing." Years later, Trip Fontaine was irritated by our suggestion that Lux's passion might have come from a misplaced need. "What are you saying, that I was just a vehicle? You can't fake that, man. It was real." We even managed to bring up the subject with Mrs. Lisbon during our single interview with her in a bus station cafeteria, but she grew rigid. "None of my daughters lacked for any love. We had plenty of love in our house."

It was hard to tell. As October came, the Lisbon house began to look less cheerful. The blue slate roof, which in certain lights had resembled a pond suspended in the air, visibly darkened. The yellow bricks turned brown. Bats flew out of the chimney in the evening, as they did from the Stamarowski mansion the next block over. We were used to seeing bats wheeling over the Stamarowskis', zigzagging and diving as girls screamed and covered their long hair. Mr. Stamarowski wore black turtlenecks and stood on his balcony. At sunset he let us roam his big lawn, and once in the flower bed we found a dead bat with its face of a shrunken old man with two prize teeth. We always thought the bats had come with the Stamarowskis from Poland; they made sense swooping over that somber house with its velvet curtains and Old World decay, but not over the practical double chimneys of the Lisbon house. There were other signs of creeping desolation. The illuminated doorbell went out. The bird feeder fell in the backyard and was left on the ground. On the milk box Mrs. Lisbon left a curt note to the milkman: "Stop bringing bad milk!" Recalling that time, Mrs. Higbie insisted that Mr. Lisbon, using a long pole, had closed the outside shutters. When we asked around, everyone agreed. Exhibit #3, however, a photograph taken by Mr. Buell, shows Chase ready to swing his new Louisville Slugger, and in the background the Lisbon house has all its shutters open (we find a magnifying glass helpful). The photo was taken on October 13, Chase's birthday and the opening of the World Series.

Other than to school or church the Lisbon girls never went anywhere. Once a week a Kroger's truck delivered groceries. Little Johnny Buell and Vince Fusilli stopped it one day by holding an imaginary rope across the street, one on each side tugging air like twin Marcel Marceaux. The driver let them climb in, and they looked through his order slips, lying that they wanted to grow up and be deliverymen themselves. The Lisbon order, which Vince Fusilli pocketed, turned out to resemble a requisition of army supplies.

| | |
|---|---|
| *1 – 5 lb.* | *Krog. flour* |
| *5 – 1 gal* | *Carnat. Dehyd. milk* |
| *18 roll* | *Wh. Cld. t. p.* |
| *24 can* | *Del. pchs. (in syr.)* |
| *24 can* | *Del. g. peas* |
| *10 lbs.* | *Gr. chuck* |
| *3* | *Won. Br.* |
| *1* | *Jif p. but.* |
| *3* | *Kell. C. Flks.* |
| *5* | *Stkst. Tu.* |
| *1* | *Krog. mayo.* |
| *1* | *iceberg* |
| *1 lb.* | *O. May. bacon* |
| *1* | *L. Lks. but.* |
| *1* | *Tang o. f.* |
| *1* | *Hersh. choc.* |

We waited to see what would happen with the leaves. For two weeks they had been falling, covering lawns, because in those days we still had trees. Now, in autumn, only a few leaves make swan dives from the tops of remaining elms, and most leaves drop four feet from saplings held up by stakes, runt replacements the city has planted to console us with the vision of what our street will look like in a hundred years. No one is sure what kind of trees these new trees are. The man from the Parks Department said only that they had been selected for their "hardiness against the Dutch elm beetle."

"Even the bugs don't like them, that means," said Mrs. Scheer.

In the past, fall began with a collective rattle in the treetops; then, in an endless profusion, the leaves snapped off and came floating down, circling and flapping in updrafts, like the world shedding itself. We let them accumulate. We stood by with an excuse to do nothing while every day the branches showed growing patches of sky.

The first weekend after leaf fall, we began raking in military ranks, heaping piles in the street. Different families used different methods. The Buells employed a three-man formation, with two rakers raking lengthwise and another sweeping in at a right angle, in imitation of a formation Mr. Buell had used over the Hump. The Pitzenbergers toiled with ten people—two parents, seven teenagers, and the two-year-old Catholic mistake following with a toy rake. Mrs. Amberson, fat, used a leaf blower. We all did our part. Afterward, the scrubbed grass, like thoroughly brushed hair, gave us a pleasure we felt all the way to our bowels. Sometimes the pleasure was so keen we raked up the grass itself, leaving patches of dirt. At the end of day we stood at the curbside surveying our lawns where every blade had been flattened, every dirt clod obliterated, and even some of the dormant crocus bulbs violated. In those days before universal pollution we were allowed to burn our leaves, and at night, in one of the last rituals of our disintegrating tribe, every father came down to the street to ignite his family's pile.

Usually Mr. Lisbon did their raking alone, singing in his soprano's voice, but from fifteen Therese had begun to help, stooping and scratching in mannish clothes, knee-high rubber boots and a fishing cap. At night Mr. Lisbon would light his pile like the rest of the fathers, but his anxiety over the fire's getting out of control would diminish his pleasure. He patrolled his pile, tossing leaves into the center, tidying the conflagration, and when Mr. Wadsworth offered him a sip from his monogrammed flask, as he did every father on his rounds, Mr. Lisbon would say, "Thanks no, thanks no."

The year of the suicides the Lisbons' leaves went unraked. On the appropriate Saturday Mr. Lisbon didn't stir from his house. From time to time as we raked, we looked over at the Lisbon house, its walls accumulating autumn's dampness, its littered and varicolored lawn hemmed in by lawns becoming increasingly exposed and green. The more leaves we swept away, the more seemed heaped over the Lisbons' yard, smothering bushes and covering the first porch step. When we lit bonfires that night, every house leaped forward, blazing orange. Only the Lisbon house remained dark, a tunnel, an emptiness, past our smoke and flames. As weeks passed, their leaves remained. When they blew onto other people's lawns there was grumbling.

"These aren't *my* leaves," Mr. Amberson said, stuffing them into a can. It rained twice and the leaves grew soggy and brown, making the Lisbon lawn look like a field of mud.

It was the growing shabbiness of the house that attracted the first reporters. Mr. Baubee, editor of the local paper, continued to defend his decision against reporting on a personal tragedy such as suicide. Instead, he chose to investigate the controversy over the new guardrails obscuring our lakefront, or the deadlock in negotiations over the cemetery workers' strike, now in its fifth month (bodies were being shipped out of state in refrigerated trailers). The "Welcome, Neighbor" section continued to feature newcomers attracted by our town's greenness and quiet, its breathtaking verandas—a cousin of Winston Churchill at his home on Windmill Pointe Boulevard, looking too thin to be related to the Prime Minister; Mrs. Shed Turner, the first white woman ever to penetrate the jungles of Papua New Guinea, holding in her lap what appeared to be a shrunken head, though the caption identified the blur as "her Yorkie, William the Conqueror."

Back in summer, the city newspapers had neglected to report on Cecilia's suicide because of its sheer prosaicness. Owing to extensive layoffs at the automotive plants, hardly a day passed without some despairing soul sinking beneath the tide of the recession, men found in garages with cars running, or twisted in the shower, still wearing work clothes. Only murder-suicides made the papers, and then only on page 3 or 4, stories of fathers shotgunning families before turning the guns on themselves, descriptions of men setting fire to their own houses after securing the doors. Mr. Larkin, publisher of the city's largest newspaper, lived only a half mile from the Lisbons, and there was no doubt he knew what had transpired. Joe Hill Conley, who fooled around with Missy Larkin every so often (she'd had a yearlong crush on him despite his frequent shaving cuts), testified to us that Missy and her mother had discussed the suicide within Mr. Larkin's hearing, but that he showed no interest as he lay on his chaise in the sun with a wet cloth over his eyes. Nevertheless, on October 15, over three months later, a letter to the editor was published describing in the sketchiest manner possible the particulars of Cecilia's suicide, and calling on the schools to address "today's teenagers' overwhelming anxiety." The letter was signed "Mrs. I. Dew Hopewell," an obvious pseudonym, but certain details pointed to someone on our street. First of all, the rest of the town had forgotten about Cecilia's suicide by that point, whereas the growing disrepair of the Lisbon house constantly reminded us of the trouble within. Years later, after there were no more daughters to save, Mrs. Denton confessed that she had written the letter, in a fit of righteous indignation under the hair dryer. She did not regret it. "You can't just stand by and let your neighborhood go down the toilet," she said. "We're good people around here."

The day after her letter appeared, a blue Pontiac drove

up to the Lisbon house and an unfamiliar woman got out. After checking the address against a piece of paper, she walked up to the front porch nobody had climbed in weeks. Shaft Tiggs, the paperboy, now lobbed papers against the door from ten feet away. He'd even stopped collecting on Thursdays (his mother made up the difference from her pocketbook, cautioning him not to tell his father). The Lisbon porch, where we'd first stood to see Cecilia on the fence, had become like a sidewalk crack: stepping on it was bad luck. The AstroTurf welcome mat curled at the edges. Unread papers lay in a waterlogged heap, red ink running from color sports photographs. The metal mailbox released an odor of rust. The young woman moved the newspapers aside with her blue pump and knocked. The door opened a crack and the woman, squinting into the darkness, launched into her spiel. At some point she realized her listener was a foot shorter than where she was looking, and readjusted her gaze. She took a pocket notebook from her jacket, waving it like the faked papers spies wave in war films. It worked. The door opened a few more inches to let her in.

Linda Perl's story appeared the next day, though Mr. Larkin would never discuss his reasons for running it. It gave a detailed account of Cecilia's suicide. From the quotations in the piece (you may read it for yourself if you like; we've included it as Exhibit #9), it's clear Ms. Perl, a staff reporter recently hired from a provincial newspaper in Mackinac, interviewed only Bonnie and Mary before Mrs. Lisbon threw her out. The story proceeds by the logic of the many "human interest" pieces that had begun to proliferate at the time. It paints the picture of the Lisbon house in the broadest terms. Phrases such as "The tony suburb known more for debutante parties than for funerals of debutante-aged girls" and "The bright bouncy girls show little sign of the recent tragedy" give an idea of Ms. Perl's style. After rendering the most cursory description of Cecilia ("She liked to paint and write in her journal"), the piece solves the mystery of her death by giving way to conclusions such as these: "Psychologists agree that adolescence is much more fraught with pressures and complexities than in years past. Often, in today's world, the extended childhood American life has bestowed on its young turns out to be a wasteland, where the adolescent feels cut off from both childhood and adulthood. Self-expression can often be frustrated. More and more, doctors say, this frustration can lead to acts of violence whose reality the adolescent cannot separate from the intended drama."

Ostensibly, the piece avoids sensationalism by informing the readership of a common social danger. The following day a general article on teenage suicide appeared, also by Ms. Perl, complete with charts and graphs, and mentioning Cecilia only in its first sentence: "The suicide of an East Side teenager last summer has increased public awareness of a national crisis." From then on it was a free-for-all. Articles came out listing teenage suicides statewide for the past year. Photographs ran, usually school portraits showing troubled youngsters in dress-up clothes, boys with wispy mustaches and necktie knots like goiters, girls with hair sprayed into meringue, their vulnerable necks tagged by gold chains spelling out "Sherri" and "Gloria." Home photos presented the teenagers smiling in happier times, often over birthday cakes flaming with conclusive candles. Because Mr. and Mrs. Lisbon refused interviews, the papers had to obtain photographs of Cecilia from our school yearbook, *Spirit*. On the torn-out page (Exhibit #4), Cecilia's penetrating face peers from between the sweatered shoulders of two cropped-out schoolmates. Television crews came by to film the increasingly dreary exterior of the Lisbon house, first Channel 2, then Channel 4, then finally Channel 7. We watched to see the Lisbon house on TV, but they didn't use the footage until months later after the rest of the girls killed themselves, and by then the season was all wrong. Meanwhile, a local television show focused on the subject of teenage suicide, inviting two girls and one boy to explain their reasons for attempting it. We listened to them, but it was clear they'd received too much therapy to know the truth. Their answers sounded rehearsed, relying on concepts of self-esteem and other words clumsy on their tongues. One of the girls, Rannie Jilson, had tried to end her life by baking a pie full of rat poison so that she could eat it without attracting suspicion, but had served only to kill her eighty-six-year-old grandmother, a lover of sweets. At this point Rannie broke down weeping, the host consoled her, and we were into a commercial.

Many people objected to the articles and television

shows, coming as they did so long after the fact. Mrs. Eugene said, "Why can't they let her rest in peace," while Mrs. Larson lamented that the media attention had come "just when things were getting back to normal." Nevertheless, the coverage alerted us to danger signals we couldn't help but look for. Were the Lisbon girls' pupils dilated? Did they use nose spray excessively? Eye drops? Had they lost interest in school activities, in sports, in hobbies? Had they withdrawn from their peers? Did they suffer crying jags for no reason? Did they complain of insomnia, pains in the chest, constant fatigue? Pamphlets arrived, dark green with white lettering, sent out by our local Chamber of Commerce. "We thought green was cheerful. But not too cheerful," said Mr. Babson, who was president. "Green was also serious. So we went with it." The pamphlets made no mention of Cecilia's death, delving instead into the causes of suicide in general. We learned that there were 80 suicides per day in America, 30,000 per year, that an attempt or completion happened every minute, a completion every 18 minutes, that 3 to 4 times as many males completed suicide but 3 times as many females attempted it, that more whites than nonwhites completed suicide, that the rate of suicide among the young (15–24) had tripled in the last four decades, that suicide was the second leading cause of death among high-school students, that 25 percent of all suicides occurred in the 15–24 age group, but that, contrary to our expectations, the highest rate of suicide was found among white males over 50. Many men said afterward that the board members of the local Chamber of Commerce, Mr. Babson, Mr. Laurie, Mr. Peterson, and Mr. Hocksteder, had shown great prescience in predicting the negative publicity the suicide scare would bring to our town, as well as the subsequent fall in commercial activity. While the suicides lasted, and for some time after, the Chamber of Commerce worried less about the influx of black shoppers and more about the outflux of whites. Brave blacks had been slipping in for years, though they were usually women, who blended in with our maids. The city downtown had deteriorated to such a degree that most blacks had no other place to go. Not by choice did they pass our display windows where trim mannequins modeled green skirts, pink espadrilles, blue handbags clasped by gold frogs kissing. Even though we'd always chosen to play Indians and not cowboys, considered Travis Williams the best kickoff returner ever and Willie Horton the best hitter, nothing shocked us more than the sight of a black person shopping on Kercheval. We couldn't help but wonder if certain "improvements" in The Village hadn't been made to scare black people off. The ghost in the window of the costume shop, for instance, had an awfully pointed, hooded head, and the restaurant, without explanation, took fried chicken off its menu. But we were never sure if these developments had been planned, because as soon as the suicides began the Chamber of Commerce turned its attention to a "Campaign for Wellness." Under the guise of health education, the chamber set up tables in school gymnasia, giving out information on a variety of hazards, from rectal cancer to diabetes. The Hare Krishnas were allowed to chant bald-headed and serve sugary vegetarian food for free. Mixed in with this new approach were the green pamphlets and family therapy sessions at which kids had to stand up and describe their nightmares. Willie Kuntz, whose mother took him to one, said, "They weren't going to let me out of there until I cried and told my mom I loved her. So I did. But I faked the crying part. Just rub your eyes until they hurt. That works, sort of."

Amid the increasing scrutiny, the girls managed to keep a low profile at school. Various sightings of them at the time merged into a general image of their careful cluster moving down the central hallway. They passed beneath the great school clock, the black finger of the minute hand pointing down at their soft heads. We always expected the clock to fall, but it never did, and soon the girls had skipped past the danger, their skirts growing transparent in the light coming from the hall's far end, revealing the wishbones of their legs. If we followed, however, the girls would vanish, and, looking into classrooms they might have entered, we would see every other face but theirs, or would overshoot their trail and end up in the Lower School amid a meaningless swirl of finger paintings. The smell of egg tempera still brings back those useless pursuits. The halls, cleaned by lonely janitors at night, were silent, and we would follow a pencil arrow some kid had drawn on the wall for fifty feet, telling ourselves that this would be the time we spoke to the Lisbon girls and asked them what was troubling them. Sometimes we caught sight of tattered kneesocks rounding a corner, or came upon them doubled over, shoving books into a cubbyhole, flicking the hair out of their eyes. But it was always the same: their white faces drifting in slow motion past us, while we pretended we hadn't been looking for them at all, that we didn't know they existed.

We have a few documents from the time (Exhibits #13–#15)—Therese's chemistry write-ups, Bonnie's history paper on Simone Weil, Lux's frequent forged excuses from phys. ed. She always used the same method, faking the rigid *t*'s and *b*'s of her mother's signature and then, to distinguish her own handwriting, penning her signature, Lux Lisbon, below, the two beseeching *L*'s reaching out for each other over the ditch of the *u* and the barbed-wire *x*. Julie Winthrop also used to skip gym and spent many classes with Lux in the girls' locker room. "We used to climb up on the lockers and smoke," she told us. "You couldn't see us from the ground, and if any teachers came by, they couldn't tell where the smoke was coming from. They usually thought whoever was smoking had already left." According to Julie Winthrop, she and Lux were only "cig friends" and didn't talk much on top of the lockers, too busy inhaling or listening for footsteps. She did say that Lux had an affected hardness that might have been a reaction to pain. "She was always saying, 'Fuck this school,' or 'I can't wait until I get out of here.' But so did lots of kids." Once, however, after they were finished smoking, Julie jumped down off the lockers and started out. When

Lux didn't follow, she called her name. "She still didn't answer, so I went back and looked on top of the lockers. She was just lying there, hugging herself. She wasn't making any sound. She was just shaking like she was really cold."

Our teachers remembered the girls during this period in various ways, depending on the subject they taught. Mr. Nillis said of Bonnie, "It was pre-cal. We didn't exactly get touchy-feely"; while Señor Lorca said of Therese, "A big girl! I think smaller, maybe happier. That is the way of the world and men's hearts." Apparently, though not a natural at languages, Therese spoke in a credible Castilian accent and had a great capacity for memorizing vocabulary. "She could speak Spanish," Señor Lorca said, "but not *feel* it."

In her written response to our questions (she wanted time to "ponder and deliberate"), Miss Arndt, the art teacher, said, "Mary's watercolors did possess what, for lack of a better word, I will call a 'mournfulness.' But in my experience, there are really only two kinds of children: the empty-headed ones (Fauvist flowers, dogs, and sailboats) and the intelligent ones (gouaches of urban decay, gloomy abstractions)—much like my own painting in college, and during those three heady years in 'the Village.' Could I foresee she would commit suicide? I regret to say, no. At least ten percent of my students were born with modernist tendencies. I ask you: is dullness a gift? intelligence a curse? I'm forty-seven years old and live alone."

Day by day, the girls ostracized themselves. Because they stayed in a group, other girls found it difficult to talk or walk with them, and many assumed they wanted to be left alone. And the more the Lisbon girls were left alone, the more they retreated. Sheila Davis told of being in an English study group with Bonnie Lisbon. "We were discussing this book *Portrait of a Lady*. We had to do a character sketch on Ralph. Bonnie didn't say much at first. But then she reminded us how Ralph always keeps his hands in his pockets. Then, like a jerk, I go, 'It's really sad when he dies.' I wasn't even thinking. Grace Hilton elbowed me and I turned purple. It got totally quiet."

It was Mrs. Woodhouse, the headmaster's wife, who came up with the idea for the "Day of Grieving." She had majored in psychology in college and now, twice a week, volunteered at a Head Start program in the inner city. "They kept writing about the suicide in the paper, but do you know we hadn't mentioned it once in school all that year?" she told us nearly twenty years later. "I'd wanted Dick to address the matter at Convocation, but he felt otherwise and I had to defer. But little by little, as the volume rose, he came around to my view." (In fact, Mr. Woodhouse had addressed the subject, if obliquely, during his speech of welcome at Convocation. After introducing the new teachers, he had said, "It has been a long, hard summer for some of us here today. But today begins a new year of hopes and goals.") Mrs. Woodhouse broached her idea to a few departmental heads during dinner at the modest ranch-style house that came with her husband's position, and the following week proposed it at a full teachers' meeting. Mr. Pulff, who left shortly thereafter to pursue a job in advertising, recalled a few of Mrs. Woodhouse's words that day. "'Grief is natural,' she said. 'Overcoming it is a matter of choice.' I remember it because I used it later for a diet product: 'Eating is natural. Gaining weight is your choice.' Maybe you saw it." Mr. Pulff voted against the Day of Grieving but was in the minority. The date was set.

Most people remember the Day of Grieving as an obscure holiday. The first three hours of school were canceled and we remained in our homerooms. Teachers passed out mimeographs related to the day's theme, which was never officially announced, as Mrs. Woodhouse felt it inappropriate to single out the girls' tragedy. The result was that the tragedy was diffused and universalized. As Kevin Tiggs put it, "It seemed like we were supposed to feel sorry for everything that ever happened, ever." Teachers had latitude to present material of their own choosing. Mr. Hedlie, the English teacher who rode his bicycle to school with his trouser cuffs secured in metal clips, handed out a collection of poems by the Victorian poet Christina Rossetti. Deborah Ferentell remembered a few lines from one poem entitled "Rest":

> *O Earth, lie heavily upon her eyes;*
> *Seal her sweet eyes weary of watching, Earth;*
> *Lie close around her; leave no room for mirth*
> *With its harsh laughter, nor for sound of sighs.*
> *She hath no questions, she hath no replies.*

The Reverend Pike spoke of the Christian message of death and rebirth, working in a story of his own heartrending loss when his college football team failed to clinch the division title. Mr. Tonover, who taught chemistry and still lived with his mother, was at a loss for words on the occasion, and let his students cook peanut brittle over a Bunsen burner. Other classes, dividing into groups, played games where they envisioned themselves as architectural structures. "If you were a building," the leader would ask, "what kind of building would you be?" They had to describe these structures in great detail and then make improvements. The Lisbon girls, stranded in separate homerooms, declined to play, or kept asking to be excused to go to the bathroom. None of the teachers insisted on their participating, with the result that all the healing was done by those of us without wounds. At midday, Becky Talbridge saw the Lisbon girls together in the girls' bathroom in the Science Wing. "They'd brought chairs in from the hall and they were just sitting there, waiting it out. Mary had a run in her nylon—can you believe she wore nylons?— and she was fixing it with fingernail polish. Her sisters were sort of watching her but they seemed pretty bored. I went into the stall, but I could feel them out there and I couldn't, you know, go."

Mrs. Lisbon never learned about the Day of Grieving. Neither her husband nor her daughters mentioned it when they returned home that day. Mr. Lisbon had of course been present at the teachers' meeting when Mrs. Woodhouse made her proposal, but accounts differ as to his reaction. Mr. Rodriguez remembered him as "nodding his head, but not saying anything," while Miss Shuttleworth recalled that he left the meeting shortly after it began and never returned. "He never heard about the Day of Grieving. He left in a state of distraction and a winter coat," she said, still quizzing us on rhetorical constructions (in this case, zeugma) which we had to identify before being excused from her presence. When Miss Shuttleworth came into the room for her interview, we stood in respect as we always had, and even though we were approaching middle age, a few of us balding, she still referred to us as "infants," as she had in her classroom so long ago. She still had the plaster bust of Cicero on her desk and the imitation Grecian urn we had given her upon graduation, and still exuded the air of a powdered celibate polymath. "I don't think Mr. Lisbon knew about the *Dies Lacrimarum* until it was well under way. I passed by his classroom during second period and he was at the blackboard, in his chair, instructing. I don't think anyone had had the fortitude to acquaint him with the day's activities." Indeed, when we spoke to him years later, Mr. Lisbon possessed only a vague memory of the Day of Grieving. "Try decade," he told us.

For a long time no one agreed on the success of the various attempts to address Cecilia's suicide. Mrs. Woodhouse thought the Day of Grieving had served a vital purpose, and many teachers were pleased that the silence around the subject had been broken. A psychological counselor came on staff once a week, sharing the small office of the school nurse. Any student feeling the need to talk was encouraged to go. We never did, but every Friday peeked in to see if any of the Lisbon girls met with the counselor. Her name was Miss Lynn Kilsem, but a year later, after the rest of the suicides, she disappeared without a word. Her degree in social work turned out to be fake, and no one is sure if her name was really Lynn Kilsem, or who she was, or where she went off to. In any case, she is one of the few people we haven't been able to track down, and in the characteristic irony of fate, one of the few people who might have been able to tell us something. For apparently the girls went to see Miss Kilsem regularly on Fridays, though we never saw them amid the paltry medical supplies of that poor excuse for a nurse's office. Miss Kilsem's patient records were lost in an office fire five years later (a coffeemaker, an old extension cord) and we have no exact information regarding the sessions. Muffie Perry, however, who had been using Miss Kilsem as a sports psychologist, often recalled seeing Lux or Mary in the office, and sometimes Therese and Bonnie as well. We had a great deal of trouble locating Muffie Perry herself, owing to the many rumors involving her married name. Some said she was now Muffie Friewald, others Muffie von Rechewicz, but when we finally dug her up, tending the rare orchids her grandmother had bequeathed to the Belle Isle Botanical Garden, she told us her name was still Muffie Perry, period, as it had been in the days of her field hockey triumphs. We didn't recognize her at first, what with the sucking vines and thick creepers, the misty hothouse air, and even when we cajoled her to stand under the artificial grow lamp, we saw that she had swelled and puckered, that her great goal-scoring back was hunched, but that her tiny teeth in their bright gums were unchanged. The decadence of Belle Isle contributed to our gloomy reappraisal. We remembered the delicate fig-shaped island, stranded between the American Empire and peaceful Canada, as it had been years ago, with its welcoming red-white-and-blue flag-shaped flower bed, splashing fountains, European casino, and horse paths leading through woods where Indians had bent trees into giant bows. Now grass grew in patches down to the littered beach where children fished with pop tops tied to string. Paint flaked from once-bright gazebos. Drinking fountains rose from mud puddles laid with broken-brick stepping stones. Along the road the granite face of the Civil War Hero had been spray-painted black. Mrs. Huntington Perry had donated her prize orchids to the Botanical Garden in the time before the riots, when civic moneys still ran high, but since her death the eroding tax base had forced cutbacks that had laid off one skilled gardener a year, so that plants that had survived transplantation from equatorial regions to bloom again in that false paradise now withered, weeds sprang up amid scrupulous identification tags, and fake sunlight flowed for only a few hours per day. The only thing that remained was the steam vapor, beading the sloping greenhouse windows and filling our nostrils with the moisture and aroma of a rotting world.

It was the decay that brought Muffie Perry back. Her grandmother's cycnoches had nearly died of blight; parasites overran her three extraordinary dendrobiums; and the bank of miniature masdevallias, whose purple velvet petals tipped in blood Mrs. Huntington Perry had herself bred through elaborate hybridization, looked for all the world like a rack of cheap nursery pansies. Her granddaughter had been volunteering her time in the hope of restoring the flowers to former glory, but she told us it was hopeless, hopeless. The plants were expected to grow in the light of a dungeon. Hoodlums jumped the back fence and ran through the greenhouse, uprooting plants for the fun of it. Muffie Perry had wounded one vandal by wielding a garden trowel. We had a hard time directing her attention back from the world of cracked windows, heaped dirt, unpaid admissions, and rats nesting in Egyptian bulrushes. Gradually, however, feeding the tiny faces of the orchids with an eyedropper filled with what looked like milk, she told us how the girls had appeared during their sessions with Miss Kilsem. "At first they were still pretty depressed-looking. Mary had these huge circles under her eyes. Like a mask." Muffie Perry could still remember the office's superstitious smell of antiseptic, which she always thought was the odor of the girls' grief. They would be just leaving when she came in, their eyes downcast, their shoes untied, but they always remembered to take a chocolate mint from the dish the nurse kept on a table by the door. They left Miss Kilsem bobbing in the wake of whatever they'd told her. Often she sat at her desk, eyes closed, thumbs to acupressure points, and didn't speak for a full minute. "I've always had a hunch that Miss Kilsem was the one they confided in," Muffie Perry said. "For whatever reason. Maybe that's why she took off."

Whether the girls confided in Miss Kilsem or not, the therapy seemed to help. Almost immediately their moods brightened. Coming in for her appointment, Muffie Perry heard them laughing or talking excitedly. The window would sometimes be open, and both Lux and Miss Kilsem would be smoking against the rules, or the girls would have raided the candy dish, strewing Miss Kilsem's desk with wadded wrappers.

We noticed the change, too. The girls seemed less tired. In class they stared out the window less, raised their hands more, spoke up. They momentarily forgot the stigma attached to them and took part again in school activities. Therese attended Science Club meetings in Mr. Tonover's bleak classroom with its fire-retardant tables and deep black sinks. Mary helped the divorced lady sew costumes for the school play two afternoons a week. Bonnie even showed up at a Christian fellowship meeting at the house of Mike Firkin, who later became a missionary and died of malaria in Thailand. Lux tried out for the school musical, and because Eugie Kent had a crush on her, and Mr. Oliphant the theater director had a crush on Eugie Kent, she got a small part in the chorus, singing and dancing as though she were happy. Eugie said later that Mr. Oliphant's blocking always kept Lux onstage while Eugie was off, so that he could never find her in the darkness backstage to wrap himself up in the curtains with her. Four weeks later, of course, after the girls' final incarceration, Lux dropped out of the play, but those who saw it performed said that Eugie Kent sang his numbers in his usual strident unremarkable voice, more in love with himself than with the chorus girl whose absence no one noticed.

By this time autumn had turned grim, locking the sky in steel. In Mr. Lisbon's classroom, the planets shifted a few inches each day, and it was clear, if you looked up, that the earth had turned its blue face away from the sun, that it was sweeping down its own dark alley in space, over where cobwebs collected in the ceiling corner, out of reach of the janitor's broom. As summer's humidity became a memory, the summer itself began to seem unreal, until we lost sight of it. Poor Cecilia appeared in our consciousness at odd moments, most often as we were just waking up, or staring out a car-pool window streaked with rain—she rose up in her wedding dress, muddy with the afterlife, but then a horn would honk, or our radio alarms would unleash a popular song, and we snapped back to reality. Other people filed Cecilia's memory away even more easily. When they spoke of her, it was to say that they had always expected Cecilia to meet a bad end, and that far from viewing the Lisbon girls as a single species, they had always seen Cecilia as apart, a freak of nature. Mr. Hillyer summed up the majority sentiment at the time: "Those girls have a bright future ahead of them. That other one was just going to end up a kook." Little by little, people ceased to discuss the mystery of Cecilia's suicide, preferring to see it as inevitable, or as something best left behind. Though Mrs. Lisbon continued her shadowy existence, rarely leaving the house and getting her groceries delivered, no one objected, and some even sympathized. "I feel sorriest for the mother," Mrs. Eugene said. "You would always wonder if there was something you could have done." As for the suffering, surviving girls, they grew in stature like the Kennedys. Kids once again sat next to them on the bus. Leslie Tompkins borrowed Mary's brush to tame her long red hair. Julie Winthrop smoked with Lux atop the lockers, and said the shaking episode was not repeated. Day by day, the girls appeared to be getting over their loss.

It was during this convalescent period that Trip Fontaine made his move. Without consulting anyone or confessing his feelings for Lux, Trip Fontaine walked into Mr. Lisbon's classroom and stood at attention before his desk. He found Mr. Lisbon alone, in his swivel chair, staring vacantly at the planets hanging above his head. A youthful cowlick sprang from his gray hair. "It's fourth period, Trip," he said wearily. "I don't have you until fifth."

"I'm not here for math today, sir."

"You're not?"

"I'm here to tell you that my intentions toward your daughter are entirely honorable."

Mr. Lisbon's eyebrows rose, but his expression was used up, as though six or seven boys had made the same declaration that very morning.

"And what might those intentions be?"

Trip brought his boots together. "I want to ask Lux to Homecoming."

At that point, Mr. Lisbon told Trip to sit down, and for the next few minutes, in a patient voice, he explained that he and his wife had certain rules, they had been the same rules for the older girls and he couldn't very well change them now for the younger ones, even if he wanted to his wife wouldn't let him, ha ha, and while it was fine if Trip wanted to come over to watch television again, he could not, repeat not, take Lux out, especially in a car. Mr. Lisbon spoke, Trip told us, with surprising sympathy, as though he, too, recalled the below-the-belt pain of adolescence. He could also tell how starved Mr. Lisbon was for a son, because as he spoke he got up and gave Trip's shoulders three sporting shakes. "I'm afraid it's just our policy," he said, finally.

Trip Fontaine saw the doors closing. Then he saw the family photograph on Mr. Lisbon's desk. Before a Ferris wheel, Lux held in one red fist a candy apple whose polished surface reflected the baby fat under her chin. One side of her sugar-coated lips had come unstuck, showing a tooth.

"What if it was a bunch of us guys?" Trip Fontaine said. "And we took out your other daughters, too, like in a group? And we had them back by whatever time you say?"

Trip Fontaine made this new offer in a controlled voice, but his hands shook and his eyes grew moist. Mr. Lisbon looked at him a long time.

"You on the football squad, son?"

"Yes, sir."

"What position?"

"Offensive tackle."

"I played safety in my day."

"Crucial position, sir. Nothing between you and the goal line."

"Exactly."

"Thing is, sir, we've got the big Homecoming game against Country Day, and then the dance and everything, and all the guys on the team are going with dates."

"You're a good-looking young fella. Lots of girls would go with you, I bet."

"I'm not interested in lots of girls, sir," Trip Fontaine said. Mr. Lisbon sat back down in his chair. He drew a long breath. He looked at the photograph of his family, one face of which, smiling dreamily, no longer existed. "I'll take it up with their mother," he said, finally. "I'll do what I can."

That was how a few of us came to take the girls on the only unchaperoned date they ever had. As soon as he left Mr. Lisbon's classroom, Trip Fontaine began assembling his team. At football practice that afternoon, during wind sprints, he said, "I'm taking Lux Lisbon to Homecoming. All I need is three guys for the other chicks. Who's it going to be?" Running twenty-yard intervals, gasping for breath, in clumsy pads and unclean athletic socks, we each tried to convince Trip Fontaine to pick us. Jerry Burden offered three free joints. Parkie Denton said they could take his father's Cadillac. We all said something. Buzz Romano, nicknamed "Rope" because of the astonishing trained pet he showed us in the showers, covered his protective cup with his hands and lay moaning in the end zone: "I'm dying! I'm dying! You got to pick me, Tripster!"

In the end, Parkie Denton won because of the Cadillac, Kevin Head because he'd helped Trip Fontaine tune up his car, and Joe Hill Conley because he won all the school prizes, which Trip thought would impress Mr. and Mrs. Lisbon. The next day Trip presented the slate to Mr. Lisbon, and by the end of the week Mr. Lisbon announced his and his wife's decision. The girls could go under the following conditions: (1) they would go in a group; (2) they would go to the dance and nowhere else; (3) they would be home by eleven. Mr. Lisbon told Trip it would be impossible to get around these conditions. "I'm going to be one of the chaperons," he said.

It's difficult to know what the date meant to the girls. When Mr. Lisbon gave them permission, Lux ran and hugged him, kissing him with the unself-conscious affection of a little girl. "She hadn't kissed me like that in years," he said. The other girls reacted with less enthusiasm. At the time, Therese and Mary were playing Chinese checkers while Bonnie looked on. They broke their concentration from the dimpled metal board for only a moment, asking their father the identities of the other boys in the group. He told them. "Who's taking who?" Mary asked.

"They're just going to raffle us off," Therese said, and then made six ringing jumps into her safety zone.

Their lukewarm reaction made sense in terms of family

history. In concert with other church mothers, Mrs. Lisbon had arranged group dates before. The Perkins boys had paddled the Lisbon girls in five aluminum canoes along a murky canal at Belle Isle, while Mr. and Mrs. Lisbon and Mr. and Mrs. Perkins kept a watchful distance in paddle boats. Mrs. Lisbon thought the darker urges of dating could be satisfied by frolic in the open air—love sublimated by lawn darts. On a road trip recently (no reason for going other than boredom and gray skies) we stopped in Pennsylvania and, while buying candles in a rough-hewn store, learned of the Amish courting custom wherein a boy takes his homespun date for a ride in a black buggy, followed by her parents in another. Mrs. Lisbon, too, believed in keeping romance under surveillance. But whereas the Amish boy later returns in the dead of night to throw pebbles against the girl's window (pebbles everyone agrees not to hear), no nocturnal amnesty existed in Mrs. Lisbon's doctrine. Her canoes never led to campfires.

The girls could expect only more of the same. And with Mr. Lisbon chaperoning, they would be kept on the usual short leash. It was difficult enough having a teacher for a parent, on view day after day in his three suits, making a living. The Lisbon girls received free tuition because of their father's position, but Mary had once told Julie Ford this made her feel "like a charity case." Now he would be patrolling the dance along with other teachers who had volunteered or been forced to chaperon, usually the most uncoordinated teachers who didn't coach a sport, or the most socially inept for whom the dance was a way of filling another lonely night. Lux didn't seem to mind because her thoughts were filled with Trip Fontaine. She had gone back to writing names on her underthings, using water-soluble ink so that she could wash the "Trips" off before her mother saw them. (All day, however, his name had been continuously announcing itself against her skin.) Presumably she confessed her feelings about Trip to her sisters, but no girl at school ever heard her mention his name. Trip and Lux sat together at lunch, and sometimes we saw them walking the halls, searching for a closet or bin or heating duct to lie down inside, but even at school Mr. Lisbon was on hand, and after a few suppressed circuits, they came past the cafeteria and up the rubber-matted ramp leading to Mr. Lisbon's classroom and, briefly touching hands, went their separate ways.

The other girls barely knew their dates. "They hadn't even been *asked*," Mary Peters said. "It was like an arranged marriage or something. Creepy." Nevertheless, they allowed the date to go forward, to please Lux, to please themselves, or just to break the monotony of another Friday night. When we talked to Mrs. Lisbon years later, she told us she had had no qualms about the date, mentioning in support of this claim the dresses she had sewn especially for the evening. The week before Homecoming, in fact, she had taken the girls to a fabric store. The girls wandered amid the racks of patterns, each containing the tissue-paper outline of a dream dress, but in the end it made no difference which pattern they chose. Mrs. Lisbon added an inch to the bustlines and two inches to the waists and hems, and the dresses came out as four identical shapeless sacks.

A photo survives of that night (Exhibit #10). The girls are lined up in their party dresses, shoulder to square shoulder, like pioneer women. Their stiff hairdos ("hairdon'ts," Tessie Nepi, the beautician, said) have the stoic, presumptuous quality of European fashions enduring the wilderness. The dresses, too, look frontierish, with lace-trimmed bibs and high necklines. Here you have them, as we knew them, as we're still coming to know them: skittish Bonnie, shrinking from the flash; Therese, with her braincase squeezing shut the suspicious slits of her eyes; Mary, proper and posed; and Lux, looking not at the camera but up in the air. It was raining that night, and a leak had developed just over her head, hitting her cheek a second before Mr. Lisbon said, "Cheese." Though hardly ideal (a distracting light source invades from the left), the photograph still conveys the pride of attractive offspring and liminal rites. An air of expectancy glows in the girls' faces. Gripping one another, pulling each other into the frame, they seem braced for some discovery or change of life. Of *life*. That, at least, is how we see it. Please don't touch. We're going to put the picture back in its envelope now.

After that portrait was taken, the girls waited for the boys in individual ways. Bonnie and Therese sat down to play a game of cards, while Mary stood very still in the middle of the living room, trying not to wrinkle her dress.

Lux opened the front door and wobbled onto the porch. At first we thought she had sprained her ankle, but then we saw she was wearing high heels. She walked up and down, practicing, until Parkie Denton's car appeared at the end of the block. Then she turned, rang her own doorbell to warn her sisters, and disappeared inside again.

Left out, we watched the boys drive up. Parkie Denton's yellow Cadillac floated down the street, the boys suspended in the car's inner atmosphere. Though it was raining, and the windshield wipers were going, the car's interior had a warm glow. As they passed Joe Larson's house, the boys gave us a thumbs-up.

Trip Fontaine got out first. He'd pushed up his jacket sleeves as male models did in his father's fashion magazines. He was wearing a thin tie. Parkie Denton had on a blue blazer, as did Kevin Head, and then Joe Hill Conley vaulted from the backseat, wearing an oversize tweed blazer belonging to his father the schoolteacher and Communist. At that point, the boys hesitated, standing around the car, oblivious to the drizzle, until Trip Fontaine finally headed up the front path. We lost sight of them at the door, but they told us the beginning of the date was like any other. The girls had gone upstairs, pretending not to be ready, and Mr. Lisbon took the boys into the living room.

"The girls'll be down in just a minute," he said, looking at his watch. "Jeez. I better get going myself." Mrs. Lisbon came to the archway. She was holding her temple as though she had a headache, but her smile was polite.

"Hello, boys."

"Hello, Mrs. Lisbon" (in unison).

She had the rectitude, Joe Hill Conley later said, of someone who had just come from weeping in the next room. He had sensed (this said many years later, of course, when Joe Hill Conley claimed to tap at will the energy of his chakras) an ancient pain arising from Mrs. Lisbon, the sum of her people's griefs. "She came from a sad race," he said. "It wasn't only Cecilia. The sadness had started long before. Before America. The girls had it, too." He had never noticed her bifocals before. "They cut her eyes in half."

"Which one of you is driving?" Mrs. Lisbon asked.

"I am," said Parkie Denton.

"How long have you had your license?"

"Two months. But I had my permit for a year before that."

"We don't usually like the girls to go out in cars. So many accidents nowadays. It's raining and the roads will be slick. So I hope you'll be very careful."

"We will."

"OK," Mr. Lisbon said, "third degree's over. Girls!"— delivered to the ceiling—"I've got to get going. I'll see you at the dance, boys."

"See you there, Mr. Lisbon."

He went out, leaving the boys alone with his wife. She didn't meet their eyes but scanned them generally, like a head nurse reading charts. Then she went to the bottom of the stairs and stared up. Not even Joe Hill Conley could imagine what she was thinking. Of Cecilia perhaps, climbing those same stairs four months ago. Of the stairs she had descended on her own first date. Of sounds only a mother can hear. None of the boys ever remembered seeing Mrs. Lisbon so distracted. It was as though she had suddenly forgotten they were there. She touched her temple (it *was* a headache).

At last the girls came to the top of the stairs. It was dim up there (three of twelve chandelier bulbs had burned out), and they held the banister lightly as they descended. Their loose dresses reminded Kevin Head of choir robes. "They didn't seem to notice, though. Personally, I think they liked the dresses. Or else they were just so happy to be going out they didn't care what they wore. I didn't care, either. They looked great."

Only when the girls reached the bottom did the boys realize they hadn't decided who was taking whom. Trip Fontaine, of course, had dibs on Lux, but the other three girls were up for grabs. Fortunately, their dresses and hair-dos homogenized them. Once again the boys weren't even sure which girl was which. Instead of asking, they did the only thing they could think of doing: they presented the corsages.

"We got white," Trip Fontaine said. "We didn't know what color you were wearing. The flower guy said white would go with everything."

"I'm glad you got white," said Lux. She reached out and took the corsage, which was housed in a little plastic case.

"We didn't go for wrist ones," Parkie Denton said. "Those always fall apart."

"Yeah, those are bad," said Mary. No one said anything

more. No one moved. Lux inspected her flower in its time capsule. In the background, Mrs. Lisbon said, "Why don't you let the boys pin them on?"

At that, the girls stepped forward, shyly presenting the fronts of their dresses. The boys fumbled with the corsages, taking them out of their cases and avoiding the decorative stickpins. They could sense Mrs. Lisbon watching them, and even though they were close enough to feel the Lisbon girls' breath and to smell the first perfume they had ever been allowed to wear, the boys tried not to stick the girls or even to touch them. They gently lifted the material from the girls' chests and hung white flowers over their hearts. Whichever Lisbon girl a boy pinned became his date. When they finished, they said good night to Mrs. Lisbon and led the girls outside to the Cadillac, holding the empty corsage cases over the girls' heads to protect their hair from the drizzle.

From that point on, things went better than expected. At home, each boy had pictured the Lisbon girls amid the stock scenery of our impoverished imaginations—cavorting in the surf or playfully fleeing at the ice-skating rink, dangling ski-hat pom-poms like ripe fruit before our faces. In the car, however, beside the actual living girls, the boys realized the paltriness of these images. Inverse properties were also discarded: notions of the girls as damaged or demented. (The crazy old lady in the elevator every day turns out to be, when you finally speak to her, perfectly lucid.) Something like this revelation came over the boys. "They weren't all that different from my sister," Kevin Head said. Lux, complaining she never got to, wanted to sit up front. She slid in between Trip Fontaine and Parkie Denton. Mary, Bonnie, and Therese crowded into the backseat, with Bonnie getting the hump. Joe Hill Conley and Kevin Head sat on either side against the back doors.

Even up close, the girls didn't look depressed. They settled into the seats, not minding the tight fit. Mary half sat in Kevin Head's lap. They began chattering immediately. As houses passed, they had something to say about the families in each one, which meant that they had been looking out at us as intensely as we had been looking in. Two summers ago they had seen Mr. Tubbs, the UAW middle-management boss, punch the lady who had followed his wife home after a fender bender. They suspected the Hessens had been Nazis or Nazi sympathizers. They loathed the Kriegers' aluminum siding. "Mr. Belvedere strikes again," said Therese, referring to the president of the home-improvement company in his late-night commercial. Like us, the girls had distinct memories tied to various bushes, trees, and garage roofs. They recalled the race riots, when tanks had appeared at the end of our block and National Guardsmen had parachuted into our backyards. They were, after all, our neighbors.

At first the boys said nothing, too overwhelmed by the Lisbon girls' volubility. Who had known they talked so much, held so many opinions, jabbed at the world's sights with so many fingers? Between our sporadic glimpses of the girls they had been continuously living, developing in ways we couldn't imagine, reading every book on the bowdlerized family bookshelf. Somehow, too, they'd kept up on dating etiquette, through television or observation at school, so that they knew how to keep the conversation flowing or fill awkward silences. Their dating inexperience showed only in their pinned-up hair, which looked like stuffing coming out, or exposed wiring. Mrs. Lisbon had never given the girls beauty tips, and forbade women's magazines in the house (a *Cosmo* survey, "Are you multiply orgasmic?" had been the final straw). They had done the best they could.

Lux spent the ride dialing the radio for her favorite song. "It makes me crazy," she said. "You know they're playing it somewhere, but you have to find it." Parkie Denton drove down to Jefferson Avenue, past the Wainwright house with its green historical marker, and toward the gathering lakefront mansions. Imitation gas lanterns burned on front lawns. On every corner a black maid waited for the bus. They drove on, past the glittering lake, and finally under the ragged cover of elms near the school.

"Hold on a sec," Lux said. "I want a cig before we go in."

"Dad'll smell it on you," Bonnie said from the backseat.

"Nah, I've got mints." She shook them.

"He'll smell it on our clothes."

"Just tell him some kids were smoking in the bathroom."

Parkie Denton lowered the front window while Lux smoked. She took her time, exhaling through her nose. At one point she jutted out her chin at Trip Fontaine, rounded her lips, and, with a chimpanzee profile, sent forth three perfect smoke rings.

"Don't let it die a virgin," Joe Hill Conley said. He leaned into the front seat and poked one.

"That's gross," said Therese.

"Yeah, Conley," Trip Fontaine said. "Grow up."

On the way into the dance, the couples separated. One of Bonnie's high heels got stuck in the gravel and she leaned on Joe Hill Conley while she detached it. Trip Fontaine and Lux moved on together, already an item. Kevin Head walked in with Therese, while Parkie Denton gave Mary his arm.

The light rain had stopped for a moment and the stars were out, in patches. As Bonnie's shoe came loose, she looked up and called attention to the sky. "It's always the Big Dipper," she said. "You look at those charts and they have stars all over the place, but if you look up, all you see is the Big Dipper."

"It's because of the lights," Joe Hill Conley said. "From the city."

"Duh," Bonnie said.

The girls were smiling as they entered the gymnasium amid the glowing pumpkins and scarecrows dressed in school colors. The Dance Committee had decided on a harvest theme. Straw was scattered over the basketball court and cornucopias spewed tumorous gourds on the cider table. Mr. Lisbon had already arrived, wearing an orange tie reserved for festive occasions. He was talking with

Mr. Tonover, the chemistry teacher. Mr. Lisbon didn't acknowledge the girls' arrival in any way, though he might not have seen them. The game lights had been covered with orange gels from the theater and the bleachers were dark. A rented disco ball hung from the scoreboard, dappling the room with light.

We had arrived with our own dates by then, and danced with them as though holding mannequins, looking over their chiffon shoulders for the Lisbon girls. We saw them come in, unsteady in their high heels. Wide-eyed, they looked around the gym, and then, conferring among themselves, left their dates while they took the first of seven trips to the bathroom. Hopie Riggs was at the sink when the girls entered. "You could tell they were embarrassed by their dresses," she said. "They didn't say anything, but you could tell. I was wearing a dress with a velvet bodice and taffeta skirt that night. I can still fit into it." Only Mary and Bonnie had to use the facilities, but Lux and Therese kept them company, Lux looking in the mirror for the instant it took to reconfirm her beauty, Therese avoiding it altogether.

"There's no paper," Mary said from her stall. "Throw me some."

Lux ripped a bunch of paper towels from the dispenser and lofted them over the stall.

"It's snowing," Mary said.

"They were really loud," Hopie Riggs told us. "They acted like they owned the place. I had something on the back of my dress, though, and Therese got it off." When we asked if the Lisbon girls had spoken about their dates in the confessional surroundings of the bathroom, Hopie answered, "Mary said she was happy her guy wasn't a total geek. That was it, though. I don't think they cared so much about their dates as just being at the dance. I felt the same way. I was there with Tim Carter, the shrimpo."

When the girls came out of the bathroom, the dance floor was getting more crowded, circulating couples slowly around the gym. Kevin Head asked Therese to dance and soon they were lost in the tumult. "God, I was so young," he said years later. "So *scared*. So was she. I took her hand and we didn't know which way to do it. To interlace fingers or not. Finally we did. That's what I remember most. The finger thing."

Parkie Denton remembers Mary's studied movements, her poise. "*She* led," he said. "She had a Kleenex balled in one hand." During the dance, she made polite conversation, the kind beautiful young women make with dukes during waltzes in old movies. She held herself very straight, like Audrey Hepburn, whom all women idolize and men never think about. She seemed to have a picture in her mind of what pattern their feet should make over the floor, of how they should look together, and she concentrated fiercely to realize it. "Her face was calm, but inside she was tense," Parkie Denton said. "Her back muscles were like piano strings." When a fast song came on, Mary danced less well. "Like old people at weddings trying it out."

Lux and Trip didn't dance until later, and instead moved about the gymnasium looking for a place to be alone.

Bonnie followed. "So I followed her," Joe Hill Conley said. "She pretended she was just walking around, but she kept track of Lux from the corner of her eye." They went in one side of the dance mob and out the other. They hugged the far wall of the gym, passing beneath the decorated basketball net, and ended up by the bleachers. Between songs, Mr. Durid, Dean of Students, opened the voting for Homecoming King and Queen, and while everyone was looking toward the glass ballot jar on the cider table, Trip Fontaine and Lux Lisbon slipped underneath the bleachers.

Bonnie pursued them. "It was like she was afraid of being left alone," Joe Hill Conley said. Though she hadn't asked him to, he followed her. Underneath, in the stripes of light coming through the slats, he saw Trip Fontaine holding a bottle up to Lux's face so she could read the label. "Did anybody see you come in?" Lux asked her sister.

"No."

"What about you?"

"No," Joe Hill Conley said.

Then no one spoke. Everyone's attention returned to the bottle Trip Fontaine held in his hand. Reflections from the disco ball glittered on the bottle's surface, illuminating the inflamed fruit on the label.

"Peach schnapps," Trip Fontaine explained years later, in the desert, drying out from that and everything else. "Babes love it."

He had purchased the liqueur with a fake I.D. that afternoon, and had carried it in the lining of his jacket all evening. Now, as the other three watched, he unscrewed the bottle cap and sipped the syrup that was like nectar or honey. "You have to taste it with a kiss," he said. He held the bottle to Lux's lips, saying, "Don't swallow." Then, taking another swig, he brought his mouth to Lux's in a peach-flavored kiss. Her throat gurgled with captive mirth. She laughed, a trickle of schnapps dripped down her chin where she caught it with one ringed hand, but then they grew solemn, faces pressed together, swallowing and kissing. When they stopped, Lux said, "That stuff's really good."

Trip handed the bottle to Joe Hill Conley. He held it to Bonnie's mouth, but she turned away. "I don't want any," she said.

"Come on," Trip said. "Just a taste."

"Don't be a goody-goody," said Lux.

Only the strip of Bonnie's eyes was visible, and in the silver light they filled with tears. Below, in the dark where her mouth was, Joe Hill Conley thrust the bottle. Her moist eyes widened. Her cheeks filled. "Don't swallow it," Lux commanded. And then Joe Hill Conley spilled the contents of his own mouth into Bonnie's. He said she kept her teeth together throughout the kiss, grinning like a skull. The peach schnapps passed back and forth between his mouth and hers, but then he felt her swallowing, relaxing. Years later, Joe Hill Conley boasted that he could analyze a woman's emotional makeup by the taste of her mouth, and insisted he'd stumbled on this insight that night under the bleachers with Bonnie. He could sense her whole being through the kiss, he said, as though her soul escaped through her lips, as the Renaissance believed. He tasted first the grease of her ChapStick, then the sad Brussels-sprout flavor of her last meal, and past that the dust of lost afternoons and the salt of tear ducts. The peach schnapps faded away as he sampled the juices of her inner organs, all slightly acidic with woe. Sometimes her lips grew strangely cold, and, peeking, he saw she kissed with her frightened eyes wide open. After that, the schnapps went back and forth. We asked the boys if they had talked intimately with the girls, or asked them about Cecilia, but they said no. "I didn't want to ruin a good thing," Trip Fontaine said. And Joe Hill Conley: "There's a time for talk and a time for silence." Even though he tasted mysterious depths in Bonnie's mouth, he didn't search them out because he didn't want her to stop kissing him.

We saw the girls come out from underneath the bleachers, dragging their dresses and wiping their mouths. Lux moved sassily to the music. It was then Trip Fontaine finally got to dance with her, and years later he told us the baggy dress had only increased his desire. "You could feel how slim she was under all those drapes. It killed me." As the night wore on, the girls became accustomed to their dresses and learned to move in them. Lux found a way of arching her back that made her dress tight in front. We walked past them whenever we could, going to the bathroom twenty times and drinking twenty glasses of cider. We tried to grill the boys in order to participate vicariously in the date, but they wouldn't leave the girls alone for a minute. When the balloting for King and Queen was finished, Mr. Durid mounted the portable stage and announced the winners. Everyone knew the King and Queen could only be Trip Fontaine and Lux Lisbon, and even girls in hundred-dollar dresses applauded as they made their way forward. Then they danced, and we all danced, cutting in on Head and Conley and Denton to dance with the Lisbon girls ourselves. They were flushed by the time they got to us, damp under the arms and giving off heat from their high necklines. We held their sweaty palms, turning them under the mirrored ball. We lost them in the vastness of their dresses and found them again, squeezed the pulp of their bodies and inhaled the perfume of their exertion. A few of us grew brave enough to insert our legs between theirs and to press our agony against them. In the dresses the Lisbon girls looked identical again, as they flowed from hand to hand, smiling, saying thank you, thank you. A loose thread got caught in David Stark's wristwatch, and as Mary untangled it, he asked, "Are you having a good time?"

"I'm having the best time of my life," she said.

She was telling the truth. Never before had the Lisbon girls looked so cheerful, mixed so much, or talked so freely. After one dance, while Therese and Kevin Head got some cool air in the doorway, Therese asked, "What made you guys ask us out?"

"What do you mean?"

"I mean, do you feel sorry for us?"

"No way."

"Liar."

"I think you're pretty. That's why."

"Do we seem as crazy as everyone thinks?"

"Who thinks that?"

She didn't reply, only stuck her hand out the door to test for rain. "Cecilia was weird, but we're not." And then: "We just want to live. If anyone would let us."

Later, going to the car, Bonnie stopped Joe Hill Conley to look for the stars again. Everything was clouded over. As they gazed up at the dull sky, she asked, "Do you think there's a God?"

"Yeah."

"Me too."

By that time it was ten-thirty and the girls had only a half hour to get back home. The dance was breaking up, and Mr. Lisbon's car emerged from the faculty parking lot, heading home. Kevin Head and Therese, Joe Hill Conley and Bonnie, Parkie Denton and Mary all converged at the Cadillac, but Lux and Trip didn't follow. Bonnie ran back into the gymnasium to check, but they couldn't be found.

"Maybe they went home with your dad," Parkie Denton said.

"I doubt it," said Mary, looking off into the dark and fingering her crushed corsage. The girls took off their high heels so they could walk better, and searched in among the parked cars and by the flagpole that had flown at half-mast the day Cecilia died, though it had been summer and no one but the lawn crew had noticed. The girls, so happy moments before, grew quiet, and forgot about their dates. They moved in a pack, separating and coming back together. They searched over near the theater, behind the

Science Wing, and even in the courtyard where the small statue of a girl stood, donated in memory of Laura White, her bronze skirt just beginning to oxidize. Scars crossed her welded wrists, symbolically, but the Lisbon girls didn't notice, or say anything when they returned to the car at 10:50 P.M. They got in to be taken home.

The ride back happened mostly in silence. Joe Hill Conley and Bonnie sat in back beside Kevin Head and Therese. Parkie Denton drove, later complaining that this afforded him no chance to make his move on Mary. Mary, however, spent the ride fixing her hair in the sun-visor mirror. Therese said to her, "Forget it. We're cooked."

"Luxie is. Not us."

"Anyone have some mints or some gum?" Bonnie asked. No one did, and she turned to Joe Hill Conley. She scrutinized him a moment, then, using her fingers, combed his part over to the left side. "That looks better," she said. Nearly two decades later, the little hair he has left remains parted by Bonnie's invisible hand.

Outside the Lisbon house, Joe Hill Conley kissed Bonnie for the last time and she let him. Therese gave Kevin Head her cheek. Through steamed windows the boys looked up at the house. Mr. Lisbon had already returned and a light was on in the master bedroom.

"We'll walk you to the door," Parkie Denton said.

"No, don't," said Mary.

"Why not?"

"Just don't." She got out without so much as a handshake.

"We had a really good time," Therese said in back. Bonnie whispered into Joe Hill Conley's ear, "Will you call me?"

"Absolutely."

The car doors creaked open. The girls climbed out, adjusted themselves, and went into the house.

Uncle Tucker had just gone out to the garage refrigerator to get another six-pack when the taxi drove up two hours later. He saw Lux get out and reach into her purse for the five-dollar bill Mrs. Lisbon had given each daughter before leaving that evening. "Always have cab fare" was her dictum, even though that night was the first time she had allowed the girls to go out, and, hence, to need any. Lux didn't wait for her change. She started up the driveway, lifting her dress to walk and staring at the ground. The back of her coat was smudged white. The front door opened and Mr. Lisbon stepped onto the porch. His jacket was off but he was still wearing the orange necktie. He came down the steps and met Lux halfway. Lux began making excuses with her hands. When Mr. Lisbon cut her off, she hung her head and then, grudgingly, nodded. Uncle Tucker couldn't recall the exact moment Mrs. Lisbon joined the scene. At some point, however, he became conscious of music playing in the background and, looking up at the house, saw Mrs. Lisbon in the open doorway. She was dressed in a plaid robe and held a drink in her hand. Behind her, music filtered out, full of reverberating organs and seraphic harps. Having started drinking at noon, Uncle Tucker had almost finished the case of beer he consumed each day. He began to weep, looking out from the garage, as music filled the street like air. "It was the kind of music they play when you die," he said.

It was church music, a selection from among the three albums Mrs. Lisbon liked to play over and over again on Sundays. We knew about the music from Cecilia's diary ("Sunday morning. Mom's playing that crap again"), and months later, when they were moving out, we found the albums in the trash they put at the curb. The albums are—as we've listed in the Record of Physical Evidence—*Songs of Faith*, by Tyrone Little and the Believers, *Eternal Rapture*, by the Toledo Baptist Choir, and *Singing Thy Praises*, by the Grand Rapids Gospelers. Beams of light pierce clouds on each cover. We haven't even played the records through once. It's the same music we pass by on the radio, in between the Motown and rock and roll, a beacon of light in a world of darkness, and totally shitty. Choirs sing in blond voices, scales ascend toward harmonic crescendos, like marshmallow foaming into the ears. We'd always wondered who listened to such music, picturing lonely widows in rest homes, or pastors' families passing plates of ham. Never once did we imagine those pious voices drifting up through floorboards to churchify niches where the Lisbon girls knelt to pumice calluses on their big toes. Father Moody heard the music the few times he visited for coffee on Sunday afternoons. "It wasn't my cup of tea," he said to us later. "I go in for the more august stuff. Handel's *Messiah*. Mozart's Requiem. This was basically, if I may say so, what you might expect to hear in a Protestant household."

As the music played, Mrs. Lisbon stood in the doorway, unmoving. Mr. Lisbon herded Lux inside. Lux came up the steps and crossed the porch, but her mother did not let her enter. Mrs. Lisbon said something Uncle Tucker couldn't hear. Lux opened her mouth. Mrs. Lisbon bent forward and held her face motionless near Lux's. "Breathalizer," Uncle Tucker explained to us. The test lasted no more than five seconds before Mrs. Lisbon reared back to strike Lux across the face. Lux flinched, but the blow never came. Arm raised, Mrs. Lisbon froze. She turned toward the dark street, as though a hundred eyes and not only Uncle Tucker's two were watching. Mr. Lisbon also turned. As did Lux. The three of them stared into the largely lightless neighborhood, where trees continued to drip, and cars slept in garages and carports, engines pinging all night as they cooled. They stayed very still, and then Mrs. Lisbon's hand fell limply to her side, and Lux saw her chance. She shot by her, up the stairs, into her room.

We learned only years later what had happened to Lux and Trip Fontaine. Even then Trip Fontaine told us with extreme reluctance, insisting, as the Twelve Steps mandated, that he was a changed man. After their dance as Homecoming King and Queen, Trip had ushered Lux through the knot of applauding subjects to the very door where Therese and Kevin Head had gone to get some air. "We were hot from dancing," he said. Lux was still wearing the Miss America tiara Mr. Durid had placed on her head. They both bore royal ribbons across their chests. "What do we do now?" Lux had asked.

"Whatever we want."

"I mean as King and Queen. Do we have to do something?"

"This is it. We danced. We got ribbons. It only lasts for tonight."

"I thought it was for all year long."

"Well, it is. But we don't do anything."

Lux took this in. "I think it stopped raining," she said.

"Let's go outside."

"I better not. We've got to go in a minute."

"We can keep an eye on the car. They won't leave without us."

"My dad," Lux said.

"Just say you had to put your crown in your locker."

It had indeed stopped raining, but the air was misty when they crossed the street and walked hand in hand over the soggy football field. "See that divot," Trip Fontaine said. "That's where I reamed this guy today. Cross-body block."

They walked past the fifty, the forty, and into the end zone, where no one saw them. The white stripe Uncle Tucker later saw on Lux's coat came from the goal line she lay down upon. Throughout the act, headlights came on across the field, sweeping over them, lighting up the goalpost. Lux said, in the middle, "I always screw things up. I always do," and began to sob. Trip Fontaine told us little more.

We asked him if he put her in the cab, but he said no. "I walked home that night. I didn't care how she got home. I just took off." Then: "It's weird. I mean, I liked her. I really liked her. I just got sick of her right then."

As for the other boys, they spent the rest of the night driving around our suburb. They drove past the Little Club, the Yacht Club, the Hunt Club. They drove through The Village, where Halloween displays had given way to Thanksgiving. At 1:30 A.M., unable to stop thinking about the girls whose presence still filled the car, they decided to make one final pass by the Lisbon house. They stopped for Joe Hill Conley to relieve himself behind a tree, then proceeded down Cadieux, speeding past the smallish houses that had once been cottages for summer help. They passed a subdivision where one of our great mansions had stood, its ornamental gardens replaced by redbrick houses with antiqued doors and mammoth garages. They turned onto Jefferson, passing the War Memorial and the black gates of the remaining millionaires, and rode in silence toward the girls who had become real to them at last. As they approached the Lisbons' house, they saw a light burning in a bedroom window. Parkie Denton held up his hand for the other boys to slap. "Pay dirt," he said. But their jubilation was short-lived. For even before the car stopped they knew what had happened. "It hit me in the pit of my stomach that those girls weren't going on any more dates," Kevin Head told us years later. "The old bitch had locked them up again. Don't ask me how I knew. I just did." The window shades had closed like eyelids and the shaggy flower beds made the house look abandoned. In the window where the one light burned, however, the shade rippled. A hand peeled it back, revealing a hot yellow slice of face—Bonnie, Mary, Therese, or even Lux—looking down the street. Parkie Denton tooted his horn, a short hopeful blast, but just as the girl put her palm to the glass, the light went out.

# FOUR

A few weeks after Mrs. Lisbon shut the house in maximum-security isolation, the sightings of Lux making love on the roof began.

Following the Homecoming dance, Mrs. Lisbon closed the downstairs shades. All we could see were the girls' incarcerated shadows, which ran riot in our imaginations. Moreover, as fall turned to winter, the trees in the yard drooped and thickened, concealing the house, even though their leaflessness should have revealed it. A cloud always seemed to hover over the Lisbons' roof. There was no explanation except the psychic one that the house became obscured because Mrs. Lisbon willed it to. The sky grew darker, and light abandoned the daytime, so that we found ourselves always moving in a timeless murk, the only way to discern the hour the taste of our burps, tooth-pasty in the morning, redolent in the afternoon of the jellied beef of school cafeteria meals.

Without explanation, the girls were taken out of school. They merely failed to show up one morning, and then again the next. When Mr. Woodhouse asked about the matter, Mr. Lisbon seemed to have no idea the girls were gone. "He kept saying, 'Have you checked out back?'"

Jerry Burden picked the combination on Mary's locker to find most of her books left behind. "She had postcards taped up inside. Weird stuff. Couches and shit." (Actually art museum postcards showing a Biedermeier chair and a pink chintz Chippendale sofa.) Her notebooks were piled on the top shelf, each one bearing the name of a bright new subject she never got to study. Inside *American History*, amid spasmodic notes, Jerry Burden found the following doodle: a girl with pigtails is bent under the weight of a gigantic boulder. Her cheeks puff out, and her rounded lips expel steam. One widening steam cloud contains the word *Pressure*, darkly retraced.

Given Lux's failure to make curfew, everyone expected a crackdown, but few anticipated it would be so drastic. When we spoke to her years later, however, Mrs. Lisbon maintained that her decision was never intended to be punitive. "At that point being in school was just making things worse," she said. "None of the other children were speaking to the girls. Except boys, and you knew what they were after. The girls needed time to themselves. A mother knows. I thought if they stayed at home, they'd heal better." Our interview with Mrs. Lisbon was brief. She met us at the bus station in the small town she now lives in, because the station was the only place that served coffee.

Her hands were red-knuckled and her gums had receded. Her tragedy hadn't made her more approachable, and in fact lent her the unknowable quality of a person who had suffered more than could be expressed. Nevertheless, we wanted to talk to her most of all because we felt that she, being the girls' mother, understood more than anyone why they had killed themselves. But she said, "That's what's so frightening. I don't. Once they're out of you, they're different, kids are." When we asked her why she had never pursued the psychological counseling Dr. Hornicker offered, Mrs. Lisbon became angry. "That doctor wanted to blame it on us. He thought Ronnie and I were to blame." A bus came into the station then, and through the open doorway at Gate 2 a gust of carbon monoxide blew over the counter with its stacks of fried doughnuts. Mrs. Lisbon said she had to leave.

She had done more than take the girls out of school. The next Sunday, arriving home after a spirited church sermon, she had commanded Lux to destroy her rock records. Mrs. Pitzenberger (who happened to be redecorating a room next door) heard the fierce argument. "Now!" Mrs. Lisbon kept repeating, while Lux tried to reason, to negotiate, and finally burst into tears. Through the upstairs hall window, Mrs. Pitzenberger saw Lux stomp to her bedroom, returning with a collection of peach crates. The crates were heavy and Lux slid them down the stairs like sleds. "She acted like she was going to whiz them down. But she always grabbed them before they got out of control." In the living room, Mrs. Lisbon had the fire going, and Lux, now crying without sound, began to consign her records one by one to the flames. We never learned which albums were condemned at that auto-da-fé, but apparently Lux held up album after album, appealing for Mrs. Lisbon's mercy. The smell quickly grew overpowering, and the plastic melted over the andirons, so that Mrs. Lisbon told Lux to stop. (She threw out the rest of the albums with that week's trash.) Still, Will Timber, who was getting a grape pop, said he could smell burning plastic all the way to Mr. Z's, the party store on Kercheval.

For the next few weeks we hardly saw the girls at all. Lux never spoke to Trip Fontaine again, nor did Joe Hill Conley call Bonnie, as he had promised. Mrs. Lisbon took the girls to their grandmother's house to get advice from an old woman who had lived through everything. When we called her in Roswell, New Mexico, where she had moved after living forty-three years in the same single-story house, the old lady (Mrs. Lema Crawford) did not respond to questions about her involvement in the punishment, either out of stubbornness or because of the feedback her hearing aid picked up over the phone. She did refer, however, to her own misfortune at the hands of love some sixty years earlier. "You never get over it," she said. "But you get to where it doesn't bother you so much." And then, before hanging up: "Lovely weather down here. Best thing I ever did was to throw down the old shovel and hoe and get out of that town."

The smoky sound of her voice brought the scene to life for us: the old woman at the kitchen table, her skimpy hair up in an elasticized turban; Mrs. Lisbon tight-lipped and grim in a chair opposite; and the four penitents, heads lowered, fingering knickknacks and porcelain figurines. There is no discussion of how they feel or what they want out of life; there is only the descending order—grandmother, mother, daughters—with the backyard outside under rain, and the dead vegetable garden.

Mr. Lisbon continued to go to work in the mornings and the family continued to attend church on Sundays, but that was it. The house receded behind its mists of youth being choked off, and even our own parents began to mention how dim and unhealthy the place looked. Raccoons were attracted by its miasmic vapors at night, and it wasn't unusual to find a dead one squashed by a car as it had tried to make its getaway from the Lisbons' trash cans. One week, on the front porch, Mrs. Lisbon set off tiny smoke bombs that gave off a sulfurous stench. No one had ever seen the gadgets before, but it was rumored they were a defense against the raccoons. Then, about the time the first cold spell hit, people began to see Lux copulating on the roof with faceless boys and men.

At first it was impossible to tell what was happening. A cellophane body swept its arms back and forth against the slate tiles like a child drawing an angel in the snow. Then another darker body could be discerned, sometimes in a fast-food restaurant uniform, sometimes wearing an assortment of gold chains, once in the drab gray suit of an accountant. Through the bronchioles of leafless elm branches, from the Pitzenbergers' attic, we finally made out Lux's face as she sat wrapped in a Hudson's Bay blanket, smoking a cigarette, impossibly close in the circle of our binoculars because she moved her lips only inches away but without sound.

We wondered how she could do such a thing on her own house, with her parents sleeping nearby. True, it was impossible for Mr. and Mrs. Lisbon to see their own roof, and, once installed, Lux and her partners enjoyed relative safety; but there was the unavoidable prior noise of sneaking down to let the boys and men in, of leading them up creaking stairs in a darkness charged with anxious vibrations, night noises humming in their ears, the men sweating, risking statutory rape charges, the loss of their careers, divorce, just to be led up the stairway, through a window, to the roof, where in the midst of their passion they chafed their knees and rolled in stagnant puddles. We never knew how Lux met them. From what we could tell, she didn't leave the house. She didn't even leave at night, sneaking out to do it in a vacant lot or down by the lake, but preferred to make love on the premises of her confinement. For our own part, we learned a great deal about the techniques of love, and because we didn't know the words to denote what we saw, we had to make up our own. That was why we spoke of "yodeling in the canyon" and "tying the tube," of "groaning in the pit," "slipping the turtle's head," and "chewing the stinkweed." Years later, when we lost our own virginities, we resorted in our panic to pantomiming Lux's gyrations on the roof so long ago; and even now, if we were to be honest with ourselves, we would have to admit that it is always that pale wraith we make love to, always her feet snagged in the gutter, always her single blooming hand steadying itself against the chimney, no matter what our present lovers' feet and hands are doing. And we'd have to admit, too, that in our most intimate moments, alone at night with our beating hearts, asking God to save us, what comes most often is Lux, succubus of those binocular nights.

We received reports of her erotic adventures from the most unlikely sources, kids from working-class neighborhoods with feathered haircuts who swore they'd gone to the roof themselves with Lux, and though we quizzed them, trying to find inconsistencies in their stories, we never succeeded. They said it was always too dark inside the house to see, the only thing alive Lux's hand, urgent and bored at once, tugging them forward by their belt buckles. The floor was an obstacle course. Dan Tyco, with his tackle's neck, stepped in something soft at the top of the landing and picked it up. Only after Lux led him out the window and up to the roof could he see by moonlight what he held: the half-eaten sandwich Father Moody had encountered five months earlier. Other kids found congealed bowls of spaghetti, empty tin cans, as though Mrs. Lisbon had stopped cooking for the girls and they lived by foraging.

According to the boys' descriptions, Lux had lost weight, though we couldn't tell through the binoculars. All sixteen mentioned her jutting ribs, the insubstantiality of her thighs, and one, who went up to the roof with Lux dur-

ing a warm winter rain, told us how the basins of her collarbones collected water. A few boys mentioned the acidic
taste of her saliva—the taste of digestive fluids with nothing to do—but none of these signs of malnourishment or
illness or grief (the small cold sores at the corners of her
mouth, the patch of hair missing above her left ear) de-
tracted from Lux's overwhelming impression of being a
carnal angel. They spoke of being pinned to the chimney as
if by two great beating wings, and of the slight blond fuzz
above her upper lip that felt like plumage. Her eyes shone,
burned, intent on her mission as only a creature with no
doubts as to either Creation's glory or its meaninglessness
could be. The words the boys used, their shifty eyebrows,
fright, bafflement, made it clear they had served as only the
most insignificant footholds in Lux's ascent, and, in the
end, even though they had been carried to the peak, they
couldn't tell us what lay beyond. A few of them remarked
on the overriding sense of Lux's measureless charity.

Though she carried on few extended conversations, we
got an idea of her state of mind from the little that got
back to us of the little she said. She told Bob McBrearley
that she couldn't live without "getting it regular," though
she delivered the phrase with a Brooklyn accent, as though
imitating a movie. A sense of playacting permeated
much of her behavior. Willie Tate admitted that, despite
her eagerness, "she didn't seem to like it much," and many
boys described similar inattention. Lifting their heads
from the soft shelf of Lux's neck, they found her eyes
open, her brow knitted in thought; or at the height of

passion they felt her pick a pimple on their backs. Nevertheless, on the roof, Lux reportedly said pleading things like, "Put it in. Just for a minute. It'll make us feel close." Other times she treated the act like some small chore, positioning the boys, undoing zippers and buckles with the weariness of a checkout girl. She oscillated wildly in her contraceptive vigilance. Some reported her administering complex procedures, inserting three or four jellies or creams at once, topping them off with a white spermicide she referred to as "the cream cheese." Occasionally she sufficed with her "Australian method," which involved shaking up a Coke bottle and hosing down her insides. In stricter moods she laid down her catchphrase ultimatum: "No erection without protection." Often she used sanitized pharmaceutical products; other times, presumably cut off by Mrs. Lisbon's blockade, she fell back on the ingenious methods devised by midwives in centuries past. Vinegar proved useful, as did tomato juice. Love's tiny seacraft foundered in acidic seas. Lux kept an assortment of bottles, as well as one foul rag, behind the chimney. Nine months later, when the roofers hired by the new young couple found the bottles, they called down to the young wife, "Looks like somebody was having salad up here."

It was crazy to make love on the roof at any time, but to make love on the roof in winter suggested derangement, desperation, self-destructiveness far in excess of any pleasure snatched beneath the dripping trees. Though some of us saw Lux as a force of nature, impervious to chill, an ice goddess generated by the season itself, the majority knew she was only a girl in danger, or in pursuit, of catching her death of cold. Therefore we were not surprised when, three weeks into Lux's airborne displays, the EMS truck appeared yet again. By this, its third rescue, the truck had become as familiar as Mrs. Buell's hysterical voice calling Chase home. When it rocketed up the drive, familiarity blinded us to its new snow tires, the rings of salt encrusting each fender. We saw Sheriff—the skinny one with the mustache—leaping from the driver's seat even before he did so, and after that every sight had déjà vu written all over it. We were prepared for the nightgowned girls to streak past the windows, for lights to chart the paramedics' progress toward the victim, first the foyer light going on, then the hall light, the upstairs hall, the bedroom on the right, until the pinball-machine house was lit up in sectors. It was after 9 P.M. and no moon showed. Birds had built nests in the old streetlamps, so that light filtered down through straw and moulted feathers. The birds had flown south long ago, but in dappled beams Sheriff and the fat one appeared once again in the doorway of the Lisbon house. They were carrying the stretcher, just as we expected, but when the porch light came on we were not prepared for what we saw: Lux Lisbon, sitting up, very much alive.

She appeared to be in pain, but as they carried her out of the house she had the presence of mind to snatch up a *Reader's Digest*, which she later read cover to cover in the hospital. In fact, despite her convulsions (she was clutching her stomach), Lux had dared to put on a coat of the forbidden pink lipstick that tasted—so the boys on the roof told us—like strawberries. Woody Clabault's sister had the same brand, and once, after we got into his parents' liquor cabinet, we made him put on the lipstick and kiss each one of us so that we, too, would know what it tasted like. Beyond the flavor of the drinks we improvised that night—part ginger ale, part bourbon, part lime juice, part scotch—we could taste the strawberry wax on Woody Clabault's lips, transforming them, before the artificial fireplace, into Lux's own. Rock music blared from the tape player; we threw ourselves about in chairs, bodilessly floating to the couch from time to time to dip our heads into the strawberry vat, but the next day we refused to remember that any of this had happened, and even now it's the first time we've spoken of it. At any rate, the memory of that night was superseded by that of Lux's being hoisted into the EMS truck, because, despite discrepancies of time and space, it was Lux's lips we tasted, not Clabault's.

Her hair clearly needed washing. George Pappas, who reached the truck before Sheriff closed the door, described how blood had pooled in Lux's cheeks. "You could see veins," he said. Holding the magazine in one hand, clutching her midsection with the other, she rode the stretcher as though it were a bobbing lifeboat. Her thrashing, cries, scowls of agony only emphasized the inertness of Cecilia, whom we now saw in memory as even deader than she had actually been. Mrs. Lisbon didn't jump into the truck as she had previously but remained on the lawn, waving as though

Lux had boarded a bus to summer camp. Neither Mary, Bonnie, nor Therese came outside. Discussing it later, many of us felt we suffered a mental dislocation at that moment, which only grew worse through the course of the remaining deaths. The prevailing symptom of this state was an inability to recall any sound. Truck doors slammed silently; Lux's mouth (eleven fillings, according to Dr. Roth's records) screamed silently; and the street, the creaking tree limbs, the streetlight clicking different colors, the electric buzz of the pedestrian crossing box—all these usually clamorous voices hushed, or had begun shrieking at a pitch too high for us to hear, though they sent chills up our spines. Sound returned only once Lux had gone. Televisions erupted with canned laughter. Fathers splashed, soaking aching backs.

It was half an hour before Mrs. Patz's sister called from Bon Secours with the preliminary report that Lux had suffered a burst appendix. We were surprised to hear the damage was not self-inflicted, though Mrs. Patz said, "It's the stress. That poor girl's under so much stress, her appendix just blew up. Same thing happened to my sister." Brent Christopher, who had nearly cut off his right hand with a power saw that night (he was installing a new kitchen), saw Lux being wheeled into the emergency room. Though his arm was bandaged and his brain stupefied with painkiller, he remembers the interns lifting Lux onto the cot next to his. "She was breathing out of her mouth, hyperventilating, and holding her stomach. She kept saying, 'Ouch,' exactly the way you'd spell it." Apparently, after the interns hurried off to get the doctor, there came a moment when Brent Christopher and Lux were left alone. She stopped crying and looked his way. He held up his gauze-wrapped hand. She looked at it without interest. Then she reached up and closed the curtain separating the beds.

A Dr. Finch (or French—the records are illegible) examined Lux. He asked her where it hurt, took blood, thumped her, gagged her with a tongue depressor, and peered in her eyes, ears, and nose. He checked her side and found no swelling. She no longer showed signs of pain, in fact, and after the first few minutes, the doctor stopped asking questions relating to her appendix. Some people said that to an experienced medical eye the signs were obvious: a look of anxiety, a frequent touching of the belly. Whatever it was, the doctor knew right away. "How long since your last period?" he asked.

"A while."

"A month?"

"Forty-two days."

"Don't want your parents to know?"

"No, thank you."

"Why all the commotion? Why the ambulance?"

"Only way I could get out of the house."

They were whispering, the doctor leaning over the bed, Lux sitting up. Brent Christopher heard a sound he identified as teeth chattering. Then Lux said, "I just want a test. Can you give me one?"

The doctor didn't verbally agree to the test, but for some reason, when he stepped into the hall, he told Mrs.

Lisbon, who had just arrived, leaving her husband home with the girls, "Your daughter's going to be fine." He then went into his office, where a nurse later found him chain-smoking his pipe. We've imagined various possibilities of what went through Dr. Finch's mind that day: that he had fallen in love with a fourteen-year-old with a late period, that he was estimating in his head how much money he had in the bank, how much gas in the car, how far they could get before his wife and kids found out. We never understood why Lux went to the hospital instead of to Planned Parenthood, but most people agreed she was telling the truth and that, in the end, she could devise no other way to see a doctor. When Dr. Finch came back, he said, "I'm going to tell your mother we're running gastrointestinal tests." Brent Christopher stood up then, silently vowing to help Lux escape himself. He heard her say, "How long will it take to find out?"

"About half an hour."

"Do you really use a rabbit?"

The doctor laughed.

Upright, Brent Christopher felt his hand throb, his eyes blurred, he became dizzy; but before he fell back into unconsciousness, he saw Dr. Finch pass by, heading toward Mrs. Lisbon. She heard about it first, and then the nurses heard about it, and then we did. Joe Larson ran across the street to hide in the Lisbons' bushes, and it was then he heard Mr. Lisbon's girlish weeping, a sound quite musical, he said. Mr. Lisbon was sitting in his La-Z-Boy, his feet up on the footrest, his hands over his face. The phone rang.

He looked at it. He picked it up. "Thank God," he said, "thank God." Lux, it turned out, had only a bad case of indigestion.

In addition to a pregnancy test, Dr. Finch gave Lux a complete gynecological exam. It was from Ms. Angelica Turnette, a hospital clerical worker, that we later received the documents that we hold among our most prized possessions (her nonunion pay hardly made ends meet). The doctor's report, in a series of titillating numbers, presents Lux in a stiff paper gown stepping onto the scale (99), opening her mouth for the thermometer (98.7), and urinating into a plastic cup (WBC 6–8 occ. clump; mucus heavy; leukocytes 2+). The simple appraisal "mild abrasions" reports the condition of her uterine walls, and in an advancement that has since been discontinued, a photograph was taken of her rosy cervix, which looks like a camera shutter set on an extremely low exposure. (It stares at us now like an inflamed eye, fixing us with its silent accusation.)

"The pregnancy test was negative, but it was clear she was sexually active," Ms. Turnette told us. "She had HPV [human papilloma virus, a precursor to genital warts]. The more partners you have, the more HPV. It's that simple."

Dr. Hornicker happened to be on call that night and managed to see Lux for a few minutes without Mrs. Lisbon's knowledge. "The girl was still waiting for the test results, so she was understandably tense," he said. "Still, though, there was something else about her, an additional unease." Lux had gotten dressed and was sitting on the edge of the emergency room cot. When Dr. Hornicker introduced himself, she said, "You're the doctor who talked to my sister."

"That's right."

"Are you going to ask me questions?"

"Only if you want me to."

"I'm just here"—she lowered her voice—"to see the gyno."

"So you don't want me to ask you questions?"

"Ceel told us all about your tests. I'm just not in the mood right now."

"What kind of mood are you in?"

"No mood. I'm just kind of tired is all."

"Not getting enough sleep?"

"I sleep all the time."

"And yet you're still tired?"

"Yeah."

"Why do you think that is?"

Up to this point, Lux had answered briskly, swinging her feet, which didn't reach the floor. Now she paused and regarded Dr. Hornicker. She settled back, retracting her head so that the slight chubbiness swelled beneath her chin.

"Iron-poor blood," she said. "Runs in the family. I'm going to ask the doctor for some vitamins."

"She was in deep denial," Dr. Hornicker told us later. "She was obviously not sleeping—a textbook symptom of depression—and was pretending that her problem, and by association her sister Cecilia's problem, was of no real consequence." Dr. Finch came in with the test results soon after that, and Lux jumped happily off the cot. "But even her delight had a manic quality to it. She bounced off the walls."

Shortly after that meeting, in the second of his many reports, Dr. Hornicker began to revise his view of the Lisbon girls. Citing a recent study by Dr. Judith Weisberg that examined "the bereavement process of adolescents who have lost a sibling by suicide" (see *List of Funded Studies*), Dr. Hornicker gave an explanation for the Lisbon girls' erratic behavior—their withdrawal, their sudden fits of emotion or catatonia. The report maintained that as a result of Cecilia's suicide the surviving Lisbon girls suffered from Post-Traumatic Stress Disorder. "It's not unusual," Dr. Hornicker wrote, "for the sibling of an A.L.S. [adolescent lost to suicide] to act out suicidal behavior in an attempt to come to grips with their grief. There is a high incidence of repetitive suicide in single families." Then, in a marginal aside, he dropped his medical manner and jotted: "Lemmings."

As it circulated in the next few months, this theory convinced many people because it simplified things. Already Cecilia's suicide had assumed in retrospect the stature of a long-prophesied event. Nobody thought it shocking anymore, and accepting it as First Cause removed any need for further explanation. As Mr. Hutch put it, "They made Cecilia out to be the bad guy." Her suicide, from this perspective, was seen as a kind of disease infecting those close at hand. In the bathtub, cooking in the broth of her own blood, Cecilia had released an airborne virus which the other girls, even in coming to save her, had contracted. No one cared how Cecilia had caught the virus in the first place. Transmission became explanation. The other girls, safe in their own rooms, had smelled something strange, sniffed the air, but ignored it. Black tendrils of smoke had crept under their doors, rising up behind their studious backs to form the evil shapes smoke or shadow take on in cartoons: a black-hatted assassin brandishing a dagger; an anvil about to drop. Contagious suicide made it palpable. Spiky bacteria lodged in the agar of the girls' throats. In the morning, a soft oral thrush had sprouted over their tonsils. The girls felt sluggish. At the window the world's light seemed dimmed. They rubbed their eyes to no avail. They felt heavy, slow-witted. Household objects lost meaning. A bedside clock became a hunk of molded plastic, telling something called time, in a world marking its passage for some reason. When we thought of the girls along these lines, it was as feverish creatures, exhaling soupy breath, succumbing day by day in their isolated ward. We went outside with our hair wet in the hopes of catching flu ourselves so that we might share their delirium.

At night the cries of cats making love or fighting, their caterwauling in the dark, told us that the world was pure emotion, flung back and forth among its creatures, the agony of the one-eyed Siamese no different from that of the Lisbon girls, and even the trees plunged in feeling. The first slate tile slid off their roof, missing the porch by an inch and embedding itself in the soft turf, and from a distance we could see the tar underneath, letting in water. In the living room, Mr. Lisbon positioned an old paint can underneath a leak, then watched as it filled with the midnight-blue shade of Cecilia's bedroom ceiling (she'd chosen the shade to look like the night sky; the can had been in the closet for years). In the days following, other cans caught streams, on top of the radiator, the mantel, the dining room table, but no roofer showed up, most likely, people believed, because the Lisbons could no longer bear anyone intruding into their house. They endured their leaks on their own, staying in the rain forest of their living room. Mary kept up appearances by getting the mail (heating bills, advertisements, never anything personal anymore), coming out in bright green or pink sweaters emblazoned with red hearts. Bonnie wore a kind of smock we took to calling her hair shirt, largely because of the spiky feathers that covered it. "Her pillow must leak," said Vince Fusilli. The plumage, not white, as one would expect, but dun-colored, came from low-grade ducks, farmed creatures whose cooped-up smell drifted downwind whenever Bonnie appeared stuck all over with quills. But no one got very near. No one ventured to the house anymore, not any of our mothers or fathers, not the priest; and even the mailman, rather than touching the mailbox, lifted the lid with the spine of Mrs. Eugene's *Family Circle*. Now the soft decay of the house began to show up more clearly. We noticed how tattered the curtains had become, then realized we weren't looking at curtains at all but at a film of dirt, with spy holes wiped clean. The best thing was to see them make one: the pink heel of a hand flattening against the glass, then rubbing back and forth to uncover the bright mosaic of an eye, looking out at us. Also, the gutters sagged.

Mr. Lisbon alone left the house, and our only contact with the girls was through the signs they left on him. His hair looked excessively combed, as though the girls, unable to preen for anybody else, preened him. His cheeks no longer sported banners of tissue paper, blood-spotted like tiny Japanese flags, suggesting to many people that his daughters had begun to shave him with considerably more care than Joe the Retard's brothers lavished on him. (Mrs. Loomis, however, maintained he'd gotten an electric razor after what had happened with Cecilia.) Whatever the details, Mr. Lisbon became the medium through which we glimpsed the girls' spirits. We saw them through the toll they exacted on him: his puffy red eyes that hardly opened anymore to see his daughters wasting away; his shoes scuffed from climbing stairs forever threatening to lead to another inert body; his sallow complexion dying in sympathy with them; and his lost look of a man who realized that all this dying was going to be the only life he ever had. As he set off for work, Mrs. Lisbon no longer fortified him with a mug of coffee. Nevertheless, at the wheel, he automatically reached for the mug in its dashboard holder . . . and brought last week's cold coffee to his lips. At school, he walked the halls with a fake smile and welling eyes, or in shows of boyish spirits shouted, "Hip check!" and pinned students against the wall. He held on too long, though, freezing until the kids said, "Face-off," or, "You're in the penalty box now, Mr. Lisbon," anything to snap him out of it. Kenny Jenkins got in a headlock with Mr. Lisbon and spoke only of the serenity that came over the two of them. "It was weird. I could smell his breath and everything, but I didn't try to get away. It was like being on the bottom of a nigger pile, when you're getting squashed but it's all peaceful and everything." Some people admired his continuing to work; others condemned it as hardness of heart. He began to look skeletal beneath his green suit, as though Cecilia, in dying, had tugged him briefly to the other side. He reminded us of Abraham Lincoln, loose-limbed, silent, carrying around the world's pain. He never passed a drinking fountain without sampling its small relief.

Then, abruptly, less than six weeks after the girls left school, Mr. Lisbon resigned. From Dini Fleisher, the headmaster's secretary, we learned that Mr. Woodhouse had called Mr. Lisbon in for a meeting over Christmas vacation. Dick Jensen, chairman of the Board of Trustees, also attended. Mr. Woodhouse asked Dini to serve eggnog from the carton in the small office refrigerator. Before accepting, Mr. Lisbon asked, "This isn't spiked, is it?"

"It's Christmas," Mr. Woodhouse said.

Mr. Jensen spoke about the Rose Bowl. He said to Mr. Lisbon, "You're a U. of M. man yourself, right?"

At this point Mr. Woodhouse indicated that Dini should leave, but before she was out the door, she heard

Mr. Lisbon say, "I am. But I don't think I've ever told you that, Dick. Sounds like you've been looking into my file."

The men laughed, without mirth. Dini shut the door.

On January 7, when school resumed, Mr. Lisbon was no longer on staff. Technically, he had taken a leave of absence, but the new math teacher, Miss Kolinski, evidently felt secure enough about her position to remove the planets from their ceiling orbit. The fallen globes sat in the corner like the final trash heap of the universe, Mars embedded in Earth, Jupiter cracked in half, Saturn's rings slicing poor Neptune. We never learned exactly what was said in the meeting, but the gist was clear: Dini Fleisher told us that parents had begun making complaints shortly after Cecilia killed herself. They maintained that a person who couldn't run his own family had no business teaching their children, and the chorus of disapproval had grown steadily louder as the Lisbon house deteriorated. Mr. Lisbon's behavior hadn't helped, his eternal green suit, his avoidance of the faculty lunch room, his piercing tenor cutting through the male singing group like the keening of a bereaved old woman. He was dismissed. And returned to a house where, some nights, lights never went on, not even in the evening, nor did the front door open.

Now the house truly died. For as long as Mr. Lisbon had gone back and forth to school, he circulated a thin current of life through the house, bringing the girls treats—Mounds bars, orange push-ups, rainbow-colored Kool-Pops. We could imagine what the girls felt inside because we knew what they were eating. We could share their headaches from wolfing ice cream. We could make ourselves sick on chocolate. When Mr. Lisbon stopped going out, however, he stopped bringing home sweets. We couldn't be sure the girls were eating at all. Offended by Mrs. Lisbon's note, the milkman had stopped delivering milk, good *or* bad. Kroger's stopped bringing groceries. Mrs. Lisbon's mother, Lema Crawford, mentioned during that same crackling phone call to New Mexico that she had given Mrs. Lisbon most of her summer pickles and preserves (she had hesitated saying "summer" because that had been the summer Cecilia had died, and all the while the cucumbers, strawberries, and even she herself, seventy-one years old, had gone on growing and living). She also told us that Mrs. Lisbon kept an abundant supply of canned goods downstairs, as well as fresh water and other preparations against nuclear attack. They had a kind of bomb shelter downstairs, apparently, just off the rec room from which we had watched Cecilia climb to her death. Mr. Lisbon had even installed a propane camping toilet. But that was in the days when they expected perils to come from without, and nothing made less sense by that time than a survival room buried in a house itself becoming one big coffin.

Our concern increased when we saw Bonnie visibly wasting away. Just after dawn, as Uncle Tucker was going to bed, he used to see her come onto the front porch, under the mistaken notion that everyone on the street was asleep. She always wore the feathered smock and sometimes carried the pillow Uncle Tucker referred to as a

"Dutch wife" because of the way she hugged it. One ripped corner spewed feathers, fleecing the air around her head. She sneezed. Her long neck was thin and white and she had the rickety painful walk of a Biafran, as though her hip joints lacked lubrication. Because he was so skinny himself from his liquid beer diet, we believed Uncle Tucker's statements about Bonnie's weight. It wasn't as if Mrs. Amberson had said Bonnie was wasting away. Compared to her, everyone was. But Uncle Tucker's turquoise-and-silver belt buckle looked as big on him as the jeweled belt of a heavyweight champ. He knew what he was talking about. And, peering from his garage, one hand on the refrigerator, he watched as with uncoordinated movements Bonnie Lisbon came down the two front steps, proceeded across the lawn to the small dirt mound left from the digging months ago, and, at the site of her sister's death, began to say the rosary. Holding the pillow in one hand, she told her beads with the other, making sure to finish before the first house light came on down the block and the neighborhood awoke.

We didn't know whether it was asceticism or starvation. She looked peaceful, Uncle Tucker said, without the feverish appetite of Lux, or the tight-lipped, tight-assed expression of Mary. We asked if she had carried a laminated picture of the Virgin, but he didn't think so. She came out every morning, though sometimes, if a Charlie Chan movie was on, Uncle Tucker would forget to check.

It was Uncle Tucker, too, who first detected the smell we could never identify. One morning, as Bonnie came out to the dirt mound, she left the front door open, and Uncle Tucker became aware of an odor unlike any other he had ever encountered. At first he thought it was merely an intensification of Bonnie's wet-bird aroma, but it persisted even after she returned inside, and when we woke up, we smelled it, too. For even as the house began to fall apart, casting out whiffs of rotten wood and soggy carpet, this other smell began wafting from the Lisbons', invading our dreams and making us wash our hands over and over again. The smell was so thick it seemed liquid, and stepping into its current felt like being sprayed. We tried to locate its source, looking for dead squirrels in the yard or a bag of fertilizer, but the smell contained too much syrup to be death itself. The smell was definitely on the side of life, and reminded David Black of a fancy mushroom salad he'd eaten on a trip with his parents to New York.

"It's the smell of trapped beaver," Paul Baldino said, sagely, and we didn't know enough to disagree, but we found it hard to imagine such an aroma issuing from the ventricles of love. The smell was partly bad breath, cheese, milk, tongue film, but also the singed smell of drilled teeth. It was the kind of bad breath you get used to the closer you go in, until you can't really notice because it's your own breath, too. Over the years, of course, the open mouths of women have blown into our faces ingredients of that original smell, and occasionally, poised over unfamiliar bedsheets, in the dark of that night's betrayal or blind date, we've greedily welcomed any new particular reek because of its partial connection to the fumes that began blowing from the Lisbon house shortly after it was closed up, and never really stopped. Right now, if we concentrate, we can smell it still. It found us in our beds, and on the playground as we played Kill the Man with the Ball; it came down the stairs of the Karafilises' so that Old Mrs. Karafilis dreamed she was back in Bursa cooking grape leaves. It reached us even over the stink of Joe Barton's grandfather's cigar, as he showed us the photo album of his Navy days, explaining that the plump women in petticoats were only his cousins. Strangely enough, even though the smell was overpowering, we didn't once think of holding our breaths, or, as a last resort, breathing through our mouths, and after the first few days we sucked in the aroma like mother's milk.

Dim dormant months followed: ice-bound January; unrelenting February; soiled, slushy March. We still had winters in those days, vast snowdrifts, days of canceled school. At home on snowy mornings, listening to school closings on the radio (a parade of Indian county names, Washtenaw, Shiawassee, until our own Anglo-Saxon Wayne), we still knew the vivifying feeling of staying warm inside a shelter like pioneers. Nowadays, because of shifting winds from the factories and the rising temperature of the earth, snow never comes in an onslaught anymore but by a slow accretion in the night, momentary suds. The world, a tired performer, offers us another half-assed season. Back in the days of the Lisbon girls, snow fell every week and we shoveled our driveways into heaps higher than our cars. Trucks dumped salt. Christmas lights went up, and old man

Wilson sprang for his annual extravagant display: a twenty-foot snowman, with three mechanized reindeer pulling a fat Santa in his sleigh. The display always brought a line of cars up our street, but that year the traffic slowed down twice. We could see families pointing and smiling at Santa, then growing still and avid before the Lisbons' house like rubberneckers at a crash site. The fact that the Lisbons put up no lights until after Christmas made their house look even bleaker. On the Pitzenbergers' lawn next door, three snowbound angels blew red trumpets. At the Bateses' on the other side, multicolored gumdrops glowed within the frosted bushes. It was only in January, after Mr. Lisbon had been out of work a week, that he came out to string lights. He covered the front bushes, but when he plugged in the lights he wasn't pleased with the result. "One of these is a blinker," he said to Mr. Bates as the latter walked to his car. "The box says it's got a red tip, but I've checked them all and can't find the culprit. I hate blinking lights." Perhaps he did, but they stayed blinking, whenever he remembered to plug them in at night.

All winter, the girls remained elusive. Sometimes one or another would come outside, hugging herself in the cold, her breath clouding her face, and after a minute would go back in. At night, Therese continued to use her ham radio, tapping out messages that took her away from her house, to warm southern states and even to the tip of South America. Tim Winer searched the radio waves for Therese's frequency and a few times claimed to have found it. Once she was talking to a man in Georgia about his dog (arthritic hips, operate or not?), and another time she spoke, in that genderless, nationless medium, to a human being whose few responses Winer managed to record. It was all dots and dashes, but we made him put it into English. The exchange went something like this:

"You too?"

"My brother."

"How old?"

"Twenty-one. Handsome. Beautiful on violin."

"How?"

"Bridge nearby. Swift current."

"How get over?"

"Never will."

"What is Colombia like?"

"Warm. Peaceful. Come."

"Like to."

"You are wrong about *bandidos*."

"Have to go. Mom calling."

"Painted roof blue like you said."

"Bye."

"Bye."

That was it. The interpretation is, we think, quite obvious, and shows that as late as March, Therese was reaching out toward a freer world. About this time she sent away for application materials from a list of colleges (the reporters would make much of this later). The girls also ordered catalogues for items they could never buy, and the Lisbons' mailbox filled up once again: furniture catalogues from Scott-Shruptine, high-end clothing, exotic vacations. Unable to go anywhere, the girls traveled in their imaginations to goldtipped Siamese temples, or past an old man with bucket and leaf broom tidying a moss-carpeted speck of Japan. As soon as we learned the names of these brochures we sent for them ourselves to see where the girls wanted to go. *Far East Adventures. Footloose Tours. Tunnel to China Tours. Orient Express.* We got them all. And, flipping pages, hiked through dusty passes with the girls, stopping every now and then to help them take off their backpacks, placing our hands on their warm, moist shoulders and gazing off at papaya sunsets. We drank tea with them in a water pavilion, above blazing goldfish. We did whatever we wanted to, and Cecilia hadn't killed herself: she was a bride in Calcutta, with a red veil and the soles of her feet dyed with henna. The only way we could feel close to the girls was through these impossible excursions, which have scarred us forever, making us happier with dreams than wives. Some of us abused the catalogues, taking them off into rooms alone, or sneaking them out under our shirts. But we had little else to do, and the snow came down, and the sky was unremittingly gray.

We'd like to tell you with authority what it was like inside the Lisbon house, or what the girls felt being imprisoned in it. Sometimes, drained by this investigation, we long for some shred of evidence, some Rosetta stone that would explain the girls at last. But even though that winter was certainly not a happy one, little more can be averred.

Trying to locate the girls' exact pain is like the self-examination doctors urge us to make (we've reached that age). On a regular basis, we're forced to explore with clinical detachment our most private pouch and, pressing it, impress ourselves with its anatomical reality: two turtle eggs bedded in a nest of tiny sea grapes, with tubes snaking in and out, knobbed with nodules of gristle. We're asked to find in this dimly mapped place, amid naturally occurring clots and coils, upstart invaders. We never realized how many bumps we had until we went looking. And so we lie on our backs, probing, recoiling, probing again, and the seeds of death get lost in the mess God made us.

It's no different with the girls. Hardly have we begun to palpate their grief than we find ourselves wondering whether this particular wound was mortal or not, or whether (in our blind doctoring) it's a wound at all. It might just as well be a mouth, which is as wet and as warm. The scar might be over the heart or the kneecap. We can't tell. All we can do is go groping up the legs and arms, over the soft bivalvular torso, to the imagined face. It is speaking to us. But we can't hear.

Every night we scanned the girls' bedroom windows. Around dinner tables our conversations inevitably turned to the family's predicament. Would Mr. Lisbon get another job? How would he support his family? How long could the girls endure being cooped up? Even Old Mrs. Karafilis made one of her rare journeys to the first floor (it not being bath day) just to stare down the street at the Lisbon house. We couldn't remember another instance where Old Mrs. Karafilis had taken interest in the world, because ever since we had known her, she had lived in the basement waiting to die. Sometimes Demo Karafilis took us downstairs to play Foosball, and, moving among the heating ducts, spare cots, battered luggage, we would tunnel through to the small room Old Mrs. Karafilis had decorated to resemble Asia Minor. Artificial grapes hung from a ceiling lattice; decorative boxes housed silkworms; the cinder-block walls were painted the precise cerulean blue of the old country's air. Taped-up postcards served as windows into another time and place where Old Mrs. Karafilis still lived. Green mountains rose in the background, giving way to chipped Ottoman tombs, red-tiled roofs, a puff of steam rising in one Technicolor corner from a man selling hot bread. Demo Karafilis never told us what was wrong with his grandmother, nor did he think it odd they kept her in the basement amid the vast boiler and gurgling drains (our lowland suburb was prone to flooding). Still, the way she stopped before the postcards, licking one thumb and pressing it to the same whitened spot, the way she smiled with her golden teeth, nodding toward the vistas as though greeting passersby, all this told us that Old Mrs. Karafilis had been shaped and saddened by a history we knew nothing about. When she did see us, she said, "Close the light, dolly *mou*," and we did, leaving her in the dark, fanning herself with the complimentary fan the funeral parlor that had buried her husband sent every Christmas. (The fan, cheap cardboard stapled to a Popsicle stick, showed Jesus praying at Gethsemane, portentous clouds piling up behind him, and on the flip side advertised mortuary services.) Other than to take a bath, Old Mrs. Karafilis came upstairs—a rope tied to her waist, Demo's father lightly pulling, Demo and his brothers assisting behind—only when *Train to Istanbul* came on television every two years. Then she'd sit, excited as a girl, leaning forward on the couch and waiting for the ten-second scene where the train passed a few green hills that held her heart. She'd raise both arms, let out a vulture's cry, just as the train—same way every time—disappeared into the tunnel.

Old Mrs. Karafilis never cared much about neighborhood gossip, mostly because she couldn't understand it, and the part she did understand seemed trivial. As a young woman, she had hidden in a cave to escape being killed by the Turks. For an entire month she had eaten nothing but olives, swallowing the pits to fill herself up. She had seen family members butchered, men strung up in the sun eating their own privates, and now hearing how Tommy Riggs totaled his parents' Lincoln, or how the Perkinses' Christmas tree caught fire, killing the cat, she didn't see the drama. The only time she perked up was when someone mentioned the Lisbon girls, and then it wasn't to ask questions or get details but to enter into telepathy with them. If we were talking about the girls within her hearing, Old Mrs. Karafilis would lift her head, then raise herself painfully from her chair and cane across the cold cement floor. At one end of the basement a window well let in weak light, and, going up to its cold panes, she stared at a patch of sky visible through a lace of spiderweb. That was as much of the girls' world as she could see, just the same sky above their house, but it told her enough. It occurred to us that she and the girls read secret signs of misery in cloud formations, that despite the discrepancy in their ages something timeless communicated itself between them, as though she were advising the girls in her mumbling Greek, "Don't waste your time on life." Mulch and blown leaves filled the window well, a broken chair from when we'd made a fort. Light shone through Old Mrs. Karafilis's housedress, as thin and drably patterned as paper toweling. Her sandals were right for wearing to a *hammam*, some steaming place, not across that drafty floor. On the day she heard about the girls' new incarceration, she jerked her head up, nodded, didn't smile. But had known already, it seemed.

From her weekly bath of Epsom salts, she talked of the girls, or to them, we couldn't tell which. We didn't get too close, or listen at the keyhole, because the few contradictory glimpses we'd gotten of Old Mrs. Karafilis, with her sagging breasts from another century, her blue legs, her undone hair shockingly long and glossy as a girl's, filled us with embarrassment. Even the sound of the tub running made us blush, her muffled voice coming over it, complaining of aches while the black lady, none too young herself, coaxed her in, the two of them alone with their decrepitude behind the bathroom door, crying out, singing, first the black lady, then Old Mrs. Karafilis singing some Greek song, and finally just the sound of water we couldn't imagine the color of, sloshing around. Afterward, she'd appear just as pale as before, her head wrapped in a towel. We could hear her lungs inflating as the black lady fitted the rope around Old Mrs. Karafilis's waist and began lowering her down the stairs. Despite her wish to die as soon as possible, Old Mrs. Karafilis always looked fearful during these descents, gripping the banister, eyes magnified behind rimless glasses. Sometimes as she passed we'd tell her the latest about the girls, and she'd cry, "*Mana!*," which meant something like "Holy shit!," Demo said, but she never really seemed surprised. Out past the weekly glimpsed windows, out past the street, lived the world, which had, Old Mrs. Karafilis knew, been dying for years.

In the end, it wasn't death that surprised her but the stubbornness of life. She couldn't understand how the Lisbons kept so quiet, why they didn't wail to heaven or go mad. Seeing Mr. Lisbon stringing Christmas lights, she shook her head and muttered. She let go of the special geriatric banister installed along the first floor, took a few steps at sea level without support, and for the first time in seven years suffered no pain. Demo explained it to us like this: "We Greeks are a moody people. Suicide makes sense to us. Putting up Christmas lights after your own daughter does it—that makes no sense. What my *yia yia* could never understand about America was why everyone pretended to be happy all the time."

Winter is the season of alcoholism and despair. Count the drunks in Russia or the suicides at Cornell. So many exam-takers threw themselves into the gorge of that hilly campus that the university declared a midwinter holiday to ease the tension (popularly known as "suicide day," the holiday popped up in a computer search we ran, along with "suicide ride" and "suicide-mobile"). We don't understand those Cornell kids any better, some Bianca with her first diaphragm and all life ahead of her plunging off the footbridge, cushioned only by her down vest; dark existential Bill, with his clove cigarettes and Salvation Army overcoat, not leaping as Bianca did, but easing himself over the rail and hanging on for dear death before letting go (shoulder muscles show tears in 33 percent of people choosing bridges; the other 67 percent just jump). We mention this now only to show that even college students, free to booze and fornicate, bring about their own ends in large numbers. Imagine what it was like for the Lisbon girls, shut up in their house with no blaring stereo or ready bong around.

The newspapers, later writing about what they termed a "suicide pact," treated the girls as automatons, creatures so barely alive that their deaths came as little change. In the sweep of Ms. Perl's accounts, which boiled two or three months and the suffering of four individuals into a paragraph with a heading "When Youth Sees No Future," the girls appear as indistinguishable characters marking black *x*'s on a calendar or holding hands in self-styled Black Masses. Suggestions of satanism, or some mild form of black magic, haunt Ms. Perl's calculations. She made much of the record-burning incident, and often quoted rock lyrics that alluded to death or suicide. Ms. Perl befriended a local deejay and spent an entire night listening to the records that Lux's schoolmates listed among her favorites. From this "research," she came up with the find she was most proud of: a song by the band Cruel Crux, entitled "Virgin Suicide." The chorus follows, though neither Ms. Perl nor we have been able to determine if the album was among those Mrs. Lisbon forced Lux to burn:

> *Virgin suicide*
> *What was that she cried?*
> *No use in stayin'*
> *On this holocaust ride*
> *She gave me her cherry*
> *She's my virgin suicide*

The song certainly ties in nicely with the notion that a dark force beset the girls, some monolithic evil we weren't responsible for. Their behavior, however, was anything but monolithic. While Lux trysted on the roof, Therese grew fluorescent sea horses in a drinking glass, and, down the hall, Mary spent hours looking into her portable mirror. Set in an oval of pink plastic, the mirror was surrounded by exposed bulbs like a mirror in an actress's dressing room. A switch allowed Mary to simulate various times and weathers. There were settings for "morning," "afternoon," and "evening," as well as one for "brite sun" and "overcast." For hours Mary would sit before the mirror, watching her face swim through the alterations of counterfeit worlds. She wore dark glasses in sunshine, and bundled up under clouds. Mr. Lisbon sometimes saw her flipping the switch back and forth, passing through ten or twenty days at once, and she often got one of her sisters to sit before the mirror so that she could dispense advice. "See, the circles under your eyes come out in overcast. That's because we've got pale skin. In sunlight . . . just a minute . . . see, like this, they're gone. So you should wear more base or concealer on cloudy days. On sunny days, our complexions tend to wash out, so we need color. Lipstick and even eyeshadow."

The searchlight of Ms. Perl's prose also tends to wash out the girls' features. She uses catchphrases to describe the girls, calling them "mysterious" or "loners," and at one point goes so far as to say they were "attracted to the pagan aspect of the Catholic Church." What that phrase meant exactly we were never sure, but many people felt it had to do with the girls' attempt to save the family elm.

Spring had finally arrived. Trees budded. The frozen streets, in thawing, cracked. Mr. Bates recorded new potholes, as he did every year, sending a typed list to the Department of Transportation. In early April, the Parks Department returned to replace ribbons around condemned trees, this time using not red but yellow ribbons printed with the words "This tree has been diagnosed with Dutch elm disease and will be removed in order to inhibit further spread. By order of Parks Dept." You had to circle a tree three times to read the whole sentence. The elm in the Lisbons' front yard (see Exhibit #1) was among the condemned, and with the weather still cool a truckful of men arrived to cut it down.

We knew the technique. First a man in a fiberglass cage ascended into the treetop and, after boring a hole into the bark, put his ear to it as though listening for the tree's failing pulse; then, without ceremony, he began clipping smaller branches, which fell into the grasping orange gloves of the men below. They stacked the branches neatly, as though they were two-by-fours, and then fed them into the buzz saw in the truck's back. Showers of sawdust shot into the street, and years later, when we found ourselves in old-fashioned bars, the sawdust on the floors always brought back to us the cremation of our trees. After denuding the trunk, the men left to denude others, and for a time the tree stood blighted, trying to raise its stunted arms, a creature clubbed mute, only its sudden voicelessness making us realize it had been speaking all along. In that death-row state, the trees resembled the Baldinos' barbecue, and we understood that Sammy the Shark had fashioned his escape tunnel with great foresight, to look not as trees did now but as they were coming to look, so that if he was ever forced to escape in the future, he could leave through one of a hundred identical stumps.

Normally, people came out to say good-bye to their trees. It wasn't uncommon to see a family gathered on the lawn at a safe distance from the chain saws, a tired mom and dad with two or three long-haired teenagers, and a poodle with a ribbon in its hair. People felt they owned the trees. Their dogs had marked them daily. Their children had used them for home plate. The trees had been there when they'd moved in, and had promised to be there when they moved out. But when the Parks Department came to cut them down, it was clear our trees were not ours but the city's, to do with as it wished.

The Lisbons, however, didn't come out during the de-branching. The girls looked on from an upstairs window, their faces cold-cream white. Lunging and retreating, the elevated man sheared off the elm's great green crown. He chopped off the sick limb that had sagged and sprouted yellow leaves last summer. He proceeded to cut off the healthy limbs, too, and left the tree trunk rising like a gray pillar in the Lisbons' front yard. When the men drove away, we weren't sure whether it was dead or alive.

For the next two weeks we waited for the Parks Department to finish the job, but it took them three weeks to return. This time two men with chain saws climbed out of the truck. They circled the trunk, taking its measure, then steadied saws on thighs and pulled the starter cords. We were down in Chase Buell's basement at the time, playing bumper pool, but the whine reached us through the exposed rafters overhead. The aluminum heating vents rattled. The bright balls trembled on the green felt. The sound of the chain saws filled our heads like a dentist's drill, and we ran outside to see the men moving in on the elm. They wore goggles against flying chips, but otherwise dragged about with the boredom of men accustomed to slaughter. They lifted the snarling guide bars. One spit out tobacco juice. Then, revving the motors, they were just about to tear the tree apart when the foreman jumped out of the truck, furiously waving his arms. Across the lawn, in a phalanx, the Lisbon girls were running toward the men. Mrs. Bates, who was looking on, said she thought the girls were going to fling themselves on the chain saws. "They were heading straight for them. And their eyes looked wild." The Parks Department men didn't know what the foreman was jumping up and down about. "I was blind-sided," one said. "The girls ducked right under my saw. Thank God I saw them in time." Both men did, and held their saws in the air, backing off. The Lisbon girls ran past them. They might have been playing a game. They looked behind them as though afraid of being tagged. But then they reached the safety zone. The men turned off their chain saws and the pulsing air subsided into silence. The girls surrounded the tree, linking hands in a daisy chain.

"Go away," said Mary. "This is our tree."

They weren't facing the men but the tree itself, pressing their cheeks against the trunk. While Therese and Mary had shoes on, Bonnie and Lux had run out barefoot, which led many to believe the rescue had been a spontaneous idea. They hugged the trunk, which rose above them into nothingness.

"Girls, girls," the foreman said. "You're too late. The tree's already dead."

"That's what you say," said Mary.

"It's got beetles. We have to take it down so they won't spread to other trees."

"There's no scientific evidence that removal limits

infestation," said Therese. "These trees are ancient. They have evolutionary strategies to deal with beetles. Why don't you just leave it up to nature?"

"If we left it up to nature, there'd be no trees left."

"That's what it's going to be like anyway," said Lux.

"If boats didn't bring the fungus from Europe in the first place," Bonnie said, "none of this would have ever happened."

"You can't put the genie back in the bottle, girls. Now we've got to use our own technology to see what we can save."

Actually, none of this might have been spoken. We've pieced it together through partial accounts, and can attest only to the general substance. The girls did feel the trees would survive better on their own, and did place the blame for the disease on human arrogance. But many people felt this was a smoke screen. That particular elm, as everyone knew, had been Cecilia's favorite. Its tarred knothole still retained her small handprint. Mrs. Scheer recalled Cecilia often standing under the tree in springtime, trying to catch the whirling propellers of its seeds. (For our own part, we recall those green seeds housed in a single fibrous wing, and how they helicoptered to the ground, but we can't be sure whether they came from the elms or from, say, the chestnuts, and none of us has a botany handbook handy, so popular with rangers and realists.) At any rate, many people in our neighborhood found it easy to imagine why the girls might connect the elm with Cecilia. "They weren't saving *it*," said Mrs. Scheer. "They were saving her memory."

Three rings formed around the tree: the blond ring of the Lisbon girls, the forest green of the Parks Department men, and, farther out, the ring of onlookers. The men reasoned with the girls, grew stern, tried to bribe them with a ride on the truck, and finally threatened them. The foreman had his men break for lunch, thinking the girls would give up, but after forty-five minutes they remained belted around the tree. Finally he went up to the house to talk with Mr. and Mrs. Lisbon, but, to our surprise, they offered no help. They answered the door together, Mr. Lisbon with his arm around his wife in a rare display of physical affection. "We've got an order to cut down your elm," the foreman said. "But your kids won't let us."

"How do you know that tree's sick?" Mrs. Lisbon said.

"Believe me. We know. It's got yellow leaves. It *had* yellow leaves. We cut that branch off already. The tree's dead, for Christ's sake."

"We're for aritex," Mr. Lisbon said. "Are you familiar with that? Our daughter showed us an article. It's a less aggressive therapy."

"And it doesn't work. Look, we leave this tree and the others will all be gone by next year."

"Will be anyway, way things are going," said Mr. Lisbon.

"I don't want to have to call the police."

"The police?" Mrs. Lisbon asked. "The girls are just standing in their own front yard. Since when is that a crime?"

The foreman gave up then, but he never followed through on his threat. By the time he got back to the truck,

Ms. Perl's blue Pontiac had pulled up behind it. A staff photographer was already snapping the shots that would later appear in the newspaper. Less than an hour had elapsed between the time the girls surrounded the tree and Ms. Perl's Weegee-like arrival, but she would never divulge the source who had tipped her off. Many people believe the girls did it themselves to get publicity, but there's no way of telling. As the photographer continued shooting, the foreman told his men to get into the truck. The next day, a short article appeared, accompanied by a grainy picture of the girls embracing the tree (Exhibit #8). They seem to be worshipping it like a group of Druids. In the picture, you can't tell that the tree ends starkly twenty feet above their inclined heads.

"Four sisters of Cecilia Lisbon, the East Side teen whose suicide last summer focused awareness on a national problem, put their own bodies in jeopardy Wednesday in an attempt to save the elm Cecilia had so dearly loved. The tree was diagnosed with Dutch elm disease last year and was scheduled to be removed this spring." From the above, it's clear Ms. Perl accepted the theory that the girls saved the tree in memory of Cecilia, and from what we've read in Cecilia's journal, we see no reason to disagree. Years later, however, when we spoke to Mr. Lisbon, he denied this. "Therese was the one who was into trees. She knew everything about them. All the varieties. How deep the roots went. I never remember Cecilia taking much interest in plant life, to be honest."

Only after the Parks Department drove away did the

girls break their daisy chain. Rubbing sore arms, they went back inside the house without so much as looking at any of us gathered on neighboring lawns. Chase Buell heard Mary say, "They'll be back," as they went inside. Mr. Patz, who had been standing in a group of ten or so people, offered, "I was on their side. When the Parks men left, I felt like applauding."

The tree survived, temporarily. The Parks Department moved down their list, removing other trees on our block, but no one else was courageous or misled enough to oppose them. The Buells' elm, with its car tire swing, was taken down; the Fusillis' disappeared one day while we were at school; and the Shalaans' vanished, too. Soon the Parks Department moved on to other blocks, though the incessant whine of their chain saws never let us, or the girls, forget about them.

Baseball season began and we lost ourselves in green fields. In the old days, Mr. Lisbon would sometimes bring the girls to a home game, and they would sit in the bleachers, rooting like everybody else. Mary would talk to the cheerleaders. "She always wanted to be one. But her mother wouldn't let her," Kristi McCulchan told us. "I used to teach her some of the cheers and she was really good." We didn't doubt it. We always watched the Lisbon girls instead of our dizzy cheerleaders. In close games they chewed their fists, and thought every ball hit to the outfield would be a home run. They bounced up and down, then rose to their feet just as the ball descended, too soon, into the outfielder's mitt. The year of the suicides the girls didn't come to a single game, nor did we expect them to. Gradually, we stopped scanning the bleachers for their excited faces, and stopped walking underneath to see what we could see of them, cut up in slices from behind.

Though we felt for the Lisbon girls, and continued to think about them, they were slipping away from us. The images we treasured of them—in bathing suits, jumping through a sprinkler, or running from a garden hose charmed by water pressure into a giant snake—began to fade, no matter how religiously we meditated on them in our most private moments, lying in bed beside two pillows belted together to simulate a human shape. We could no longer evoke with our inner ears the precise pitches and lilts of the Lisbon girls' voices. Even the jasmine soap from Jacobsen's, which we kept in an old bread box, had gotten damp and lost its aroma, smelling now like a wet matchbook. At the same time, the fact that the girls were slowly sinking hadn't completely penetrated our minds, and on some mornings we awoke to a world still unruptured: we stretched, we got out of bed, and only after rubbing our eyes at the window did we remember the rotting house across the street, and the moss-blackened windows hiding the girls from our sight. The truth was this: we were beginning to forget the Lisbon girls, and we could remember nothing else.

The colors of their eyes were fading, the location of moles, dimples, centipede scars. It had been so long since the Lisbon girls had smiled we could no longer picture their crowded teeth. "They're just memories now," Chase Buell said sadly. "Time to write them off." But even as he uttered these words, he rebelled against them, as we all did. And rather than consign the girls to oblivion, we gathered their possessions once more, everything we'd gotten hold of during our strange curatorship: Cecilia's high-tops; Therese's microscope; a jewelry box in which a strand of Mary's dishwater-blond hair lay bedded on cotton; the photocopy of Cecilia's laminated picture of the Virgin; one of Lux's tube tops. We piled everything in the middle of Joe Larson's garage, opening the automatic door halfway to see out. The sun had set and the sky was dark. With the Parks Department gone, the street was ours again. For the first time in months, a light came on in the Lisbon house, then winked out. Another light, in an adjoining room, flickered in answer. Around the aureolae of streetlights we noticed a dim swirling we didn't recognize at first because we knew it so well, a senseless pattern of ecstasy and madness: the massing of the first fish flies of the season.

A year had passed and still we knew nothing. From five the girls had reduced themselves to four, and they were all—the living and the dead—becoming shadows. Even their assorted possessions arrayed at our feet didn't reassert their existence, and nothing seemed more anonymous than a certain vinyl go-go purse, covered with gold chain, that could have belonged to any of the girls, or to any girl in the world. The fact that we had once been close enough to pass through the aromas of the girls' separate shampoos (through herbal garden, to lemon glade, and into a grove of green apples) began to seem more and more unreal.

How long could we remain true to the girls? How long could we keep their memory pure? As it was, we didn't know them any longer, and their new habits—of opening a window, for instance, to throw out a wadded paper towel—made us wonder if we had ever really known them, or if our vigilance had been only the fingerprinting of phantoms. Our talismans ceased to work. Lux's school tartan, when touched, summoned only a hazy memory of her wearing it in class—one bored hand fiddling with the silver kilt pin, undoing it, leaving the folds unfastened on her bare knees, about to fall open any minute, but never, never . . . We had to rub the skirt for minutes to see it clearly. And every other slide in our carousel began to fade in the same way, or we clicked and absolutely nothing fell into the projection slot, leaving us staring at goose bumps on a white wall.

We would have lost them completely if the girls hadn't contacted us. Just as we had begun to despair of ever being near them again, more laminated pictures of the Virgin began showing up. Mr. Hutch found one tucked into the windshield wiper of his car and, not recognizing its significance, crumpled it up and threw it into the ashtray. Ralph Hutch found it later under a layer of ash and cigarette butts. When he brought it to us the picture was burned in three spots. Still, we could see right away that it was identical to the picture of the Virgin Cecilia had clutched in the bathtub, and when we wiped off the soot, the 555-MARY telephone number emerged on the back.

Hutch wasn't the only one to find a picture. Mrs. Hessen found one pierced among her rose bushes. Joey Thompson heard an unfamiliar whirring in his bicycle tires one day, and looked down to see a Virgin picture taped between the spokes. Finally, Tim Winer found a picture stuck into the grout of his study windows, facing in at him. The picture had been there for some time, he told us, because moisture had penetrated the laminated surface, giving the Virgin's face a touch of gangrene. Otherwise she looked the same: dressed in a blue cloak with a butterfly collar of gold lamé. On her head sat an Imperial margarine crown. A rosary girded her waist, and, as usual, the Holy Mother had that beatific expression of someone on lithium. No one ever saw the girls placing the cards, nor did anyone know why they would do so. Even now, though, so many years later, we can easily recall the tingling that overtook us whenever someone came bearing a new find. The pictures were invested with significance we couldn't quite fathom, and their sorry state—rips, mildew—made them seem ancient. "The feeling," Tim Winer wrote in his own journal, "was akin to unearthing the anklet of some poor smothered girl in Pompeii. She had just put it on, and was dandling it before the window, admiring how the jewels glittered, when they suddenly lit up red with the volcano's eruption." (Winer read Mary Renault a lot.)

In addition to the Virgin cards, we became convinced the girls were signaling to us in other ways. Sometime in

May, Lux's Chinese lantern began to blink an indecipher-able Morse code. Every night, as the street grew dark, her lantern flicked on, the bulb's heat turning an inner magic lantern that projected shadows on the walls. We thought the shadows spelled out a message, and binoculars con-firmed this, but the messages turned out to be written in Chinese. The lantern usually went off and on in varying patterns—three short, two long, two long, three short—after which the overhead light blazed, revealing the room like a museum exhibit. We respected the velvet ropes as we made our brief tour, past the late-twentieth-century furnishings: a headboard from Sears with matching night table; Therese's *Apollo 11* lamp casting light on Lux's life-size poster of Billy Jack in flat-brimmed black hat and Navajo belt. The viewing lasted only thirty seconds be-fore Lux and Therese's room went dark. Then Bonnie and Mary's room lit up twice, as though in response. No figures passed before the windows, nor did the length of the illuminations correspond to any habitual activity. The girls' lights went off and on for no reason we could see.

Each night we tried to break the code. Tim Winer be-gan recording the girls' flashes with his mechanical pencil, but somehow we knew they wouldn't correspond to any established mode of communication. Some nights, the lights hypnotized us so that we came back to conscious-ness having forgotten where we were or what we were doing, only the bordello glow of Lux's Chinese lantern lighting the back room of our brains.

It took us a while to notice the lights in Cecilia's old room. Distracted by flashes at either end of the house, we failed to see the red and white pinpricks glowing at the window from which she'd jumped ten months before. Once we did, we couldn't agree what they were. Some believed they were incense sticks glowing in a secret ceremony, while others claimed they were only cigarettes. The cigarette theory caved in as soon as we detected more red lights than possible smokers, and by the time we counted sixteen, we understood at least a portion of the mystery: the girls had created a shrine to their dead sister. Those who attended church said the window resembled the Grotto at St. Paul's Catholic Church on the Lake, but instead of neat ascending rows of votive candles, each alike in size and importance like the souls they pilot-lighted, the girls had engineered a phantasmagoria of beacons. They had fused drippings from dinner candles into a single paraffin bundle wrapped with its own wick. They had fashioned ten torches from a psychedelic "craft candle" Cecilia had bought at a street art fair. They had lit the box of six squat emergency candles Mr. Lisbon kept in the upstairs closet in case of power failures. They had ignited three tubes of Mary's lipstick, which burned surprisingly well. From the windowsill, from cups suspended on clothes hangers, from old flowerpots, from cut-out milk cartons, the candles burned. At night we saw Bonnie tending the flames. Occasionally, finding candles drowning in their own wax, she dug runoff trenches with a pair of scissors;

but most often she watched the candles as if their outcome held her own, the flames almost extinguishing themselves, but, by some greed of oxygen, persisting.

In addition to God, the candles beseeched us. The Chinese lantern sent out its untranslatable S.O.S. The overhead light showed us the shabby state of the Lisbon house, and showed us Billy Jack, who had avenged his girlfriend's rape using forsworn karate. The girls' signals reached us and no one else, like a radio station picked up by our braces. At night, afterimages flashed on our inner eyelids, or hovered over our beds like a swarm of fireflies. Our inability to respond only made the signals more important. We watched the show nightly, always on the verge of discovering the key, and Joe Larson even tried flashing his own bedroom light in answer, but this made the Lisbon house go dark, and we felt reprimanded.

The first letter arrived on May 7. Slipped into Chase Buell's mailbox with the rest of the day's mail, the letter bore no stamp or return address, but when we opened it, we recognized at once the purple Flair Lux liked to write with.

> Dear whoever,
> Tell Trip I'm over him.
> He's a creep.
> Guess Who

That was all it said. In the next few weeks, other letters arrived, expressing various moods, each envelope delivered to our houses by the girls themselves in the dead of night. The idea of their sneaking out and moving about our street excited us, and a few nights we tried to stay up long enough to see them. We always awoke in the morning realizing that we'd fallen asleep at our posts. In the mailbox, like a quarter deposited under our pillows by the Tooth Fairy, a letter would be waiting. There were eight letters in all. Not all of them were written by Lux. All were unsigned. All were brief. One letter said: "Remember us?" Another said: "Down with unsavory boys." Another: "Watch for our lights." The longest said: "In this dark, there will be light. Will you help us?"

In the daytime, the Lisbon house looked vacant. The trash the family put out once a week (also in the middle of the night because no one saw them, not even Uncle Tucker) looked more and more like the refuse of people resigned to a long siege. They were eating canned lima beans. They were flavoring rice with sloppy-joe mix. At night, when the lights signaled, we racked our brains for a way of contacting the girls. Tom Faheem suggested flying a kite with a message alongside the house, but this was voted down on logistical grounds. Little Johnny Buell offered the recourse of tossing the same message on a rock through the girls' windows, but we were afraid the breaking glass would alert Mrs. Lisbon. In the end, the answer was so simple it took a week to come up with.

We called them on the telephone.

In the Larsons' sun-faded phone book, right between Licker and Little, we found the intact listing for Lisbon,

Ronald A. It sat halfway down the right-hand page, unmarked by any code or symbol, not even an asterisk referring to an appendix of pain. We stared at it for some time. Then, three index fingers at once, we dialed.

The telephone tolled eleven times before Mr. Lisbon answered. "What's it going to be today?" he said right away in a tired voice. His speech was slurred. We covered the phone and said nothing.

"I'm waiting. Today I'll listen to all your crap."

Another click sounded on the line, like a door opening onto a hollow corridor.

"Look, give us a break, will you?" Mr. Lisbon muttered.

There was a pause. Assorted breathing, mechanically reformulated, met in electronic space. Then Mr. Lisbon spoke in a voice unlike his own, a high screech . . . Mrs. Lisbon had grabbed the receiver.

"Why won't you leave us alone!" she shouted, and slammed down the phone.

We stayed on. For five more seconds her furious breath blew through the receiver, but just as we expected, the line didn't go dead. On the other end, an obscure presence waited.

We called out a tentative hello. After a moment, a faint, crippled voice returned, "Hi."

We hadn't heard the Lisbon girls speak in a long time, but the voice didn't jog our memories. It sounded— perhaps because the speaker was whispering—irreparably altered, diminished, the voice of a child fallen down a well. We didn't know which girl it was, and didn't know what to say. Still, we hung on together—her, them, us—and at some adjacent recess in the Bell telephone system another line connected. A man began talking underwater to a woman. We could half hear their conversation ("I thought maybe a salad" . . . "A salad? You're killing me with these salads"), but then another circuit must have freed, because the couple were shunted off suddenly, leaving us in buzzing silence, and the voice, raw but stronger now, said, "Shit. See you later," and the phone was hung up.

We called again next day, at the same time, and were answered on the first ring. We waited a moment for safety's sake, then proceeded with the plan we'd devised the night before. Holding the phone to one of Mr. Larson's speakers, we played the song which most thoroughly communicated our feelings to the Lisbon girls. We can't remember the song's title now, and an extensive search through records of the period has proved unsuccessful. We do, however, recall the essential sentiments, which spoke of hard days, long nights, a man waiting outside a broken telephone booth hoping it would somehow ring, and rain, and rainbows. It was mostly guitars, except for one interlude where a mellow cello hummed. We played it into the phone, and then Chase Buell gave our number and we hung up.

Next day, same time, our phone rang. We answered it immediately, and after some confusion (the phone was dropped), heard a needle bump down on a record, and the voice of Gilbert O'Sullivan singing through scratches. You may recall the song, a ballad which charts the misfortunes of a young man's life (his parents die, his fiancée stands him up at the altar), each verse leaving him more and more alone. It was Mrs. Eugene's favorite, and we knew it well from hearing her singing along over her simmering pots. The song never meant much to us, speaking as it did of an age we hadn't reached, but once we heard it playing tinily through the receiver, coming from the Lisbon girls, the song made an impact. Gilbert O'Sullivan's elfin voice sounded high enough to be a girl's. The lyrics might have been diary entries the girls whispered into our ears. Though it wasn't their voices we heard, the song conjured their images more vividly than ever. We could feel them, on the other end, blowing dust off the needle, holding the telephone over the spinning black disk, playing the volume low so as not to be overheard. When the song stopped, the needle skated through the inner ring, sending out a repeating click (like the same time lived over and over again). Already Joe Larson had our response ready, and after we played it, the Lisbon girls played theirs, and the evening went on like that. Most of the songs we've forgotten, but a portion of that contrapuntal exchange survives, in pencil, on the back of Demo Karafilis's *Tea for the Tillerman*, where he jotted it. We provide it here:

|  |  |
|---|---|
| the Lisbon girls | "Alone Again, Naturally," Gilbert O'Sullivan |
| us | "You've Got a Friend," James Taylor |
| the Lisbon girls | "Where Do the Children Play?" Cat Stevens |

| | |
|---:|:---|
| us | "Dear Prudence," |
| | The Beatles |
| the Lisbon girls | "Candle in the Wind," |
| | Elton John |
| us | "Wild Horses," |
| | The Rolling Stones |
| the Lisbon girls | "At Seventeen," Janice Ian |
| us | "Time in a Bottle," |
| | Jim Croce |
| the Lisbon girls | "So Far Away," |
| | Carole King |

Actually, we're not sure about the order. Demo Karafilis scribbled the titles haphazardly. The above order, however, does chart the basic progression of our musical conversation. Because Lux had burned her hard rock, the girls' songs were mostly folk music. Stark plaintive voices sought justice and equality. An occasional fiddle evoked the country the country had once been. The singers had bad skin or wore boots. Song after song throbbed with secret pain. We passed the sticky receiver from ear to ear, the drumbeats so regular we might have been pressing our ears to the girls' chests. Occasionally, we thought we heard them singing along, and it was almost like being at a concert with them. Our songs, for the most part, were love songs. Each selection tried to turn the conversation in a more intimate direction. But the Lisbon girls kept to impersonal topics. (We leaned in and commented on their perfume. They said it was probably the magnolias.) After a while, our songs turned sadder and sappier. That was when the girls played "So Far Away." We noted the shift at once (they had let their hand linger on our wrist) and followed with "Bridge over Troubled Water," turning up the volume because the song expressed more than any other how we felt about the girls, how we wanted to help them. When it finished, we waited for their response. After a long pause, their turntable began grinding again, and we heard the song which even now, in the Muzak of malls, makes us stop and stare back into a lost time:

> *Hey, have you ever tried*
> *Really reaching out for the other side*
> *I may be climbing on rainbows,*
> *But, baby, here goes:*

> *Dreams, they're for those who sleep*
> *Life, it's for us to keep*
> *And if you're wondering what this song is leading to*
> *I want to make it with you.*

The line went dead. (Without warning, the girls had thrown their arms around us, confessed hotly into our ears, and fled the room.) For some minutes, we stood motionless, listening to the buzz of the telephone line. Then it began to beep angrily, and a recording told us to hang up our phone and hang it up now.

We had never dreamed the girls might love us back.

The notion made us dizzy, and we lay down on the Larsons' carpet, which smelled of pet deodorizer and, deeper down, of pet. For a long time no one spoke. But little by little, as we shifted bits of information in our heads, we saw things in a new light. Hadn't the girls invited us to their party last year? Hadn't they known our names and addresses? Rubbing spy holes in grimy windows, hadn't they been looking out to see us? We forgot ourselves and held hands, smiling with closed eyes. On the stereo Garfunkel began hitting his high notes, and we didn't think of Cecilia. We thought only of Mary, Bonnie, Lux, and Therese, stranded in life, unable to speak to us until now, in this inexact, shy fashion. We went over their last months in school, coming up with new recollections. Lux had forgotten her math book one day and had to share with Tom Faheem. In the margin, she had written, "I want to get out of here." How far did that wish extend? Thinking back, we decided the girls had been trying to talk to us all along, to elicit our help, but we'd been too infatuated to listen. Our surveillance had been so focused we missed nothing but a simple returned gaze. Who else did they have to turn to? Not their parents. Nor the neighborhood. Inside their house they were prisoners; outside, lepers. And so they hid from the world, waiting for someone—for us—to save them.

But in the following days we tried to call the girls back without success. The phone rang on hopelessly, forlornly. We pictured the device howling under pillows while the girls reached for it in vain. Unable to get through, we

bought *The Best of Bread*, playing "Make It with You" over
and over. There was grand talk of tunnels, of starting from
the Larsons' basement and going beneath the street. The
dirt could be carried out in our pant legs and emptied during strolls like in *The Great Escape*. The drama of this
pleased us so much we momentarily forgot that our tunnel
had already been built: the storm sewers. We checked the
sewers, however, and found them full of water: the lake
had risen again this year. It didn't matter. Mr. Buell had an
extension ladder we could easily prop against the girls'
windows. "Just like eloping," Eugie Kent said, and the
words made our minds drift, to a red-faced, small-town
justice of the peace, and a sleeper compartment in a train
passing through blue wheat fields at night. We imagined all
sorts of things, waiting for the girls to signal for us.

None of this—the record-playing, the flashing lights,
the Virgin cards—ever got into the papers, of course. We
thought of our communication with the Lisbon girls as a
sacred confidence, even after such fidelity ceased to make
sense. Ms. Perl (who later published a book with a chapter
dedicated to the Lisbon girls) described their spirits sinking further and further in an inevitable progression. She
shows their pathetic last attempts to make a life—Bonnie's
tending the shrine, Mary's wearing bright sweaters—but
every stone the girls built shelter with has, for Ms. Perl,
an underside of mud and worms. The candles were a two-
way mirror between worlds: they called Cecilia back, but
also called her sisters to join her. Mary's pretty sweaters

only showed a desperate adolescent urge to be beautiful, while Therese's baggy sweatshirts revealed a "lack of self-esteem."

We knew better. Three nights after the record playing, we saw Bonnie bring a black trunk into her bedroom. She put it on her bed and began filling it with clothes and books. Mary appeared and threw in her climate mirror. They argued about the trunk's contents and, in a huff, Bonnie took out some of the clothes she'd put in, giving Mary more room for her things: a cassette player, a hair dryer, and the object we didn't understand until later, a cast-iron doorstop. We had no idea what the girls were doing, but we noticed the change in their demeanor at once. They moved with a new purpose. Their aimlessness was gone. It was Paul Baldino who interpreted their actions:

"Looks like they're going to make a break for it," he said, putting down the binoculars. He made this conclusion with the confident air of someone who had seen relatives disappear to Sicily or South America, and we believed him at once. "Five dollars gets you ten those girls are out of here by the end of the week."

He was right, though not in the way he intended. The last note, written on the back of a laminated picture of the Virgin, arrived in Chase Buell's mailbox on June 14. It said simply: "Tomorrow. Midnight. Wait for our signal."

By this time of year, fish flies coated our windows, making it difficult to see out. The next night, we gathered in the vacant lot beside Joe Larson's house. The sun had fallen below the horizon, but still lit the sky in an orange chemical streak more beautiful than nature. Across the street the Lisbon house was dark except for the red haze of Cecilia's shrine, nearly hidden. From the ground we couldn't see the upper story well, and tried to go up to the Larsons' roof. Mr. Larson stopped us. "I just got finished retarring it," he said. We wandered back to the lot, then walked down to the street, putting our palms against the asphalt still warm from the day's sun. The sodden smell of the Lisbon house reached us, then faded, so that we thought we'd imagined it. Joe Hill Conley began climbing trees, as usual, though the rest of us had outgrown it. We watched him shinny up a young maple. He couldn't climb far because the thin limbs wouldn't support his weight. Still, Chase Buell called up to him, "See anything?" and Joe Hill Conley squinted, then pulled the skin at the corners of his eyes taut, which he thought worked better than squinting, but finally shook his head. It gave us an idea, however, and we moved to the old tree house. Gazing up through foliage, we determined its condition. Part of the roof had been blown off in a storm years ago, and our crowning touch, the doorknob, was missing, but the structure still looked habitable.

We climbed up to the tree house the way we always had, stepping in the knothole, then on the nailed board, then on two bent nails, before grasping the frayed rope and pulling ourselves through the trapdoor. We were so much bigger now we could barely squeeze through, and once we were inside, the plywood floor sagged under our weight. The oblong window we'd cut with a handsaw years ago still looked onto the front of the Lisbon house. Next to it were five spotted photographs of the Lisbon girls, pinned with rusty tacks. We didn't remember putting them up, but there they were, dim from time and weather so that all we could make out were the phosphorescent outlines of the girls' bodies, each a different glowing letter of an unknown alphabet. Outside and below, a few people had come out to water lawns or flower beds, tossing silver lassos. The cracker voice of our local baseball announcer rose from a score of radios, describing a slow drama we couldn't see, and homerun cheers rose, too, converging above the trees and then dispersing. It grew still darker. People went inside. We tried the wick of the ancient kerosene lamp, which lit, burning on invisible residue, but within a minute, fish flies began streaming through the window, and we put the lamp out. We could hear their bodies battering street-lamps, a hail of hair balls, and popping under the tires of passing cars. A few bugs exploded as we leaned back against the tree-house walls. Inert unless detached, they flapped furiously between our fingers, then flew away to cling again, on anything, inert. The scum of their dead or dying bodies darkened street- and headlights, turned house windows into theater scrims poking out light. We settled back, pulling up a warm six-pack on a rope, and drank, and waited.

Each of us had said he was sleeping over at a friend's house, so we had all night to sit and drink, unmolested by adults. But neither at twilight nor thereafter did we see any lights in the Lisbon house other than the candles. They seemed to burn more dimly, and we suspected that despite their ministrations, the girls were running out of wax. Cecilia's window had the dank glow of an unclean fish tank. Angling Carl Tagel's telescope out the tree-house window, we managed to see the pockmarked moon steaming silently across space, then blue Venus, but when we turned the telescope on Lux's window it brought us so close we couldn't see a thing. What at first appeared the xylophone of her spine, curled in bed, turned out to be a decorative molding. A stringy peach pit, left on her bed-side table from a time of fresh food, gave rise to a number of lurid conjectures. Any time we caught sight of her, or of something moving, the piece was too small to put the puzzle together, and in the end we gave up, retracting the telescope and relying on our eyes.

Midnight passed in silence. The moon set. A bottle of Boone's Farm strawberry wine materialized, was passed around, and set on a tree limb. Tom Bogus rolled to the tree-house door and dropped from sight. A minute later, we heard him retching in the bushes of the vacant lot. We stayed up late enough to see Uncle Tucker emerge, hold-ing a piece of linoleum from the thirteenth layer he was installing to fill up the hours of his life. After getting a beer from the garage refrigerator, he walked to the front yard and surveyed his nighttime territory. Moving behind a tree, he waited for Bonnie to appear, rosary in hand.

From his vantage point he couldn't see the flashlight come on in the bedroom window, and he had gone back inside before we heard the window open. By that time we were fixed on it. The flashlight waved through the darkness. Then the light went on and off three times in succession.

A breeze arose. In the blackness, the leaves of our tree began to flutter, and the air filled with the crepuscular scent of the Lisbon house. None of us remembers thinking anything, or deciding anything, because at that moment our minds had ceased to work, filling us with the only peace we've ever known. We were above the street, aloft, at the same height as the Lisbon girls in their crumbling bedrooms, and they were calling to us. We heard wood scrape. Then, for an instant, we saw them—Lux, Bonnie, Mary, and Therese—framed in a single window. They looked our way, looked across the void at us. Mary blew us a kiss, or wiped her mouth. The flashlight went off. The window closed. And they were gone.

We didn't even stop to discuss it. In single file, like paratroopers, we dropped from the tree. It was an easy jump, and only on impact did we realize how close the ground was: no more than ten feet down. Jumping from the grass, we could nearly touch the tree-house floor. Our new height astounded us, and later many said this contributed to our resolve, because for the first time ever we felt like men.

We advanced on the house from different directions,

hiding in shadows of surviving trees. As we approached, some of us crawling army-style, others still on two feet, the smell grew stronger. The air thickened. Soon we reached an invisible barrier: no one had gotten this close to the Lisbon house in months. We hesitated, and then Paul Baldino held his hand in the air, giving the signal, and we went in closer. We grazed the brick walls, crouching under windows and getting spiderweb in our hair. We came into the damp mess of the backyard. Kevin Head tripped on the bird feeder, which was still lying there. It cracked in half, the remaining seed spilling out onto the ground. We froze, but no lights came on. After a minute, we inched in closer. Mosquitoes dive-bombed past our ears, but we paid no attention. We were too busy gazing up into the darkness for a ladder of knotted bedsheets and a descending nightgown. We saw nothing. The house rose above us, its windows reflecting dark masses of leaves. In a whisper, Chase Buell reminded us that he had just gotten his driver's license, and held up the keys to his mother's Cougar. "We can use my car," he said. Tom Faheem searched the overgrown flower beds for pebbles to ping against the girls' windows. Any second an upstairs window might open, breaking its seal of fish flies, and a face would look down at us for the rest of our lives.

At the back window, we grew brave enough to look in. Through a scrub of dead windowsill plants, we made out the interior of the house: a seascape of confused objects, advancing and retreating as our eyes adjusted to the light. Mr. Lisbon's La-Z-Boy rolled forward, its footrest raised like a snow shovel. The brown vinyl sofa slunk back against the wall. As they moved apart, the floor seemed to rise like a hydraulic stage, and in the room's only light, coming from a small shaded lamp, we saw Lux. She was lying back in a beanbag chair, her knees lifted and spread apart, her upper half sunk into the bag, which closed over her like a straitjacket. She was wearing blue jeans and suede clogs. Her long hair fell over her shoulders. She had a cigarette in her mouth, the long ash about to fall.

We didn't know what to do next. We had no instructions. We pressed our faces against the windows, using our hands as goggles. The glass panes conducted sound vibrations, and as we leaned forward, we could feel the other girls moving about above us. Something slid, stopped, slid again. Something bumped. We drew our faces away and everything went still. Then we returned to the buzzing glass.

Now Lux was groping for an ashtray. Finding none within reach, she flicked her ash onto her blue jeans, rubbing it in with her hand. As she moved, she rose out of the beanbag, and we saw that she was wearing a halter top. Tied behind her neck in a bow, the halter descended on two thin straps over her pale shoulders and sculpted collarbones, swelling finally into two yellow slings. The halter was slightly askew on the right side, revealing a soft white plumpness as she stretched. "July, two years ago," said Joe Hill Conley, identifying the last time we'd seen the halter. On a very hot day, Lux had worn it outside for five minutes before her mother had called her back in to change. Now the halter spoke of all the time in between, of everything that had happened. Most of all, it said that the girls were leaving, that from now on they'd wear whatever they liked.

"Maybe we should knock," Kevin Head whispered, but none of us did. Lux settled back in the beanbag chair. She ground out her cigarette on the floor. Behind her, on the wall, a shadow swelled. She turned abruptly, then smiled as a stray cat we'd never seen before climbed into her lap. She hugged its unresponsive body until the animal struggled free (that's one more thing we have to include: right up to the end, Lux loved the stray cat. It ran off then, out of this report). Lux lit another cigarette. In the match's flare, she looked up at the window. She lifted her chin so that we thought she'd seen us, but then she ran her hand through her hair. She was only examining her re- flection. The light inside the house made us invisible out- side, and we stood inches from the window but unseen, as though looking in at Lux from another plane of existence. The faint glow of the window flickered against our faces. Our trunks and legs descended into darkness. On the lake a freighter sounded its horn, on a fogless night. Another freighter responded at a deeper pitch. That halter could have come undone with one quick yank.

Tom Faheem went first, disproving his shy reputation. He climbed onto the back porch, quietly opened the door, and let us, at last, back into the Lisbon house.

"We're here" was all he said.

Lux looked up, but didn't rise from the chair. Her sleepy eyes showed no surprise that we were there, but at the base of her white neck a lobstery blush spread. "About time," she said. "We've been waiting for you guys." She took another drag.

"We've got a car," Tom Faheem continued. "Full tank. We'll take you wherever you want to go."

"It's just a Cougar," said Chase Buell, "but it's got a pretty big trunk."

"Can I sit in front?" Lux asked, screwing her mouth up to exhale to one side, politely away from us.

"Sure can."

"Which one of you studs is going to sit up front next to me?"

She tilted her head toward the ceiling and blew a series of smoke rings. We watched them rise, and this time Joe Hill Conley didn't run forward to stick his finger in them. For the first time, we looked around the house. The smell, now that we were inside, was stronger than ever. It was the smell of wet plaster, drains clogged with the endless tangle of the girls' hair, mildewed cabinets, leaking pipes. Paint cans were still stationed under leaks, each full of a weak solution of other times. The living room had a plundered look. The television sat at an angle, its screen removed, Mr. Lisbon's toolbox open in front of it. Chairs were missing arms or legs, as though the Lisbons had been using them for firewood.

"Where are your parents?"

"Asleep."

"What about your sisters?"

"They're coming."

Something thudded downstairs. We retreated to the back door. "Come on," Chase Buell said. "We better get out of here. It's getting late." But Lux only exhaled again, shaking her head. She pulled a halter strap away from her skin, where it left a red mark. Everything was quiet again. "Wait," she said. "Five more minutes. We're not finished packing. We had to wait until my parents were asleep. They take forever. Especially my mom. She's an insomniac. She's probably awake right now."

She got up then. We saw her rise from the beanbag chair, leaning forward to get enough momentum. The halter, on its flimsy strings, hung completely away from her body so that we saw dark air between material and skin, and then the soft flash of her flour-dusted breasts.

"My feet are all swollen," she said. "Weirdest thing. That's why I'm wearing clogs. Do you like them?" She dangled one on the end of her toes.

"Yeah."

Now she stood at full height, which wasn't tall. We had to keep telling ourselves that this was happening, that this was really Lux Lisbon, that we were in the same room with her. She looked down at herself, adjusted the halter, tucked with one thumb the exposed plumpness on her right side. Then she looked up again as though into each of our eyes at once, and began walking forward. She shuffled in the clogs, moving into the shadows, and as she approached we could hear her printing the dusty floor. From the darkness she said, "We won't all fit in a Cougar." She took one more step and her face reappeared. For a second it didn't seem alive: it was too white, the cheeks too perfectly carved, the arched eyebrows painted on, the full lips made of wax. But then she came closer and we saw the light in her eyes we have been looking for ever since.

"We better take my mom's car, don't you think? It's bigger. Which one of you can drive?"

Chase Buell raised his hand.

"Think you can drive a station wagon?"

"Sure." And then: "It's not a stick, is it?"

"No."

"Sure. No problem."

"Will you let me steer some?"

"Sure. But we should get out of here. I just heard something. Maybe it's your mom."

She came up to Chase Buell. She came so close her breath stirred his hair. And then, in front of us all, Lux unbuckled his belt. She didn't even need to look down. Her fingers saw their way, and only once did something snag, at which point she shook her head, like a musician missing an easy note. All the while she stared into his eyes, rising up on the balls of her feet, and in the quiet house we heard the pants unsnap. The zipper opened all the way down our spines. None of us moved. Chase Buell didn't move. Lux's eyes, burning and velvet, glowed in the dim room. A vein on her neck was softly pulsing, the one you're supposed to put perfume on for that reason. Even though she was doing it to Chase Buell, we could all feel Lux undoing us, reaching out for us and taking us as she knew we could be taken. Just at the last second, another soft thud came from downstairs. Upstairs, Mr. Lisbon coughed in his sleep. Lux stopped. She looked away, consulting with herself, and then she said, "We can't do this now."

She let go of Chase Buell's belt and crossed to the back door. "I've got to get some fresh air. You guys have got me all worked up." She smiled then, a loose, clumsy smile, genuine, unpretty. "I'll go wait in the car. You guys wait here for my sisters. We've got a lot of stuff." She fished in a bowl by the back door for the car keys. She made to leave, but stopped again.

"Where will we go?"

"Florida," Chase Buell said.

"Cool," said Lux. "Florida."

A minute later, we heard a car door slam shut in the garage. A few of us recall hearing the faint strains of a popular song drifting through the night, which told us she was playing the radio. We waited. We weren't sure where the other girls were. We could hear sounds of packing upstairs, a closet door opening, a suitcase jangling bedsprings. Feet moved above and below. Something was being dragged across the basement floor. Though the nature of the sounds eluded us, a precision surrounded them; every movement seemed exact, part of an elaborate escape plan. We understood that we were only pawns in this strategy, useful for a time, but this didn't lessen our exhilaration. The knowledge welled in us that we would soon be in the car with the girls, driving them out of our green neighborhood and into the pure, free desolation of back roads we didn't even know yet. We played paper, scissors, rock to see who would go along, who would stay behind. And all the while the sense that the girls would soon join us filled us with a quiet happiness. Who knew how accustomed we might get to those sounds? Of elastic satin suitcase pockets snapping closed? Of jewelry rattling? Of the hunchback foot-dragging sound of the girls carrying suitcases down an anonymous corridor? Unknown roads took shape in our minds. We saw ourselves cutting swaths through cattails, freshwater inlets, old boatyards. At some gas station we would ask for the ladies' room key because the girls would be too shy. We would play the radio with the windows open.

Sometime during this reverie, the house went silent. We assumed the girls had finished packing. Peter Sissen took out his penlight and made a shallow foray into the dining room, coming back to say, "One of them is still downstairs. There's a light on in the stairway."

We stood, we waved the penlight, we waited for the girls, but no one came. Tom Faheem tried the first stair, but it creaked so loudly he came back down again. The silence of the house rang in our ears. A car passed, sending a shadow sweeping across the dining room, momentarily lighting up the painting of the Pilgrims. The dining table was heaped with winter coats wrapped in plastic. Other hulking bundles loomed. The house had the feel of an attic where junk collects, establishing revolutionary relationships: the toaster in the birdcage; ballet slippers protruding from a wicker creel. We snaked our way amid the clutter, passing into spaces cleared for games—a backgammon board, Chinese checkers—then moving again into thickets of eggbeaters and rubber boots. We entered the kitchen. It was too dark to see, but we heard a small hiss, like someone sighing. A trapezoid of light projected up from the basement. We went to the stairs and listened. Then we started down to the rec room.

Chase Buell led the way, and as we descended, holding on to one another's belt loops, we traveled back to the day a year earlier when we had descended those same steps to attend the only party the Lisbon girls were ever allowed to throw. By the time we reached bottom, we felt we'd literally traveled back in time. For despite the inch of floodwater covering the floor, the room was just as we had left it: Cecilia's party had never been cleaned up. The paper tablecloth, spotted with mice droppings, still covered the card table. A brownish scum of punch lay caked in the cut-glass bowl, sprinkled with flies. The sherbet had melted long ago, but a ladle still protruded from the gummy silt, and cups, gray with dust and cobwebs, remained neatly stacked in front. A profusion of withered balloons hung from the ceiling on thin ribbons. The domino game still called for a three or a seven.

We didn't know where the girls had gone. Ripples

spread across the water's surface as though something had just swum by or dived down. The gurgling drain sucked intermittently. The water lapped the walls, reflecting our pink faces, and the red and blue streamers overhead. The room's changes—water bugs adhering to walls, one bobbing dead mouse—only heightened what hadn't changed. If we half closed our eyes and held our noses, we could trick ourselves into thinking the party was still going on. Buzz Romano waded out to the card table, and as we all watched, began to dance, to box-step, as his mother had taught him in the papal splendor of their living room. He held only air, but we could see her—them—all five, clasped in his arms. "These girls make me crazy. If I could just feel one of them up just once," he said, as his shoes filled and emptied with silt. His dancing kicked up the sewage smell, and after that, stronger than ever, the smell we could never forget. Because it was then we saw, over Buzz Romano's head, the only thing that had changed in the room since we left it a year before. Hanging down amid the half-deflated balloons were the two brown-and-white husks of Bonnie's saddle shoes. She had tied the rope to the same beam as the decorations.

None of us moved. Buzz Romano, oblivious, kept dancing. Above him, in a pink dress, Bonnie looked clean and festive, like a piñata. It took a minute to sink in. We gazed up at Bonnie, at her spindly legs in their white confirmation stockings, and the shame that has never gone away took over. The doctors we later consulted attributed our response to shock. But the mood felt more like guilt, like coming to attention at the last moment and too late, as though Bonnie were murmuring the secret not only of her death but of her life itself, of all the girls' lives. She was so still. She had such enormous weight. The soles of her wet shoes were embedded with bits of mica, shining and dripping.

We had never known her. They had brought us here to find that out.

How long we stayed like that, communing with her departed spirit, we can't remember. Long enough for our collective breath to start a breeze through the room that made Bonnie twist on her rope. She spun slowly, and at one point her face broke out of the seaweed of balloons, showing us the reality of the death she'd chosen. It was a world of blackening eye sockets, blood pooling in lower extremities, stiffening joints.

Already we knew the rest—though we would never be sure about the sequence of events. We argue about it still. Most likely, Bonnie died while we sat in the living room, dreaming of highways. Mary put her head in the oven shortly thereafter, on hearing Bonnie kick the trunk out from under herself. They were ready to assist one another, if need be. Mary might have still been breathing when we passed by on our way downstairs, missing her by less than two feet in the dark, as we later measured. Therese, stuffed with sleeping pills washed down with gin, was as good as dead by the time we entered the house. Lux was the last to go, twenty or thirty minutes after we left. Fleeing, screaming without sound, we forgot to stop at the garage, from which music was still playing. They found her in the front seat, gray-faced and serene, holding a cigarette lighter that had burned its coils into her palm. She had escaped in the car just as we expected. But she had unbuckled us, it turned out, only to stall us, so that she and her sisters could die in peace.

# FIVE

We knew them now. Knew the way the skinny one drove, with his bursts of acceleration midblock, his cautious turning, his habit of misjudging the Lisbons' driveway so that he ran over the lawn. We knew the bending sound a siren made as it passed, a phenomenon Therese identified correctly as the Doppler effect the third time the EMS truck came, but not the fourth because she was bent herself by then, winding down and away in slow spirals, a feeling akin to being sucked through your own intestines. We knew that the fat one had sensitive skin and was plagued with razor bumps, that he wore a metal wedge on the heel of his shoe because his left leg was shorter than his right, and that he made an uneven clicking sound as he hitched across the macadam driveway. We knew that the skinny one's hair tended to get oily, because when they came to get Cecilia his long hair had looked like Bob Seger's, but now, a year later, the fluff was gone and he looked like a drowned rat. We still didn't know their real names, but we were beginning to intuit the condition of their paramedic lives, the smell of bandages and oxygen masks, the taste of precalamity dinners on resuscitated mouths, the flavor of life ebbing away on the other side of their own puffing faces, the blood, brain spatter, blue cheeks, bulging eyes, and—on our own block—the succession of limp bodies wearing charm bracelets and gold lockets in the shape of a heart.

When they came the fourth time they were losing faith. The truck made the same jolting stop, tires skidded, doors flew open, but as they jumped out the paramedics had lost their valiant appearance and were clearly two men afraid of being humiliated. "It's those two guys again," said Zachary Larson, five. The fat one gave the skinny one a look and they started for the house, this time taking no equipment. Mrs. Lisbon, face white, answered the door. She pointed inside, saying nothing. When the paramedics entered, she remained in the doorway, tightening the belt of her robe. She straightened the welcome mat with her toe, twice. Soon the paramedics ran out again, changed and electrified, and got the stretcher. A minute later they were carrying Therese out, facedown. Her dress, hiked up around her waist, revealed her unbecoming underwear, the color of an athletic bandage. The buttons in back had popped open to reveal a slice of mushroom-colored back. Her hand kept falling off the stretcher, though each time Mrs. Lisbon replaced it. "Stay," she commanded, to the hand apparently. But the hand flopped out again. Mrs. Lisbon stopped, her shoulders sagged, she seemed to give up. In the next second she was running, holding on to Therese's arm and murmuring what some people heard as, "Not you, too," and Mrs. O'Connor, who had acted in college, as, "But too cruel."

By this time we were back in our beds, shamming sleep. Outside, Sheriff wore an oxygen mask to enter the garage and raise the automatic door. When it opened (so people told us) nothing came out, no smoke as everyone expected, not even a trace of gas that made things shimmer like a mirage—the station wagon sat vibrating, and because Sheriff had brushed another switch accidentally, the windshield wipers were going like mad. The fat one went inside to get Bonnie down from the rafters, balancing one chair on another like a circus performer. They found Mary in the kitchen, not dead but nearly so, her head and torso thrust into the oven as though she were scrubbing it. A second EMS truck came (the only time this happened) bringing two paramedics more efficient than Sheriff and the fat one. They rushed inside and saved Mary's life. For a while. For what it was worth.

Technically, Mary survived for more than a month, though everyone felt otherwise. After that night, people spoke of the Lisbon girls in the past tense, and if they mentioned Mary at all it was with the veiled wish that she would hurry up and get it over with. In fact, the final suicides surprised few people. Even we who had tried to save the girls came to consider ourselves temporarily insane. In hindsight, Bonnie's battered trunk lost its associations with travel and flight and became only what it was: a drop weight for a hanging, like sandbags in old Westerns. Still, while everyone agreed the suicides came as predictably as seasons or old age, we could never agree on an explanation for them. The final suicides seemed to confirm Dr. Hornicker's theory that the girls had been suffering from Post-Traumatic Stress Disorder, but Dr. Hornicker later distanced himself from that conclusion. Even if Cecilia's suicide led to copycatting, that still didn't explain why Cecilia had killed herself in the first place. At a hastily called Lions Club meeting, Dr. Hornicker, the guest speaker, brought up the possibility of a chemical link, citing a new study of "platelet serotonin receptor indices in suicidal children." Dr. Kotbaum of the Western Psychiatric Institute had found that many suicidal persons possessed deficient amounts of serotonin, a neurotransmitter essential for the regulation of mood. Since the serotonin study had been published after Cecilia's suicide, Dr. Hornicker had never measured her serotonin level. He did, however, examine a blood sample taken from Mary, which showed a slight deficiency of serotonin. She was put on medication, and after two weeks of psychological tests and intensive therapy, her blood was tested again. At that time her serotonin level appeared normal.

As for the other girls, autopsies were performed on each of them, in accordance with a state law requiring investigation in all deaths by suicide. As written, the law gave the police leeway in such cases, and their prior failure to order an autopsy on Cecilia led many to believe they now suspected Mr. and Mrs. Lisbon of foul play, or wished to put pressure on them to move. A single coroner, brought in from the city with two fatigued assistants, opened up the girls' brains and body cavities, peering inside at the mystery of their despair. They used an assembly-line approach, the assistants rolling each girl past the doctor as he used his table saw, his hose, his vacuum. Photographs were taken, but never released, though we wouldn't have had the stomach to look at them. We did, however, read the coroner's report, written in a colorful style that made the girls' deaths as unreal as the news. He spoke of the incredible cleanliness of the girls' bodies, the youngest he had ever worked on, showing no signs of wastage or alcoholism. Their smooth blue hearts looked like water balloons, and the rest of their organs possessed a similar textbook clarity. In older people, or the chronically ill, the organs tend to lose their shape, to distend, change color, grow connections with organs they have nothing to do with, so that most entrails look, as the coroner put it, "like a rubbish dump." The Lisbon girls, on the other hand, were "like something behind glass. Like an exhibit." Nevertheless, it saddened the coroner to pierce and shred those unblemished bodies, and a few times he was overcome with emotion. In one margin he scrawled a note to himself: "Seventeen years in this business and I'm a basket case." He persevered in his function, however, finding the mass of half-digested pills trapped in Therese's ileum, the strangulated section of Bonnie's esophagus, the riot of carbon monoxide in Lux's tepid blood.

Ms. Perl, whose story came out in the evening paper,

was the first to point out the significance of the date. The girls, it turned out, had killed themselves on June 16, the anniversary of Cecilia's wrist-slitting. Ms. Perl made much of this, speaking of "ominous foreshadowing" and "eerie coincidence," and single-handedly initiated the feeding frenzy of speculation that continues to this day. In her subsequent articles—one every two or three days for two weeks—she shifted her tone from the sympathetic register of a fellow mourner to the steely precision of what she never succeeded in being: an investigative reporter. Scouring the neighborhood in her blue Pontiac, she cobbled together reminiscences into an airtight conclusion, far less truthful than our own, which is full of holes. Fed the emetic of Ms. Perl's insistent questions, Amy Schraff, Cecilia's old friend, disgorged a memory of presuicidal days: one boring afternoon, Cecilia had made her lie on her bed beneath the zodiac mobile. "Close your eyes and keep them closed," she had said. The door opened and the other sisters entered the room. They placed their hands over Amy's face and body. "Who do you want to contact?" Cecilia asked. "My grandmother," Amy replied. The hands were cool on her face. Someone lit incense. A dog barked. Nothing happened.

From that episode, no more indicative of spiritualism than a Ouija board's turning up amid the usual Milton Bradleys, Ms. Perl based her claim that the suicides were an esoteric ritual of self-sacrifice. Her third story, under the headline "Suicides May Have Been Pact," outlines the generic conspiracy theory, which held that the girls planned the suicides in concert with an undetermined astrological event. Cecilia had merely entered first, while her sisters waited in the wings. Candles lit the stage. In the orchestra pit, Cruel Crux began to wail. The *Playbill* we held in the audience showed a picture of the Virgin. Ms. Perl choreographed it all nicely. What she could never explain, however, was why the girls chose the date of Cecilia's suicide *attempt* rather than her actual death some three weeks later on July 9.

But this discrepancy stopped no one. Once the copycat suicides occurred, the media descended on our street without letup. Our three local television stations sent news teams, and even a national correspondent showed up in a motor home. He'd heard about the suicides at a truck stop in the southwestern corner of our state, and had come up to see for himself. "I doubt I'll shoot anything," he said. "I'm supposed to be the color guy." Still, he parked the motor home down the block, and from then on we saw him lounging on its plaid seats, or cooking hamburgers on the miniature stove. Undeterred by the parents' delicate condition, the local news teams ran stories immediately. It was then we saw the footage of the Lisbon house taken months earlier, a soggy pan of roof and stark front door, leading to a recap where every night the same five faces filed by, Cecilia in her yearbook photo, followed by her sisters in theirs. Live hookups were still new at the time, and often microphones went dead, or lights burned out, leaving reporters speaking in the dark. Spectators not yet bored with television competed to get their heads into the frame. Each day the reporters attempted to interview Mr. and Mrs. Lisbon, and each day they failed. By showtime, however, they seemed to have gained access to the girls' very bedrooms, given all the intimate treasures they brought back. One reporter held up a wedding dress made the same year as Cecilia's, and except for the unshorn hem, we couldn't tell them apart. Another reporter ended his broadcast by reading a letter Therese had written to the Brown admissions office—"ironically," as he put it, "only three days before she put an end to any dreams of college . . . or of anything else." Gradually, the reporters began referring to the Lisbon girls by first names, and neglected to interview medical experts in favor of collecting reminiscences. Like us, they became custodians of the girls' lives, and had they completed the job to our satisfaction, we might never have been forced to wander endlessly down the paths of hypothesis and memory. For less and less did the reporters ask why the girls had killed themselves. Instead, they talked about the girls' hobbies and academic awards. Wanda Brown, on Channel 7, unearthed a photo of a bikinied Lux at the community swimming pool, allowing a lifeguard to reach down from his chair and apply zinc oxide to her bunnyish nose. Every night the reporters revealed a new anecdote or photo, but their discoveries bore no relation to what we knew to be true, and after a while it began to seem as though they were talking about different people. Channel 4's Pete Patillo referred to Therese's "love of horses," though we'd never seen Therese near a horse, and Tom Thomson, on Channel 2, often mixed up the girls' names. The reporters cited as fact the most apocryphal accounts, and confused details of stories they got basically right (in this way Cecilia's black underwear appeared on the wax dummy Pete Patillo passed off as Mary). Knowing the rest of the city accepted the news as gospel only demoralized us further. Outsiders, in our opinion, had no right to refer to Cecilia as "the crazy one," because they hadn't earned their shorthand by a long distillation of firsthand knowledge. For the first time ever we sympathized with the President because we saw how wildly our sphere of influence was misrepresented by those in no position to know what was going on. Even our parents seemed to agree more and more with the television version of things, listening to the reporters' inanities as though they could tell us the truth about our own lives.

After the suicide free-for-all, Mr. and Mrs. Lisbon gave up the attempt to lead a normal life. Mrs. Lisbon stopped attending church, and when Father Moody went to the house to console her, no one answered the door. "I kept ringing the bell," he told us. "No dice." During Mary's entire stay in the hospital, Mrs. Lisbon appeared only once. Herb Pitzenberger saw her come out onto the back porch with a stack of manuscript pages. Putting them into a pile, she lit them. We never learned what they were.

About this time, Ms. Carmina D'Angelo received a call from Mr. Lisbon, asking her to put the house back on the market (he'd taken it off shortly after Cecilia's suicide). Ms. D'Angelo tactfully pointed out that the present condition of the house would not facilitate the sale, but Mr. Lisbon responded, "I realize. I've got a guy coming in."

It turned out to be Mr. Hedlie, the English teacher from school. Out of work for the summer, he arrived in his VW bug, its bumper sticker still supporting the last failed Democratic candidate for President. When he got out, he was wearing not his former schoolmaster's blazer and trousers, but a bright green-and-yellow dashiki and a pair of lizard sandals. His hair covered his ears and he moved with the bohemian slouch of teachers during vacation, resuming unruly lives. Despite his look of a commune leader, he set to work in earnest, carting out over three days a mountain of refuse from the Lisbon house. While Mr. and Mrs. Lisbon went to stay in a motel, Mr. Hedlie took charge of the house, throwing away snow skis, watercolor paints, bags of clothes, a Hula Hoop. He dragged the worn-out brown sofa outside, cutting it in two when it wouldn't fit through the doorway. He filled trash bags with potholders, old coupons, heaps of accumulated twist-ties, superseded keys. We saw him attacking the overgrowth of each room, hacking away with his dustpan, and on the third day he began wearing a surgical mask because of the dust. He never spoke to us anymore in obscure Greek phrases, or took interest in our sandlot baseball games, but arrived every morning with the hopeless expression of a man draining a swamp with a kitchen sponge. As he lifted rugs and threw out towels, he unleashed the odors of the house in waves, and many people thought he wore the surgical mask to protect himself not from dust but from the exhalations of the Lisbon girls that still lived in bedding and drapes, in peeling wallpaper, in patches of carpet preserved brand-new beneath dressers and nightstands. The first day Mr. Hedlie restricted himself to the first floor, but the second day he ventured into the sacked seraglio of the Lisbon girls' bedrooms, wading ankle-deep in garments that gave off the music of a past time. Pulling Cecilia's Nepalese scarf from behind a headboard, he was greeted, at each fringy end, with the tinkling of green corroded bells. Bedsprings sang two-note plaints when stood on end. Pillows snowed dead skin.

He emptied six shelves from the upstairs closet, throwing out stacked bath towels and washcloths, frayed mattress liners bearing rose or lemon-colored stains, blankets sopped with the picnic of the girls' spilled sleep. On the top shelf he found and pitched household medical supplies—a hot-water bottle the texture of inflamed skin, a midnight-blue jar of Vicks VapoRub fingerprinted inside, a shoe box full of ointments for ringworm and conjunctivitis, salves applied to nether regions, aluminum tubes dented, squeezed, or rolled up like party favors. Also: orange baby aspirin the girls had chewed as candy, an old thermometer (oral, alas) in its black plastic case, along with a variety of other implements pressed, inserted, applied into or onto the girls' bodies; in short, all the earthly concoctions Mrs. Lisbon had used over the years to keep the girls alive and well.

This was when we found the albums of the Grand Rapids Gospelers, Tyrone Little and the Believers, and the rest. Every evening when Mr. Hedlie left, coated with a white film that aged him thirty years, we went through the mixture of treasure and junk he set out at the curb. The extraordinary latitude Mr. Lisbon had given him surprised us, for Mr. Hedlie disposed of not only replaceable items such as shoe polish tins (gouged to silver centers) but family photographs, a working Water Pik, and a strip of butcher paper marking the growth of each Lisbon daughter at one-year intervals. The last thing Mr. Hedlie threw out was the empty television set, which Jim Crotter took up to his bedroom, only to find inside the stuffed iguana Therese had taught biology with, its tail torn off and the trapdoor in its abdomen missing, exposing various numbered plastic organs. We, of course, took the family photographs and, after organizing a permanent collection in our tree house, divided the rest by choosing straws. Most of the photographs had been taken years before, in what appears to be a happier time of almost endless family cookouts. One photograph shows the girls sitting Indian style, balanced on the lawn's seesaw (the photographer has tilted the camera) by the counterweight of a smoking hibachi uphill. (We regret to say that this photograph, Exhibit #47, was recently found missing from its envelope.) Another favorite is the series of totem-pole shots, taken at a tourist attraction, with each girl substituting her face for a sacred animal.

But despite all this new evidence of the girls' lives, and of the sudden drop-off of family togetherness (the photos virtually cease about the time Therese turned twelve), we learned little more about the girls than we knew already. It felt as though the house could keep disgorging debris forever, a tidal wave of unmatched slippers and dresses scarecrowed on hangers, and after sifting through it all we would still know nothing. There came an end to the outflow, however. Three days after Mr. Hedlie forged into the house, he came out, opening the front door for the first time and proceeding down the front steps to place beside the FOR SALE sign another, smaller sign that read, GARAGE SALE. That day, and for two days following, Mr. Hedlie offered up an inventory that encompassed not only the chipped dishware of a garage sale but the heavy durable goods offered at the liquidation of an estate. Everyone went, not to buy but just to enter the Lisbon house, which had been transformed into a clean spacious area smelling of pine cleaner. Mr. Hedlie had thrown out all the linens, anything that had belonged to the girls, anything broken, leaving only furniture, tables polished with linseed oil, kitchen chairs, mirrors, beds, each item bearing a neat white tag showing the price in his effeminate handwriting. The prices were final; he did not haggle. We roamed the house, upstairs and down, touching beds the girls would never sleep on again or mirrors that would never again hold their images. Our parents didn't buy used furniture, and certainly didn't buy furniture tainted with death, but they browsed like the others who came in response to the newspaper ad. A bearded Greek Orthodox priest showed up with a group of rotund widows. After cawing like crows and turning up their noses at everything, the widows furnished the priest's new rectory bedroom with Mary's canopy bed, Therese's walnut dresser, Lux's Chinese lantern, and Cecilia's crucifix. Others arrived, carting away the contents of the house bit by bit. Mrs. Krieger found her son Kyle's retainer on a display table outside the garage, and after failing to persuade Mr. Hedlie that it belonged to her son, bought it back for three dollars. The last thing we saw was a man with a paintbrush mustache loading the sailing ship model into the trunk of his Eldorado.

Though the exterior of the house remained in disrepair, the interior was presentable once again, and within the next few weeks Ms. D'Angelo managed to sell the house to the young couple who live there now, though they can no longer be called young. Back then, however, in the first flush of having money to burn, they made an offer that Mr. Lisbon accepted, despite its being far below what he had paid. The house was almost completely empty at that point, the only thing left being Cecilia's shrine, a woolly mass of candle drippings fused to the windowsill, which Mr. Hedlie had superstitiously neglected to touch. We thought we might never see Mr. and Mrs. Lisbon again, and even then we began the impossible process of trying to forget about them. Our parents seemed better able to do this, returning to their tennis foursomes and cocktail cruises. They reacted to the final suicides with mild shock, as though they'd been expecting them or something worse, as though they'd seen it all before. Mr. Conley adjusted the tweed necktie he wore even while cutting the grass and said, "Capitalism has resulted in material well-being but spiritual bankruptcy." He went on to deliver a living room lecture about human needs and the ravages of competition, and even though he was the only Communist we knew, his ideas differed from everyone else's only in degree. Something sick at the heart of the country had infected the girls. Our parents thought it had to do with our music, our godlessness, or the loosening of morals regarding sex we hadn't even had. Mr. Hedlie mentioned that fin-de-siècle Vienna witnessed a similar outbreak of suicides on the part of the young, and put the whole thing down to the misfortune of living in a dying empire. It had to do with the way the mail wasn't delivered on time, and how potholes never got fixed, or the thievery at City Hall, or the race riots, or the 801 fires set around the city on Devil's night. The Lisbon girls became a symbol of what was wrong with the country, the pain it inflicted on even its most innocent citizens, and in order to make things better a parents' group donated a bench in the girls' memory to our school. Originally slated to commemorate just Cecilia (the project had been put in motion eight months earlier, after the Day of Grieving), the bench was rededicated just in time to include the other girls as well. It was a small bench, made from a tree from the Upper Peninsula. "Virgin timber," Mr. Krieger said, who had retooled the machinery at his air-filter factory in order to make the bench. The plaque bore the simple inscription IN MEMORY OF THE LISBON GIRLS, DAUGHTERS OF THIS COMMUNITY.

Mary was still alive at this point, of course, but the

plaque did not acknowledge that fact. She returned from the hospital a few days later, after a two-week stay. Knowing they wouldn't have come, Dr. Hornicker hadn't even asked Mr. and Mrs. Lisbon to attend the therapy sessions. He ran Mary through the same battery of tests Cecilia had taken, but found no evidence of a psychiatric illness such as schizophrenia or manic depression. "Her scores showed her to be a relatively well-adjusted adolescent. Her future wasn't bright, of course. I recommended ongoing therapy to deal with the trauma. But we had her serotonin up, and she looked good."

She came back to a house without furniture. Mr. and Mrs. Lisbon, back from the motel, were camping out in the master bedroom. Mary was also given a sleeping bag. Mr. Lisbon, understandably reticent about the days following the triple suicide, told us little about the condition Mary returned home in. Eleven years before, when the girls were just children, the family had arrived at the house one week before the moving van. They had had to camp out then, too, sleeping on the floor and reading bedtime stories by a kerosene lantern, and, oddly, that memory came back to Mr. Lisbon during his last days in the house. "Sometimes, in the middle of the night, I'd forget everything that had happened. I'd go down the hall, and for a moment, we'd just moved in again. The girls were asleep in their tent in the living room."

Left alone on the other end of those days, Mary lay in her sleeping bag, on the hard floor of the bedroom she no longer had to share. The sleeping bag was the old kind, with pilled flannel lining picturing dead ducks above red-capped hunters and a trout leaping with a hook in its mouth. She zipped the bag up so that only the top of her face showed, even though it was summer. She slept late, spoke little, and took six showers a day.

From our viewpoint, the Lisbons' sadness was beyond comprehension, and when we saw them in those last days, we were amazed at anything they did. How could they actually sit down to eat? Or come out to the back porch in the evening to enjoy the breeze? How could Mrs. Lisbon, as she did one afternoon, stagger outside, and across her uncut lawn, to pick one of Mrs. Bates's snapdragons? She held it to her nose, seemed dissatisfied with its fragrance, tucked it into her pocket like a used Kleenex, and walked to the street, squinting at the neighborhood without her glasses. Mr. Lisbon, too, every afternoon, parked the station wagon in the shade, opening the hood to pore over the engine. "You have to keep busy," Mr. Eugene said, commenting on his behavior. "What else can you do?"

Mary went down the street and took her first voice lesson from Mr. Jessup in a year. She hadn't scheduled a lesson, but Mr. Jessup couldn't turn her away. He sat at the piano, leading Mary through scales, and then put his head in a metal trash can to demonstrate how it resonated against his trained vibrato. Mary sang the Nazi song from *Cabaret*, the one she and Lux had practiced the day the tragedies began, and Mr. Jessup said that all her travails had lent her voice a dolefulness and maturity beyond her years. "She left without paying for the lesson," he said, "but it was the least I could do."

It was full-fledged summer once again, over a year from the time Cecilia had slit her wrists, spreading the poison in the air. A spill at the River Rouge Plant increased phosphates in the lake, producing a scum of algae so thick it clogged outboard engines. Our beautiful lake began to look like a lily pond, carpeted with an undulating foam. Fishermen tossed rocks from the bank, knocking holes to lower their lines through. The swamp smell that arose was outrageous amid the genteel mansions of the automotive families and the green elevated paddle tennis courts and the graduation parties held under illuminated tents. Debutantes cried over the misfortune of coming out in a season everyone would remember for its bad smell. The O'Connors, however, came up with the ingenious solution of making the theme of their daughter Alice's debutante party "Asphyxiation." Guests arrived in tuxedos and gas masks, evening gowns and astronaut helmets, and Mr. O'Connor himself wore a deep-sea diver's suit, opening the glass face mask to guzzle his bourbon and water. At the party's zenith, when Alice was rolled out in an artificial lung rented for the night from Henry Ford Hospital (Mr. O'Connor was on the board), the rotting smell pervading the air seemed only a crowning touch of festive atmosphere.

Like everyone else, we went to Alice O'Connor's coming-out party to forget about the Lisbon girls. The black bartenders in red vests served us alcohol without asking for I.D., and in turn, around 3 A.M., we said nothing when we saw them loading leftover cases of whiskey into the trunk of a sagging Cadillac. Inside, we got to know girls who had never considered taking their own lives. We fed them drinks, danced with them until they became unsteady, and led them out to the screened-in veranda. They lost their high heels on the way, kissed us in the humid darkness, and then slipped away to throw up demurely in the outside bushes. Some of us held their heads as they vomited, then let them rinse their mouths with beer, after which we got back to kissing again. The girls were monstrous in their formal dresses, each built around a wire cage. Pounds of hair were secured atop their heads. Drunk, and kissing us, or passing out in chairs, they were bound for college, husbands, child-rearing, unhappiness only dimly perceived—bound, in other words, for life.

In the party glow, adult faces grew red. Mrs. O'Connor fell out of a wing chair, her hooped skirt going over her head. Mr. O'Connor pulled one of his daughter's friends into the bathroom with him. Everyone from the neighborhood passed through the O'Connor house that night, singing the old-time songs the bald band played, or wandering back corridors, through the dusty playroom, or into the elevator that no longer worked. Raising champagne glasses, people said our industry was coming back, our nation, our way of life. Guests strolled outside beneath Venetian lanterns that led down to the lake. Under moonlight, the algae scum looked like shag carpeting, the entire lake a sunken living room. Someone fell in, was rescued, and laid on the pier. "I've had it," he said, laughing. "Good-bye, cruel world!" He tried to roll into the lake again, but his friends stopped him.

"You don't understand me," he said. "I'm a teenager. I've got problems!"

"Be quiet," a woman's voice scolded. "They'll hear you."

The back of the Lisbon house was visible through clumped trees, but no lights showed, probably because the electricity had been turned off by then. We went back inside, where people were having a good time. The waiters were serving small silver bowls of green ice cream. A tear-gas canister was set off on the dance floor, propelling a harmless mist. Mr. O'Connor danced with Alice. Everyone toasted her future.

We stayed until daybreak. As we came out into the first alcoholic dawn of our lives (a bleachy fade-in, overused through the years now by the one-note director), our lips were swollen from kissing and our mouths throbbing with the taste of girls. Already we had been married and divorced, in a sense, and Tom Faheem found a love letter left in his pants pocket by the last person to rent the tux. The fish flies that had hatched during the night were still quivering on trees and streetlights, and made the sidewalk squishy under our feet, like walking through yams. The day threatened to be muggy. We took off our jackets and shuffled along, up the O'Connors' street, around the corner, and down our own. In the distance, at the Lisbon house, the EMS truck sat, flashing its lights. They hadn't bothered to use the siren.

That was the morning the paramedics appeared for the last time, moving much too slowly in our opinion, and the fat one made the crack about its not being TV. By this time they'd been to the house so often they didn't even knock, just walked right in, past the fence that was no longer there, into the kitchen to see if the gas oven was on, then down to the basement where they found the beam clean, and finally upstairs where the second bedroom they checked contained what they were looking for: the last Lisbon daughter, in a sleeping bag, and full of sleeping pills.

She had on so much makeup that the paramedics had the odd feeling she had already been prepared for viewing by an undertaker, and this impression lasted until they saw that her lipstick and eyeshadow were smudged. She had clawed herself a little, at the end. She was dressed in a black dress and veil, which reminded some people of Jackie Kennedy's widow's weeds, and it was true: the final procession out the front door, with the two paramedics like uniformed pallbearers, and the sound of postholiday firecrackers going off on the next block over, did call to mind the solemnity of a national figure being laid to rest. Neither Mr. nor Mrs. Lisbon appeared, so it was up to us to send her off, and, for the last time, we came and stood at attention. Vince Fusilli held up his lighter as though at a rock concert. It was the best we could do for an eternal flame.

For a while we tried to accept the general explanations, which qualified the Lisbon girls' pain as merely historic, springing from the same source as other teenage suicides, every death part of a trend. We tried to go back to our old lives, to let the girls rest in peace, but a haunted quality persisted about the Lisbon house, making us see, whenever we looked, a flame shape arcing from the roof, or swinging in an upstairs window. Many of us continued to have dreams in which the Lisbon girls appeared to us more real than they had been in life, and we awoke certain that their scent of the next world remained on our pillows. Almost daily we met to go over the evidence once again, reciting portions of Cecilia's journal (the description of Lux testing a chilly sea, one knee up, flamingo-like, was popular with us then). Nevertheless, we always ended these sessions with the feeling that we were retracing a path that led nowhere, and we grew more and more sullen and frustrated.

As luck would have it, on the day of Mary's suicide, the cemetery workers' strike was settled after 409 days of arbitration. The strike's length had caused mortuaries to fill up months ago, and the many bodies awaiting burial now came back from out of state, in refrigerated trucks, or by airplane, depending on the wealth of the deceased. On the Chrysler Freeway one truck got into an accident, flipping over, and the front page of the newspaper ran a photo showing metal caskets spilling from the truck like ingots. No one attended the final mass burial of the Lisbon girls other than Mr. and Mrs. Lisbon; Mr. Calvin Honnicutt, a cemetery worker just back on the job; and Father Moody. Because of limited available space, the girls' graves did not lie side by side but widely separated, so that the funeral party had to make the rounds, going from grave to grave at the excruciatingly slow speed of cemetery traffic. Father Moody claimed the constant getting into and out of the limousine made him lose track of which girl lay at which grave. "I had to keep the eulogies sort of general," he said. "There was a lot of confusion at the cemetery that day. You're talking a year's worth of departed. The place was pretty well dug up." As for Mr. and Mrs. Lisbon, tragedy had beaten them into mindless submission. They followed the priest from graveside to graveside, saying little. Mrs. Lisbon, under sedation, kept looking up into the sky, as though at birds. Mr. Honnicutt told us, "I'd been working seventeen hours straight by that point, wired on NoDoz. I'd buried over fifty people that shift alone. Still, when I saw that lady, it broke me up."

We saw Mr. and Mrs. Lisbon when they returned from the cemetery. With dignity, they got out of the limousine and walked toward their house, each one parting the front shrubs to find access to the porch steps. They picked their way amid the broken pieces of slate. For the first time ever, we noticed a similarity between Mrs. Lisbon's face and the faces of her daughters, but that may have been due to the black veil some people recall her as wearing. We ourselves don't remember a veil and think that detail only an elaboration of romantic memory. Still, we do have the image of Mrs. Lisbon turning toward the street and showing her face as never before, to those of us kneeling at dining room windows or peering through gauzy curtains, those of us sweating in Pitzenberger's attic, the rest of us looking over car hoods or from troughs serving as first, second, and third base, from behind barbecues or from the apex of a swing's arc—she turned, she sent her blue gaze out in every direction, the same color gaze the girls had had, icy and spectral and unknowable, and then she turned back and followed her husband into the house.

Because no furniture remained, we didn't think the Lisbons would be long. Nevertheless, three hours went by and they did not reappear. With a fungo bat, Chase Buell hit a Wiffle ball into their yard, but came back saying he didn't see a single living soul inside. Later he tried to hit another Wiffle ball, but it got stuck in the trees. We didn't see Mr. and Mrs. Lisbon come out the rest of that day, or evening. It was in the middle of the night that they finally left. Nobody saw them go except Uncle Tucker. Years later, when we interviewed him, he was completely sober and recovered from his decades of abuse, and in contrast to everyone else, including ourselves, who looked much the worse for wear, Uncle Tucker looked much better. We asked him if he remembered seeing the Lisbons leave and he said he did. "I was outside, having a smoke. It was about two in the morning. I heard the door open across the street and then they came out. The mother looked bombed. The husband sort of helped her in. And then they drove away. Fast. Got the hell out."

When we awoke the next morning, the Lisbon house was empty. It looked even more run-down than ever and seemed to have collapsed from the inside, like a lung. Once the new young couple took possession of the house, we had time, amid the scraping, painting, and roofing, the uprooting of bushes and planting of Asiatic ground cover, to coalesce our intuitions and theories into a story we could live with. The new young couple knocked out the front windows (still bearing our finger- and noseprints) and installed sliding plate-glass windows with airtight seals. A team of men in white overalls and caps sandblasted the house, then over the next two weeks sprayed it with a thick white paste. The foreman, whose tag said "Mike," told us that "the new Kenitex method" would eliminate the need to repaint once and for all. "Pretty soon everybody's going to be Kenitexing," he said as the men moved about with spray guns, coating the house. When they finished, the Lisbon house was transformed into a giant wedding cake dripping frosting, but it took less than a year for chunks of Kenitex to begin falling off like gobs of bird shit. We thought it just revenge on the new young couple who had set themselves so purposefully to removing signs of the Lisbon girls we still held dear: the slate roof, where Lux had made love, covered with sandpapery shingles; the back flower bed, whose soil Therese had analyzed for lead content, laid with red bricks so that the young wife could pick flowers without getting her feet wet; the girls' rooms themselves made into private spaces for the new young couple to pursue their individual interests—a desk and computer in Lux and Therese's old room, a loom in Mary and Bonnie's. The bathtub where our naiads once floated,

Lux poking cigarettes above the water like reeds to breathe through, was ripped out to make room for a fiberglass Jacuzzi. At curbside, we examined the tub, fighting the urge to lie down in it. The little kids who did jump in couldn't appreciate the significance. The new young couple turned the house into a sleek empty space for meditation and serenity, covering with Japanese screens the shaggy memories of the Lisbon girls.

It wasn't only the Lisbon house that changed but the street itself. The Parks Department continued to cut down trees, removing a sick elm to save the remaining twenty, then removing another to save the remaining nineteen, and so on and so on until only the half-tree remained in front of the Lisbons' old house. Nobody could bear to watch when they came for it (Tim Winer compared the tree to the last speaker of Manx), but they buzz-sawed it down like the rest, saving trees farther away, on other streets. Everyone stayed inside during the execution of the Lisbons' tree, but even in our dens we could feel how blinding the outside was becoming, our entire neighborhood like an overexposed photograph. We got to see how truly unimaginative our suburb was, everything laid out on a grid whose bland uniformity the trees had hidden, and the old ruses of differentiated architectural styles lost their power to make us feel unique. The Kriegers' Tudor, the Buells' French colonial, the Bucks' imitation Frank Lloyd Wright—all just baking roofs.

Not long after, the FBI arrested Sammy the Shark Baldino, who never made it to his escape tunnel, and after a long trial, he went to prison. He reportedly continued to run his crime operation from behind bars, and the Baldino family remained in the house, though the men in bullet-proof limousines ceased to pay their respects on Sunday afternoons. The laurel trees, untrimmed, burst into odd inharmonious shapes, and the terror the family inspired decreased day by day until someone had the courage to deface the stone lions beside their front steps. Paul Baldino began to look like any other fat boy with rings around his eyes, and one day he slipped, or was pushed, in the showers at school, and we saw him lying on the tiles, nursing his foot. The convictions of other family members followed, and finally the Baldinos moved, too, carting their Renaissance art and three pool tables away in three trucks. An obscure millionaire bought the house. He made the fence a foot higher.

Everyone we spoke to dated the demise of our neighborhood from the suicides of the Lisbon girls. Though at first people blamed them, gradually a sea change took place, so that the girls were seen not as scapegoats but as seers. More and more, people forgot about the individual reasons why the girls may have killed themselves, the stress disorders and insufficient neurotransmitters, and instead put the deaths down to the girls' foresight in predicting decadence. People saw their clairvoyance in the wiped-out elms, the harsh sunlight, the continuing decline of our auto industry. This transformation in thinking went largely unnoticed, however, because we rarely ran into one another anymore. Without trees, there were no leaves to rake, no piles of leaves to burn. Winter snows continued to disappoint. We had no Lisbon girls to spy on. Now and then, of course, as we were slowly carted into the melancholic remainder of our lives (a place the Lisbon girls, wisely, it began to seem, never cared to see), we would stop, mostly alone, to gaze up at the whited sepulchre of the former Lisbon house.

The Lisbon girls made suicide familiar. Later, when other acquaintances chose to end their lives—sometimes even borrowing a book the day before—we always pictured them as taking off cumbersome boots to enter the highly associative mustiness of a family cottage on a dune overlooking the sea. Every one of them had read the signs of misery Old Mrs. Karafilis had written, in Greek, in the clouds. On different paths, with different-colored eyes or jerkings of the head, they had deciphered the secret to cowardice or bravery, whichever it was. And the Lisbon girls were always there before them. They had killed themselves over our dying forests, over manatees maimed by propellers as they surfaced to drink from garden hoses; they had killed themselves at the sight of used tires stacked higher than the pyramids; they had killed themselves over the failure to find a love none of us could ever be. In the end, the tortures tearing the Lisbon girls pointed to a simple reasoned refusal to accept the world as it was handed down to them, so full of flaws.

But this came later. Immediately following the suicides, when our suburb enjoyed its fleeting infamy, the subject of the Lisbon girls became almost taboo. "It was like picking over a corpse after a while," Mr. Eugene said. "And the liberal media distortion didn't help, either. Save the Lisbon girls. Save the snail darter. Bullshit!" Families moved away, or splintered, everybody trying out a different spot in the Sun Belt, and for a while it appeared that our only legacy would be desertion. After deserting the city to escape its rot, we now deserted the green banks of our waterlocked spit of land French explorers had named the "Fat Tip" in a three-hundred-year-old dirty joke no one ever got. The exodus was short-lived, however. One by one, people returned from their sojourns in other communities, reestablishing the faulty memory bank from which we have drawn for this investigation. Two years ago our last great automotive mansion was razed to put up a subdivision. The Italian marble lining the entrance hall—a rare rose shade found only in one quarry in the world—was cut into blocks and sold piecemeal, as were the gold-plated plumbing fixtures and ceiling frescoes. With the elms gone, too, only the runt replacements remain. And us. We aren't even allowed to barbecue any longer (city air-pollution ordinance), but if we were allowed, we might still gather, who knows, a few of us at least, to reminisce about the Lisbon house and the girls whose hair, clotted on brushes we still faithfully keep, has begun to look more and more like artificial animal fur in a natural history museum exhibit. All of it is going— Exhibits #1 through #97, arranged in five separate suitcases, each bearing a photograph of the deceased like a Coptic headstone, and kept in our refurbished tree house in one of our last trees: (#1) Ms. D'Angelo's Polaroid of the house, scummed by a greenish patina that looks like moss; (#18) Mary's old cosmetics drying out and turning to beige dust; (#32) Cecilia's canvas high-tops yellowing beyond remedy of toothbrush and dish soap; (#57) Bonnie's votive candles nibbled nightly by mice; (#62) Therese's specimen slides showing new invading bacteria; (#81) Lux's brassiere (Peter Sissen stole it from the crucifix, we might as well admit it now) becoming as stiff and prosthetic as something a grandmother might wear. We haven't kept our tomb sufficiently airtight, and our sacred objects are perishing.

In the end we had pieces of the puzzle, but no matter how we put them together, gaps remained, oddly shaped emptinesses mapped by what surrounded them, like countries we couldn't name. "All wisdom ends in paradox," said Mr. Buell, just before we left him on our last interview, and we felt he was telling us to forget about the girls, to leave them in the hands of God. We knew that Cecilia had killed herself because she was a misfit, because the beyond called to her, and we knew that her sisters, once abandoned, felt her calling from that place, too. But even as we make these conclusions we feel our throats plugging up, because they are both true and untrue. So much has been written about the girls in the newspapers, so much has been said over backyard fences, or related over the years in psychiatrists' offices, that we are certain only of the insufficiency of explanations. Mr. Eugene, who told us that scientists were on the verge of finding the "bad genes" that caused cancer, depression, and other diseases, offered his hope that they would soon "be able to find a gene for suicide, too." Unlike

Mr. Hedlie, he didn't see the suicides as a response to our historical moment. "Shit," he said, "what have kids got to be worried about now? If they want trouble, they should go live in Bangladesh."

"It was the combination of many factors," Dr. Hornicker said in his last report, written for no medical reason but just because he couldn't get the girls out of his head. "With most people," he said, "suicide is like Russian roulette. Only one chamber has a bullet. With the Lisbon girls, the gun was loaded. A bullet for family abuse. A bullet for genetic predisposition. A bullet for historical malaise. A bullet for inevitable momentum. The other two bullets are impossible to name, but that doesn't mean the chambers were empty."

But this is all a chasing after the wind. The essence of the suicides consisted not of sadness or mystery but simple selfishness. The girls took into their own hands decisions better left to God. They became too powerful to live among us, too self-concerned, too visionary, too blind. What lingered after them was not life, which always overcomes natural death, but the most trivial list of mundane facts: a clock ticking on a wall, a room dim at noon, and the outrageousness of a human being thinking only of herself. Her brain going dim to all else, but flaming up in precise points of pain, personal injury, lost dreams. Every other loved one receding as though across a vast ice floe, shrinking to black dots waving tiny arms, out of hearing. Then the rope thrown over the beam, the sleeping pill dropped in the palm with the long, lying lifeline, the window thrown open, the oven turned on, whatever. They made us participate in their own madness, because we couldn't help but retrace their steps, rethink their thoughts, and see that none of them led to us. We couldn't imagine the emptiness of a creature who put a razor to her wrists and opened her veins, the emptiness and the calm. And we had to smear our muzzles in their last traces, of mud marks on the floor, trunks kicked out from under them, we had to breathe forever the air of the rooms in which they killed themselves. It didn't matter in the end how old they had been, or that they were girls, but only that we had loved them, and that they hadn't heard us calling, still do not hear us, up here in the tree house, with our thinning hair and soft bellies, calling them out of those rooms where they went to be alone for all time, alone in suicide, which is deeper than death, and where we will never find the pieces to put them back together.